BABYLON WILL RISE

A Thriller

THE OMEGA GROUP SERIES

ALSO BY ERIC P. BISHOP

THE BODY MAN SERIES:
The Body Man
Breach Of Trust

THE OMEGA GROUP SERIES:
Ransomed Daughter
Babylon Will Rise

STANDALONE BOOKS:
Supreme Justice (Summer 2025)

THE TROY EVANS SERIES:
Untitled (Late 2025/Early 2026)

BABYLON WILL RISE

The Omega Group Series

Eric P. Bishop

BruNoe Media Publishing

BruNoe Media Publishing

eBook ISBN-979-8-9888360-9-4

Paperback ISBN-979-8-9917666-0-9

Hardcover ISBN-979-8-9917666-1-6

Library of Congress Cataloging-in-Publication Identifiers: LCCN: 2024921709

Book Cover by Momir Borocki

Author Photo by Bruce Bishop Photography

Book Formatting by Atticus

First Edition December 2024

Printed in The United States of America

10 9 8 7 6 5 4 3 2 1

Praise for Babylon Will Rise

"A gripping, fast-paced thriller, you won't be disappointed!"

--Fred Burton, Former Special Agent, NY Times Bestselling Author

"The best part of Babylon Will Rise is the character development, balanced with a great story!"

--Aida Flick

"His best work yet. Bishop knocks it out of the park! A proved leader in the thriller genre."

--Michael Carlson, Author

"Bishop's writing is like watching a Netflix thriller!"

--F.X. Regan, Retired FBI Agent, Author

"Babylon Will Rise sets a new standard in the thrillerverse with great characters and stories."

--Mikael Sandeberg (Abibliofob)

"Babylon Will Rise is fast-paced, with an excellent storyline. The intrigue and deception kept me hooked from page one. Like a fine red wine, Eric P. Bishop keeps getting better!"

--Marisia Robus

PRAISE FOR OTHER WORKS

BY ERIC P. BISHOP

"Thriller readers take note: there's a new sheriff in town."

--Ben Coes, NY Times Bestselling Author

"I loved The Body Man! A taut, torn-from-the-pages thriller that takes readers into the world of secrets and power...packed with compelling characters who are so authentic I feel I've met them."

--Adam Hamdy, Sunday Times Bestselling Author

"The Body Man is a spectacular political thriller!"

--Kashif Hussain, Best Thriller Books

"In a world of tired cliches, Eric has crafted the rip-roaring world of Troy Evans. This novella is a pure shot of intellectual adrenaline!"

--John Guarnieri, Security Director, Former USSS

"With a keen eye for details and unmatched research, Eric P. Bishop is a rising star in the thriller genre!"

--Dr. Jason Piccolo, Author, Veteran, and Retired Federal Agent

Breach Of Trust is a ride in a big block muscle car! It's raucous and will kick your a$$ backwards in the seat!

--Author Mike Mason

DEDICATION

For Andrew Reinertsen
Veteran and Friend

───◆◇◆───

"Now, I am become Death, the Destroyer of Worlds."
Bhagavad Gita 11:32

───◆◇◆───

And he cried out with a mighty voice, saying,
"Fallen, fallen is Babylon the great!
She has become a dwelling place of demons,
And a prison of every unclean spirit..."
Revelation 18:2

───◆◇◆───

Prologue

Lake Dukan, Iraq

March 17, 2003

Alwan Makki Khamas lit the Sumer king-size cigarette and took a deep drag as he breathed the pungent smoke into his lungs. After he held it in for a moment, Alwan let the plume out in a slow, methodical exhale. His weathered, thick fingers clutched the dull yellow-tinted cigarette as his other hand rested on his left hip. His wife of thirty years, Rena, despised his love of the Sumer cigarettes, but still, he smoked two packs a day no matter how much grief his nasty habit might provoke at home.

The waxing gibbous moon glowed in the night sky and illuminated the barren desert that spread out before him for miles in either direction. Alwan wondered which direction the invaders would use for their initial barrage. They were out there somewhere just beyond the distant horizon. According to intel reports, the shock and awe would soon rain down from above. Saddam met with his senior leadership three days before and assured the men gathered within the bunker located deep beneath Baghdad that the army would repulse the attack. Alwan was at the meeting with Saddam. He and the other senior military leaders knew their boisterous leader spewed forth lies, and they stood no chance against the bombardment about to be unleashed by the great Satan. It mattered not. He and the other military brass would continue to lead their men until their end.

Will this be my last glance at the bright moon before the end comes? Alwan asked himself between drags of sweet nicotine.

He rubbed a tender spot on his shoulder, and his thick hand brushed against the insignia of two swords crossing with two stars and the republican eagle above the swords. Alwan spent his entire adulthood in the Iraqi army, attaining the rank of lieutenant general two weeks before he turned fifty. He believed in the cause and the sacrifices such beliefs required. Saddam may be a madman, but Alwan was prepared to die for and with him if they were invaded.

He glanced down at his Rolex Oyster Perpetual watch; it was 1:24 a.m. The timepiece kept excellent time for a knockoff he bought a year before on the south side of the citadel in Erbil, part of Kurdistan in northern Iraq.

One of his men approached from behind. Alwan pivoted before the man reached him.

"Lieutenant General!" The junior officer spoke in a frenzied tone.

Alwan took another drag and blew it out in the officer's face. "Yes, Mohammad. What is it?"

"The sound has returned, and it's growing louder. Also, the walls are shaking."

The half-smoked cigarette dropped to the ground, and Alwan crushed it under the heel of his boot. Several weeks before the sounds and vibrations began, steadily, they grew louder and more pronounced. Alwan reported the strange occurrences up the chain of command. General An-Arbar, the man directly above him, assured Alwan it must be seismic activity, and a member of the Iraqi geologic department would come out to monitor the situation. Not surprisingly, nobody ever came.

Alwan breathed in one last gasp of fresh air before he followed the junior officer into the long tunnel that led to the underground structure hidden deep within the mountain range.

Seven minutes later, the two men arrived at the rear of the facility at the spot where the sound originated, and the vibrations were the strongest.

As he placed his hand against the wall, the vibrations shook violently. Alwan thought the wall might give way as the force grew stronger.

What is going on? Something's not right. This growing tremor isn't an earthquake.

With a concerned frown, his voice growled at the young junior officer. "Get command on the phone immediately. Whatever is happening, it's not natural." As the last few words escaped his lips, the shaking grew more intense before it stopped.

Alwan looked at the wall and back at the junior officer. Both men exchanged curious stares before they shrugged.

With the sound stopped and the shaking abated, Alwan put his ear against the wall and strained to make out a faint *tap-tap-tap* sound. After a minute, silence greeted him no matter how hard he pressed his ear against the cool concrete.

"What do you think it was?" the young officer asked. "And why did it stop?"

A sudden and vicious blast fractured the wall into a thousand pieces as chunks of concrete permeated the stale air.

The high-impact explosion violently tossed Alwan and the junior officer into the air. Both men flew across the tunnel and crashed against the opposite wall.

Alwan regained consciousness a minute later. He was slouched against the concrete wall, covered with not only his blood but also chunks of bloody flesh and skull fragments. The body parts were all that remained of the lifeless young officer, who lay at his feet in a dead heap. A massive bowling ball-sized chunk of concrete rested where his head should be instead.

A high-pierced squeal rang through Alwan's head as the force of the explosion decimated his eardrums and left him mostly deaf. As his ears rang, his eyes switched from the headless body of the junior officer to the gaping hole in the wall.

A steady stream of men poured through the opening. The putrid smell of chemicals from the explosives intertwined with burned flesh singed his nostrils.

As he looked at each person who stepped into the facility through the hole, his stare focused on one man in particular, a person he knew only too well.

The man approached where Alwan lay in a state frozen by not only the physical shock inflicted upon him by the blast but also the emotional distress caused by the sudden breach of the facility.

Alwan tried to speak, but no words would form at the corner of his lips as the metallic taste of blood filled his mouth.

The man crouched down and leaned in close enough that Alwan could smell the stench of coffee on his breath and see the yellow stains on his teeth.

The person he knew uttered only a few words. "Lieutenant General Khamas. Today, you shall see Allah in paradise."

Without the ability to reply verbally, Alwan watched as the man stood upright, raised the AK-47 slung over his shoulder, and pointed it at his face.

Alwan clenched his eyes shut and wished the last minute was only a nightmare.

The person who stood above him pulled the trigger once. The bullet split Alwan's skull, and his head slumped to the side.

A bright light permeated his vision for a fraction of a second before the shroud of darkness greeted Alwan on the other side.

PART I

1

Tacoma, Washington

Present Day

Rays of crimson streaked across the sky and reflected off the crystal-clear water as the six fatigued men tried to unwind. The members of The Omega Group took any available moments between missions to bust balls, tell stories, and give each other endless amounts of shit.

"Toss me another cold one," J.C. Kyle hollered to the person closest to the Yeti cooler. Everybody referred to J.C. as the Jackal, a handle assigned to him while he slogged through boot camp at Fort Moore.

The team lounged around the pool at Terrance Wallace's ranch-style house in the suburbs of Tacoma, Washington. Nobody called Terrance by his given name. Even his mom called him Sarge.

Everyone enjoyed the ultra-rare day off. A hot day in Tacoma proved to be the perfect time to do nothing but soak in some rays, throw down some brews, and forget about the last mission. Although none of them would ever admit it, they needed a release, an escape from the constant action. The inescapable stress, a byproduct of their perpetual missions, chipped away at their humanity and changed them in small, imperceptible ways.

Captain Troy Evans, the leader of the Omegas, who everyone called Cap, felt the drain on his soul more than the rest. His years of deployments and classified missions took their toll, and he knew deep down that his current path was not his destiny. A single act, the consequences of something that cost mere cents, altered the course of his life. Troy's smile at his surroundings concealed dark emotions just below the surface.

Troy popped the top and lobbed the glass bottle into the air. It was a slow-motion throw that would have made the beer companies salivate. The Jackal glanced up, extended his arm over the clear water, and caught the bottle by the neck without spilling a drop into the pool.

"Nice snag," Troy said as he flicked the bottle cap into the trash can beside the cooler.

The Jackal looked at the bottle from behind his mirrored, oversized sunglasses, and a toothy grin formed on the corner of his mouth. He took a drag from the Marlboro between his lips, removed it with his free hand, and let out a plume of smoke. "A Corona! Thanks Cap! I figured you would toss one of those nasty imported beers you drink."

"Hey!" Troy exclaimed. "What's wrong with my beer?"

"Nothing. But you didn't grow up in Ireland."

"Dude, you're drinking Coronas, and you sure as hell didn't live in Mexico. There's no way you're Mexican." Troy shook his head.

"I am," Jesús Soto said from the other side of the pool. He floated on a blue raft and raised his hand high. "And proud of it, you dirty gringos."

"You don't count," the Jackal said.

"Why not?" Jesús's face distorted into a quizzical look.

"Because you don't drink, and all Hispanics drink." The Jackal chuckled.

"Yo, man! That's just not right," Jesús said before he added. "And it's a little bit racist."

"Stating facts is not racism. It's the truth." The Jackal raised the bottle of Corona to his lips and chugged half it down before he took another drag from the cigarette.

"Didn't Sarge tell you not to smoke in his pool or even near it?" Troy asked.

The Jackal shrugged. "Demote me."

Sarge let out a deep sigh from over near the flaming hot grill. "You're already on the bottom of the pecking order, dipshit. There's no lower for you to go. Put that damn cancer stick out before I jump in that pool and do it for you. Unless you've got gills somewhere we can't see, it won't end well for you if I have to come in there."

"Testy, testy, testy," The Jackal replied as he mushed the cigarette against the side of the Corona bottle. "Considering what we do for a living, enjoying a few nicotine puffs should be applauded, not derided. Hell, I bet if Snoop Dogg was here, all of you choir boys would partake in whatever he passed around."

"Snoop is clean these days, dummy," Troy said.

The Jackal rolled his eyes. "Yeah, right. That's like saying the pope is no longer catholic." He flicked the extinguished cigarette butt at Jesús as his pool float drifted close to the Jackal.

"Cap!" Jesús yelled as he looked toward Troy. "I'm about to lose my cool with our resident trash talker."

Troy shook his head. "Next mission if a negligent discharge occurs in the Jackal's general direction, I got your back, Jesús. Friendly fire is a reality of war."

The Jackal laughed. "You can't pierce titanium, fellas."

Jesús splashed water towards the Jackal. "You're a filthy, rotten, piece of trash. You know that right?"

"Damn skippy," the Jackal retorted.

"Are the burgers and dogs done yet?" Dave "Digger" Riley asked from a lounge chair intentionally pushed out of the sun and far away from the splash zone of the pool.

"Keep your panties on," Sarge said. "I'm working on them. You know it's my day off, and I'm the one who bought the damn grub, right?"

"I can transfer you some Bitcoin if the food broke your budget," Digger replied.

"It's all our days off." Harrison Collins, who everyone called Harry or Doc, sat at the patio table under the oversized umbrella. "And I'm famished."

"The sun won't hurt you," Troy said as he looked at Harry relaxing under the shade. "Try coming out from under that umbrella and get some color on that pale skin of yours."

"Cap, we spend most of our days under the scorching desert sun. I'll be damned if I spend one of my few days of R&R baking under it while I'm home. You're lucky I'm out here instead of inside in the La-Z-Boy recliner with the A/C cranked."

"Man," Sarge said. "I can't remember the last time we sat around my pool and shot the shi…" He never finished the last word. The six cell phones lying in various spots around the pool area made a simultaneous, obnoxious alarm sound.

———◆———

"Dammit!" The Jackal could not hide his irritated tone as he took a final chug from his Corona. "There goes our day off." His face contorted into a snarl as he tossed the empty bottle into the grass next to the pool.

"I'll call him," Troy announced. "Maybe it's a false alarm."

"It's never a false alarm, Cap," Jesús said.

Troy dialed the colonel's number. The rest of the men could only hear one side of the conversation.

Yes, sir, we're all here. How long do we have?

Troy looked at his watch.

We can be there in ninety minutes. Yes, sir, we understand. You're right. The men are about to be royally pissed off, and for good reason, since some pre-lunch buzzes are all for naught, and we've been on rotation for the past three months without a day off.

Troy ended the call. The five other men around the pool area looked at him, their faces downtrodden.

"So?" Sarge asked. "What's the emergency?"

"He didn't say, but we need to be at the base in ninety minutes, which means we better get a move on it. That's just enough time to get quick showers at our places and grab our go bags."

"Destination?" Digger asked.

"Crystal City, VA. It's a neighborhood in Arlington."

"Northern Virginia? What the hell is there besides a bunch of bureaucrats and yuppies?" The Jackal asked.

"A meeting we must attend," Troy said.

"I guess we don't have a say in whether or not we go?" Digger asked.

"Of course, you have a choice," Troy said. "You can either walk to your cars and go get ready, or Sarge and I will drag your slack asses onto the plane in ninety minutes. Option A will work better for us all, especially my sore back."

"Lovely," Digger replied.

"Nothing like personal liberty when you're an adult in the army, huh?" The Jackal asked.

Troy shook his head. "Dude, you gave up any idea of freedom the second you signed on Uncle Sam's dotted line. Your soul may belong to the good Lord, but your ass belongs to the United States Department of Defense. At least for now."

Four of the Omegas sulked as they approached the gate leading to the driveway. Troy walked around the pool's perimeter and cleaned up discarded bottles and trash while Sarge turned off the grill before heading inside to take a fast shower.

Troy cleared his throat. "The Pentagon thanks you fine gentlemen for your splendid attitudes about giving up another stretch back home." He said this before the four men walked through the gate.

The Jackal flicked off Troy, while the others just shook their heads as they continued toward their respective vehicles.

With a toothy grin, Troy replied, "Love you boys, too. See you on the plane in eighty-seven minutes."

2

CRYSTAL CITY, VIRGINIA

The Gulfstream G450 touched down at Ronald Reagan National Airport at five p.m. EST. After he thanked the pilots, Colonel William S. Marshall stepped off the air stairs and walked toward the two black Suburbans parked to the side of the tarmac. The rest of The Omega Group followed behind the colonel with their rucksacks slung over their shoulders.

Two men in dark suits with coiled, cream-colored earpieces stood beside the vehicles. Neither man said anything as the team approached, and the men opened the doors.

"I can get used to these private jets," Digger whispered as he walked behind Troy.

Troy turned his head slightly. "Don't. The colonel only saves the best for special occasions."

"More times than not, that means we're about to be pulled into a hell of a mess," Sarge said in his commanding voice.

"Bingo," Troy said. "We're only one private jet away from military transport in a pine box covered with an American flag!"

"A pine box and flag sounds like a country hit," Harry said.

The colonel heard the banter and grinned without saying a word.

"I miss going private when we have to jump on military birds," the Jackal said.

"Yeah, nobody misses flying military jets," Sarge said.

"That would be like saying you miss the yearly prostate exam," the colonel stated.

"Eww," Troy added. "TMI, bossman."

"I kind of like the ole check-up," the Jackal replied. "Make sure the engine works right, even those hidden parts."

Jesús looked over at him. "You would, weirdo."

"I don't know how we could function without the Jackal," the colonel said.

The Jackal shrugged. "I'm God's gift to the world, I guess."

"Come now, boss," Harry said, steering the conversation away from the Jackal and his disturbing joy of having a doctor's finger stuck up his ass every year. "You must know why we got the call. They always give you the skinny. You're the man, after all."

"Not this time." The colonel shook his head. "I'm in the dark. Told you guys everything I know on the flight here. Everyone has a boss in this life, and sometimes even mine doesn't read me into what's at the end of the barrel."

"Guess we'll find out soon enough." Troy shrugged as he and the others climbed into the two vehicles.

―――――◄○►―――――

The drive from the airport was relatively quick. The vehicles turned off S Eads Street and pulled into an underground parking garage beneath a ten-story building six minutes later. As the team stepped out of the vehicles, Troy wondered why the vast subterranean garage appeared to be mostly empty. The few other vehicles parked in the spaces were like the ones that ushered them from the airport. It had the markings of a government get-together, or maybe a spook convention.

One of the security members with the coiled earpiece led the team to the elevator, which ascended one floor to the main lobby. Once inside, an older woman with streaky black and gray hair and a yellow sundress looked up from behind the marble reception desk. She nodded and motioned with her right hand to the colonel. Behind her stood three armed guards, men who looked like they could handle themselves, not your run-of-the-mill rent-a-cop security guards.

Troy took some solace knowing Paul Blart, Mall Cop, was not in charge of security.

"Take the elevator to the sixth floor, Colonel Marshall," the older woman said. "They're expecting you and your men."

"Yes, ma'am," Colonel Marshall replied, not knowing who or what they would find on the sixth floor.

Troy looked around the empty lobby. No businesspeople were visible, which seemed odd considering the time of day. It was quiet, too quiet. He saw the building directory posted just to the left of where the receptionist sat. It only had one name on it in gold letters and read *Computerized Informational Applications, Inc.* The name briefly bounced around Troy's head before it clicked: **C**omputerized **I**nformational **A**pplications, the CIA.

Troy nudged Digger, who stood beside him and pointed to the sign. "Did they want to make it that obvious?"

Digger smirked. "Guess the spooks have a sense of humor after all."

Inside the elevator, there was only one button to push on the silver control panel, the one for the sixth floor.

———◆———

When the elevator doors opened, the Omegas entered a spacious room. The walls were painted taupe, and overhead, several fluorescent lights cast too little light into the dim room. A single solid steel door was the only thing on the wall opposite the elevator. No windows, just security cameras in every corner pointed toward the elevator doors where the seven men now stood. Two men in full tactical gear, carrying MP5s, stood on either side of the room.

A man in a black suit with a red tie approached. He carried a hand-held wand in his left hand.

"We're armed." The colonel tapped his right hip. He usually did all the talking.

"Not what I'm checking for, sir," the man replied in a measured tone. His right hand held a large Faraday bag. "All cell phones and electronic equipment are to be placed in this bag, gentlemen." The man in the black suit walked from one man to the other. As he worked from right to left, he went over each of them, from the top of their heads to their toes. One hundred and ninety seconds later, after he finished with Harry, he said, "All clear."

With those two words, the locking mechanism buzzed and clicked metallically as it disengaged. The steel door swung inward with little to no sound. The man with the red tie gestured toward the opening. "That way, gentlemen. The conference room is at the end of the hallway."

Beyond the door was a long, narrow hallway that led to a single door at the far end. The door at the end of the passageway opened when they approached.

Troy could not conceal the surprised look on his face as they stepped into the conference room. He instantly recognized all the people sitting at the large mahogany table. The room was decorated with redwood panels on the walls and tan carpet on the floor. The table had fifteen plush leather chairs, seven on either side and one at the head of the table.

At the far end of the table, a man spoke in an authoritarian voice. "Thank you for traveling all the way here, gentlemen."

"No problem, sir." The colonel approached the Secretary of Defense (SecDef) Curt Wastradowski and shook his hand.

"Good to see you, William," the SecDef said.

The colonel nodded. "You as well, Mr. Secretary. It's been a little while."

"Yes, it has been. I think the last time was after the incident in Tangier, Operation Symbiosis, if I recall. We've kept you and your men busy overseas a lot since then."

"Good memory, sir. And yes, between the Department Of Defense and Section Seven, we have certainly been kept on our toes, although there aren't any complaints on our end."

"Please, take a seat." The SecDef gestured toward the plush leather chairs.

The seven seats on the left side of the table were empty. Colonel Marshall took the seat closest to the head of the table where the SecDef sat. The Omega Group took a seat in order of rank: Colonel William Marshall, Captain Troy "Cap"

Evans, Master Sergeant Terrance "Sarge" Wallace, Sergeant First Class (SFC) Jesús Soto, SFC Dave "Digger" Riley, SFC J.C. "The Jackal" Kyle, and SFC Harry "Doc" Collins.

Once settled, Troy looked across the table at the six people on the other side; the seventh seat was empty. On the right side of the table closest to SecDef Wastradowski sat the Secretary of Homeland Security (DHS), Director of National Intelligence (DNI), Chairman of Joint Chiefs of Staff (US DOD), National Security Advisor (NSC), Attorney General (AG), and the Director of the Central Intelligence Agency (DCI).

"I guess introductions would be helpful." The SecDef went around the table and pointed out who was who.

The Jackal nudged Jesús, who sat to his left and, in a quiet voice, asked, "What, the president couldn't make it?"

With a slight smile, the SecDef, who had great hearing, replied, "The president sends his regrets and wishes he could be here. Unfortunately, he's preparing to leave for Australia and the G20 summit in a few hours."

"Don't mind him." The colonel glared at the Jackal with a fierce gaze. "His lips move faster than his brain."

"Nonsense," the SecDef answered. "We value not just your abilities but also your voices. Please speak up anytime, as this meeting is an open forum."

"Now may be a good time to explain why you brought us here. Why aren't we meeting in the Pentagon or Langley?" the colonel asked. "This facility is impressive, but I expect it's not used for official gatherings."

"Good questions and an astute observation. The short version is the agency uses this building for classified meetings that require absolute discretion. This building is state-of-the-art and assures us that only those in attendance know anything we discuss in this conference room today. Langley is certainly secure, but when on the premises, people talk. There are lots of eyes always looking at the George Bush Center for Intelligence. And where there are eyes, people tend to speak about who and what they see. With so few people here at this location, the need to know becomes tiny and completely contained."

"I understand," the colonel said.

SecDef Wastradowski shook his head. "Before we get into why I brought you here, I need all of you to sign these Non-Disclosure Agreements (NDAs)." The SecDef handed the seven men to his right one-page documents and pens.

The colonel looked over the document before he raised his pen. "My men have top secret clearance, Mr. Secretary, and we are up to date on our standard non-disclosure forms."

"These NDAs aren't standard, William, and it's not a request. What we discuss today has its own set of rules. Only a handful of people in the government even know what I'm about to tell you and your men. So, I need all of you to sign these documents before I can continue. But please, by all means, read it before you sign."

"Signing away our soul?" the colonel asked rhetorically.

"Long past that, aren't we all, William!" the SecDef exclaimed.

"Touché," the colonel said. After reading every word, the colonel signed his own and gathered the documents from the six members of The Omega Group. "Okay, all signed. After all, none of us want to spend the rest of our lives at USDB."

"Leavenworth?" the SecDef asked with an audible snicker. "No, what I'm about to share is far more serious than a trip to Leavenworth if someone runs their mouth. Leaking this would get that person a one-way ticket to The Hole."

3

CRYSTAL CITY

The Hole was considered a myth by those who only heard rumors of its existence. Little did they know it was all too real and a very dangerous place. A black site prison not listed on any government document or database *The Hole* was built in absolute secrecy in a third-world nation and maintained by an autonomous entity not associated with the United States. People sent to *The Hole* disappeared, never to be seen again.

"We got it," Colonel Marshall said. "So what's our mission?"

The SecDef looked down for a moment. As his head rose, he stared at the colonel. His eyes piercing, his tone somber. "We have two empty quivers that require our immediate attention."

The expression on Colonel Marshall's face said it all. It wasn't what he expected. A moment passed before he composed himself. "Where?"

"Hmm." The SecDef bit at his lower lip. "That's why your team's here. To find them. Where they were, I can reveal, but their current location is unknown."

"Lost or stolen?"

"It's complicated. There's a bit of history intertwined in the incident."

"The abridged version will do, sir." the colonel said.

SecDef Wastradowski cleared his throat. "The DOD called it Project Nebuchadnezzar, and the short version is Saddam Hussein was obsessed with King Nebuchadnezzar, the Babylonian King ..."

Before the SecDef said anything else, the conference room door opened, and a gorgeous woman entered. All heads turned toward her as she approached the table confidently. Only one chair remained empty, which was the one at the end of the table next to the director of the CIA.

"Sorry I'm late Mr. Secretary." The woman with chestnut-colored hair and green eyes took the only remaining seat. "Traffic sucks in this hell hole we call our nation's capital." She wore a modest pair of blue pants and a white blouse with her hair pulled back into a ponytail. Her body was toned, yet her curves were pronounced. She had the figure of a model and not the waif kind.

"No problem," the SecDef said. "I was just discussing Project Nebuchadnezzar."

"I wouldn't want to miss that." Although feminine, the woman's voice had a slight rasp, which made her sound even sexier. "Please continue, Mr. Secretary. I didn't mean to interrupt."

As the SecDef spoke, the Jackal leaned toward Harry, who sat beside him. "Holy Shit! That chick's a major smoke show!"

Harry was speechless and could only nod in response.

Troy noticed the attractive woman but tried not to stare, which was hard. Like his men, he glanced over at the woman several times as the SecDef spoke.

"As I was saying," the SecDef continued. "Saddam Hussein essentially claimed he was the reincarnation of King Nebuchadnezzar II, ancient King of Babylon." He looked at The Omega Group members. "Did your team visit the ancient city of Babylon during any of your deployments in Iraq?"

"Yes, we've been there," Troy said as his eyes wandered toward the woman once more. Her lips formed a subtle smile, and she winked as they made eye contact. *What the hell? Does she know me from somewhere?*

"Did you notice the inscription Saddam demanded be etched into the bricks?" the SecDef asked.

Troy looked back at the SecDef. "Yes, it read *To King Nebuchadnezzar in the reign of Saddam Hussein, protector of Iraq, who rebuilt civilization and rebuilt Babylon.* We're aware that he fancied himself like Nebuchadnezzar. The man had an ego bigger than an elephant's ass! I was there when he swung. Still have a piece of the rope."

"This Project Nebuchadnezzar had something to do with Saddam?" the colonel asked.

The SecDef nodded. "Yes."

"But Saddam's dead," Sarge interrupted.

"He is," the SecDef replied. "And to understand your mission, I need you to know what took place during the Iran-Iraq War." He paused for a moment. "Captain Evans, I've learned you're a history buff."

"Yes, sir, I am Mr. Secretary," Troy replied.

"Do you know when the war took place between Iran and Iraq?"

Troy thought before replying. "Early eighties till late eighties, I believe, sir."

"Correct, in 1980 Saddam invaded Iran and made a land grab. It caught the Iranians by surprise, but he didn't make the progress he expected. By 1982, Iran had regained most of the land Iraq had seized, and they were on the offensive. It was a brutal war and accomplished nothing. The war ended in 1988, but not until hundreds of thousands up to possibly two million died on both sides in which the Iraqi military used chemical weapons against Iran."

"Didn't we supply them with some of those chemical weapons?" Digger asked.

The SecDef shook his head. "Officially, no, but everyone in this room knows that to be false. Of course, we did. Saddam was our ally, and we needed to do whatever was necessary to prop him up and maintain stability in the region. However, what we need to discuss is more serious than that. Project Nebuchadnezzar originated in 1985, and the after-effects are why we meet today."

He paused and looked around the room, ensuring he had everyone's undivided attention. The SecDef continued. "In late 1984, the Revolutionary Command Council (RCC) Chairman approached our government. He was sent by Saddam and met with Donald Rumsfeld, who Reagan had named his special envoy to the Middle East. The RCC Chairman presented Rumsfeld with indisputable proof that Iran had secured a nuclear weapon. The evidence beyond any doubt."

"How did Iran get a nuke?" Troy asked.

"That's just it. They didn't," the SecDef replied. "But the intel provided by Iraq falsely proved they did. Our government trusted Saddam."

"Well, that's a huge deal and something I have never been told," the colonel said.

"Few knew. Trust me, this intel is beyond your or your team's pay grade."

Colonel Marshall nodded. "No doubt."

The SecDef continued. "Because the RCC and Saddam in particular felt certain Iran would use the weapon on them in retaliation for Iraq using chemical weapons on the Iranian people, they requested something to counter the Iranian nuke."

"Couldn't blame them," the colonel said. "What did he ask for?"

The SecDef looked down for a moment before he glanced at the colonel. His face almost looked ashamed. "Saddam wanted a nuke of his own."

Complete silence filled the vacuum of the room. Mouths opened, but no words were uttered for several seconds.

Colonel Marshall's question punctured the silence. "And we didn't give him one." He could see it in the SecDef's eyes before he added. "Did we?"

"No, the president gave him two!"

"What the hell was Reagan thinking?" the colonel demanded in an irate tone.

"It's complicated, William. There's more to the story than time allows, but safeguards were implemented. The Gipper felt like it was the smart play to protect Iraq and our interests in that region of the world."

"Jesus! What safeguards would work if you gave a madman possession of two nuclear weapons?"

"We agreed to build a secure bunker east of Lake Dukan hidden in the mountains to house the two nukes and had constant eyes on the facility. Nothing went in or out without us knowing."

"Dukan? That's in the Kurds region," Troy said.

"Correct," the SecDef replied.

"Saddam wasn't a big fan of the Kurds. Weird place to hide two nukes."

SecDef nodded. "I'm sure Saddam did it out of spite."

"So we had actual personnel on-site?" Colonel Marshall asked.

"No, Saddam wouldn't allow us to keep any Americans permanently inside the complex, but we insisted quarterly inspections be performed, and he agreed."

"How kind of him," the colonel replied in a derogatory tone. "You're telling us a known tyrant gives us terms, and we accept? That's ludicrous."

The SecDef ignored the sarcasm. "We placed a device inside each of the two weapons. A safeguard of sorts."

"What kind of device?" the colonel asked.

"One that allowed the weapons to be armed, and only we had the codes."

"We gave Saddam two nukes but no way to arm them?"

"Correct."

"And yet we are sitting here today, and you've already said we have two empty quivers, so something must have gone terribly wrong."

"Bush, forty-one, intended to storm the facility during the first Gulf War in 1990," the SecDef said. "But he changed his mind at the last minute while the recovery teams were inbound. In short, the nukes stayed put."

"He left them under Saddam's control?" Troy asked. "Why?"

"The president had his reasons, Captain," The SecDef said.

"Let me guess. Those are classified?" Troy asked.

SecDef didn't answer. "During the 1990s, the inspections continued at Saddam's nuclear program sites and the facility near Lake Dukan. Fast forward to 2003 and the Iraq War. Bush, forty-three, insisted we secure the nukes as our first priority. Apparently "W" didn't like the fact Saddam tried to kill his daddy in 1993 while Bush, forty-one, was in Kuwait. It had been almost four months since the last inspection, and the president demanded that we recover the weapons before 'Shock and Awe' commenced."

"I was in theater for the bombings," the colonel said. "And felt the ground shake as the missiles struck the ground. It was a spectacular campaign."

"Members of Seal Team Six, and even an elite force part of the National Nuclear Security Administration (NNSA), a new department formed in 2000, arrived shortly before midnight on March 18, 2003."

"And let me guess, the facility was empty," the colonel said.

"Completely," the SecDef said. "The only thing that remained in the chamber were the two devices that could prevent the weapons from being armed."

"How did they get the nukes out and remove the devices to arm the weapons?" Troy asked.

"We had 24/7 satellite coverage, and they showed no suspicious activity. Someone accessed via a tunnel that ran under the facility and traveled several miles into the mountains. That's how they snuck them out. A dozen dead bodies littered the facility. The assessment was that the men guarding the facility were dead no more than a few days before our team arrived to secure the nukes. As for how they removed the devices to arm the nukes, nobody knows."

"So, two nukes have been missing since 2003. Is that what you're telling us?"

"Yes."

"And you've been looking for them ever since?" Troy asked.

"Correct, Captain."

"Why tell us now? What's changed?" the colonel asked in rapid succession.

"The situation is quite complicated, and one of those nukes has been placed on the black market for sale to the highest bidder."

"And you want us to recover it?"

"Something like that." The SecDef had a look on his face that revealed there was more to the story.

"Why not just buy it? Surely we have sources that could act as legitimate buyers?" Troy asked.

"It's not that simple," the SecDef replied.

"We'll need all the intel you have," the colonel stated.

"There's more I need to tell you. Plus, you won't be alone on this mission."

"Partnering us with another group? Seals or CAG?"

"Not exactly. We are assigning someone to your team."

"Only one person?"

"Yes, a member of Division S, Captain Martin."

"Who the hell is Division S?" Troy interrupted with a perplexed expression.

Before SecDef could answer, the colonel asked, "So where is this Captain Martin, and why is he so important that he needs to be assigned to The Omega Group?"

The Jackal leaned over to his right and whispered to Digger. "Hope this Captain Martin isn't some dick!"

"Yeah, we already have you on the team," Digger replied with a smirk.

The Jackal winked at the response.

The SecDef smiled and pointed to the woman with the chestnut hair. "I failed to introduce her as she stepped in late, but this is Captain Charlie Martin."

She stood, planted her palms on the table, and leaned inward. "My given name is Charlene, but my parents always called me Charlie. I'm a Captain in the United States Army and part of Division S."

The Jackal leaned over and whispered into Digger's ear. "Looks like the Omegas got a new cap, and this one is hot as shit."

Digger smiled. "Smoke show is right, brother."

"Division S? I've never heard of it," Troy said as he looked toward Colonel Marshall.

William shrugged as he glanced back and mouthed the words, *No Clue*.

Troy glared at the Jackal and Digger as he heard the comment before turning his attention back to the woman with a fierce gaze. "What exactly do you do for the US Army, Captain Martin?"

"Never thought you'd ask," Charlie replied.

4

— • —

NEW YORK CITY

SEPTEMBER 11, 2001

Charlie Martin's father was an investment banker at Goldman Sachs on Wall Street, while her mother worked as a neurological surgeon at New York – Presbyterian Hospital. Born into a life of privilege, she experienced an upbringing only the top one percent realize. Her parents maintained a weekend home on Long Island, while their primary residence was a three-story brownstone in the SoHo district of Manhattan.

Even with advantages most could only dream of, Charlie never felt entitled. In fact, Charlene Joy Martin went in the opposite direction. While many girls in her private school came across as arrogant and looked down upon others less fortunate, Charlie never did. She went out of her way to help those in need. The other girls in school mocked her acts of kindness, but she ignored their taunts. They ridiculed her good intentions, and behind her back, they called her *Charlie* from the late 1970s show *Charlie's Angels*, which they meant as an insult since she looked like an angel but had a man's name. She took it as a badge of courage instead of an insult.

Her mother had enrolled her little "Charlie," as she loved to call her, in gymnastics as a young child. She was a natural athlete. Her agility and speed were beyond most children her age. Her mother tried to keep her polished, refined, and well-mannered, but Charlie rebelled. Much to her mother's chagrin, she possessed an interest in contact sports at a young age and loved hand-to-hand combat. The tomboy within her continued to come out while her mother did her best to subdue those tendencies. It was a losing battle, and several boys her age paid a hefty price when they crossed her. Her dad encouraged the behavior behind her mom's back. He wanted his little girl to defend herself when she grew up.

After several years of pleading with her father, he allowed Charlie to do what she wanted and take up martial arts. Her mother resisted initially but relented after some time passed. Like gymnastics, she proved to be a natural. Charlie received her black belt in Yamabayashi Shorin ryu karate in under six years, an achievement reached faster than the seven to eight years it took most students.

Even though she could be rough around the edges, Charlie maintained a sweetness about her, a kindness that shone through no matter who she was around. She had a quick wit and ranked among her class's top students every year. Several Ivy League schools recruited her, but she rejected all the full scholarships offered. After graduating from one of New York City's elite private schools, she followed in her father's footsteps and attended New York University (NYU), majoring in finance. She had a numbers mind like her father. The first three years went by fast, and she availed herself of every opportunity she could. In her junior year, she studied abroad and spent most of that year in several European countries. Languages came naturally to her, and besides English, she was fluent in three other languages: French, Spanish, and German by the time she turned twenty-one.

Life could not have been better for Charlie. As she began her senior year back on the NYU campus, things seemed perfect until Tuesday, September 11, 2001, at 8:46 a.m. EST.

The day before, her roommate and best friend, Chloe, left NYC for Boston. Chloe and her parents departed on American Airlines Flight 175 from Logan International Airport in Boston, bound for Los Angeles to attend her grandmother's funeral. Shortly after takeoff, terrorists hijacked the plane and flew it into the South Tower of the World Trade Center at 9:03 a.m. EST.

Charlie was in her dorm room alone when the first plane struck the North Tower. She had been fast asleep, but the explosion woke her. Like many other students, she got up as word spread that an incident involving a plane had happened in lower Manhattan. Charlie went to the roof of her dorm building and watched as the smoke billowed from the upper floors of the North Tower. At that moment, while she stood mesmerized at the apparent accident, she saw the second plane fly into the South Tower. All around her, screams erupted as students watched the hellish events unfold before their eyes. Panic set in for most of the students, but not Charlie. She never screamed like the others. In fact, a resolve within her welled up, and courage amid uncertainty took over. A still, small voice within her said it would be all right.

It wasn't until later, during that horrific day, she discovered her closest friend had perished on Flight 175. She had seen her friend pass from this life to the next with her own eyes. After hearing the news, Charlie fell into a deep depression that lasted for several days. Nothing would shake her from that state, not even the tender embraces and words of encouragement from her loved ones.

A week later, she attended the funeral service for Chloe and her parents back in Boston. Charlie's family joined hundreds of others to pay their last respects. An empty casket memorialized her friend. As she passed by the casket, something inside Charlie changed. A button was pushed, a lever thrown, one that couldn't be put back in place. The next day, she returned home with her parents but didn't go back to NYU. Without telling anyone, Charlie took the subway to Times Square, where she walked into the Army recruiting station.

Her life was never the same again.

5

— • —

CRYSTAL CITY

Charlie leaned against the mahogany table, briefly thinking about that moment so many years ago that altered her path in life. The group assembled around the table brought her back to the present. Charlie cleared her throat and glanced at the SecDef. "May I, sir?" she asked.

"Absolutely," he replied. "Tell them about Division S."

She spent the next five minutes giving the people in the room a brief history of Division S. It was concise but informative, even though what she told them still left many unanswered questions.

"What you're describing about Division S is essentially The Omega Group," the Jackal said. Before he added with his trademark sarcasm, "Except injected with estrogen."

It elicited a few smiles from the team, although the colonel's sneer indicated he didn't find the statement funny.

Charlie shook her head and, in a sarcastic tone, said, "And you must be The Omega Groups resident moron!" She rolled her eyes.

Troy smiled and rapped his knuckles on the table. "Yup, this is gonna be fun mission."

The Jackal just stared, his head half-cocked. A slight smile formed at the corner of his lips. "Oh, I like you already."

Charlie ignored his retort.

Jesús leaned close to Sarge. "She's gonna kill him before we ever track down those nukes."

Sarge smirked. "One can hope."

"What's the S stand for?" Harry asked.

Charlie turned her head towards Harry. "Division S references the Egyptian goddess Sekhmet, the goddess of war and destruction. She was also closely aligned with healing. Those within the division believe it's an apt description of our capabilities. Since Division Sekhmet didn't roll off the tongue since it can be difficult for some to pronounce." She looked at the Jackal, raised her eyebrows, and added, "We decided Division S may be a better moniker."

Troy cleared his throat. "And like The Omega Group, Mr. Secretary, are we to understand that Division S rolls under the purview of Section Seven?"

The SecDef pursed his lips. "As all of you know, and your NDAs spell out, we don't really discuss Section Seven. Do we?"

"What happens in Section Seven stays in Section Seven." The Jackal looked at the colonel. "Ain't that right, sir?"

Colonel Marshall shook his head and let out an audible sigh at the exchange.

SecDef Wastradowski said nothing momentarily as he looked down at the desk before glancing back at Troy. "Let's leave it at this, Omegas. Where Division S fits into the government hierarchy has no bearing on your mission."

Troy looked first at Colonel Marshall, then at the Jackal. "I think that means Division S and The Omega Group most certainly both fall under Section Seven."

The SecDef looked at his watch, stood, and then spoke. "We need to move on, folks. In particular, we need to discuss your targets and mission parameters. You'll have plenty of time on your flight east to get to know each other and ask whatever questions you like. What Captain Martin answers or ignores is completely at her discretion."

The SecDef grabbed a remote next to his pen and clicked the button that activated the screen mounted on the wall behind him. A single photo appeared on the screen, dated and grainy.

"The man behind me is Naseefa al-Majid. He is Iraqi by birth, a second cousin of Saddam Hussein. During the 1980s and all the way until our invasion in 2003, Naseefa maintained the nuclear program in Iraq."

"The King of Clubs on the Iraqi playing cards." The colonel recognized not only the name but also the image. "One of only four men we never captured or killed."

"That's correct," the SecDef said.

"I was involved in several covert ops where we had intelligence that indicated his location. Each time, he slipped through our net."

"We've been searching for him since we toppled Saddam, but over the past decade, the trail grew cold," the SecDef said.

"And you believe he's the one who snuck the nukes out of the facility near Lake Dukan?"

"We're sure of it. From what we have pieced together from verified intel, Naseefa handled their removal. Even Saddam didn't know they were taken from the facility until after the fact."

"So, he's offering one of them for sale on the black market?"

The SecDef shook his head. "No, he's not." Then he switched the images on the screen behind him, and a different face appeared. "This man is."

As the SecDef changed the image, the colonel protested immediately. "Dammit, that is not someone I want to have a nuke." The colonel slammed his balled fist into the solid table.

"Clearly, you know Ami Sulzer," the SecDef stated.

"I've met him several times." The colonel pointed across the table at the Director of the Central Intelligence Agency (DCI). "And if it weren't for these jackasses having him on the agency payroll, I would have put a bullet in his head."

"Hey, now!" the DCI exclaimed in an angry retort. "I'm not the one that made the call on Ami. This stuff always rolls downhill, so don't take your anger management issues out on me, William."

The Director of National Intelligence (DNI) raised his arms to quell the voices. "Everybody, calm the hell down. The president alone decided to let Sulzer be …"

Colonel Marshall interrupted the DNI. "Well, that was one God-awful, stupid decision. One of many he made since he has been in office."

"Everybody, stand down!" the SecDef yelled. "Raising our voices and getting in a pissing contest over Ami Sulzer won't help us realize our objective. And for God's sake, William, show some respect when you are talking about your Commander-In-Chief."

"I respect the office, not the man currently occupying it." Colonel Marshall did nothing to mitigate the anger in his tone. He forcefully pushed his chair back from the table, stood, and walked toward the outer wall.

"You need to stop allowing your issues with the president to cloud your judgment."

"He needs to stop keeping people like Ami Sulzer on the bloated government payroll. Making deals with the devil leads all of us down the pathway to hell. There's no salvation found when you dance with Lucifer or his demons."

"Do you need a break, Colonel?" the SecDef, still seated at the head of the table, asked in a stern tone. "Maybe a few minutes to compose yourself?"

The colonel turned and shook his head. He took a deep breath and exhaled it slowly. "No, I'm fine." He sat at the table again. Several awkward seconds passed before the colonel spoke. "What's the connection between Naseefa and Ami?"

"Good question. Our intelligence indicated that Naseefa fled Iraq around the time they executed Saddam. We believe Syria provided him asylum. Intel indicates he lived a quiet life and tried his best to disappear. That is until recently when he re-emerged."

"And the nukes?"

"I'll get to that," the SecDef said.

"Why did he come out of hiding?" Troy asked.

"Naseefa was a Ba'ath party loyalist. Even after they executed Saddam, he believed they would restore power one day, and he could go home. After many years, he realized Iraq would never return to the country it once was under Saddam. According to recent intelligence, he approached Ami via a surrogate about selling a nuke several months ago."

"And you know this how?" the colonel asked.

The SecDef visibly squirmed and shifted in his chair before staring at the DNI.

"Because the agency had an asset inside Ami's inner circle," the DNI answered. "We might have made a deal with the devil as you say, Colonel Marshall, but that doesn't mean we haven't watched the devil like a hawk."

"What do you mean you *had* an asset close to him?"

"Our last correspondence with the asset was six weeks ago, then all communication stopped."

"What happened?" the colonel asked.

"Ami suspected he had a mole."

"And he eliminated your asset?"

"We believe so, but not just our asset. Six of the eight people in Ami's inner circle were found in various locations around Accra, the Capital City of Ghana."

"They were all dead?"

The DNI shook his head. "Well, if you consider being ground up in a wood chipper dead, then yes, I'd say they were all dead."

"How did you confirm the asset was one of those killed?" the colonel asked.

"We haven't, but since the asset went silent and Ami killed so many in his inner circle, we believe it's likely the asset is amongst the dead."

"Jeez, and I thought my boss could be a hard ass." The Jackal looked toward Troy.

He glared at the Jackal before he looked back at the DNI. "And so you know Ami lives primarily in Ghana?" Troy asked.

"Yes, our asset provided us a large amount of intel on a vast compound about fifty miles northeast of Accra that borders the Shai Hills Resource Reserve," the DNI said. "It is completely off the grid, has its own power source, water supply, and a farm that supplies all its food. You get the drift. It's his fortress, his solitude. He is untouchable behind those walls."

"Why Ghana, of all places?" Digger asked. "Ami is very wealthy and could have his pick of countries to hide out in."

"From what I recall, Ami is half Israeli, half German," Troy said. "Isn't Africa an unusual place for someone with his ethnic background?"

"Ghana is one of the most corrupt countries in Africa. The president of Ghana gave Ami full immunity. Let him come and go as he pleases and do what he wants while placing his own army at Ami's disposal."

"In exchange for?"

"Money, weapons, drugs, you name it. Ami takes care of whatever needs the president has."

"So we can't offer a better deal? Buy him off?"

"No, the Ghana president is not a fan of the United States. Which is ironic since he completed his undergraduate degree at Harvard and his master's at Wharton."

"Don't we have an extradition treaty with Ghana?" Troy asked.

The SecDef nodded. "We do. I've talked with the president about going that route, but there's a lot of red tape involved. Plus, it would involve us showing our hand, and in all likelihood, Ami would flee before he could be arrested. There are plenty of countries that don't have extradition deals with the United States and he could easily slip into one of them."

"We could bomb them all to the Stone Age," Sarge said. "Drop the full power of the US military on their pathetic ass-backward country."

The SecDef ignored the comment. "So, back to the nukes. Naseefa approached Sulzer to sell one on the black market."

"And the other?" Troy asked.

"The asset said Naseefa sold it to Ami personally a year ago."

"What?"

"You heard me. Ami bought one, while the other is being put up to the highest bidder in one week."

"How much did Ami pay for his?"

"We believe the payment was in the nine-figure range, lower end."

"Ami has that kind of cash?"

The SecDef nodded. "Unfortunately, yes. At least he did at the time. Global crime syndication pays handsomely."

6

CRYSTAL CITY

"Why not do what Sarge said?" Troy asked. "We are the most powerful nation on earth, so why don't we just bomb the compound to kingdom come. Won't be that hard to kill Ami, and destroy both bombs at the same time. Ghana can't do squat to us in retaliation."

The DNI shook his head. "It's not that simple. According to our asset, the bomb Ami purchased last year is not kept at the compound. In fact, our asset claims it's not even in Ghana."

"Then where is it?"

"That's why you're here." SecDef Wastradowski raised eyebrows. "We need you to find both nukes."

"Plus," the DNI said. "We can't kill Ami because we have reason to believe he has protocols in place if something were to happen to him."

"Hold up. What type of protocols?" Troy asked.

SecDef Wastradowski interrupted, "Intel indicated the nuke Ami bought will be used against Western interests if he were to be assassinated."

"You know this how?" the colonel asked.

"Nothing is for sure, but before he fell off the grid, our asset informed us of Ami's intentions. Also, we have several other sources. One of them is Naseefa's son Jalal, who, unlike his father, remained in Iraq during and then after the war. The interim Iraqi government arrested and held him in prison for several years because of his family lineage. Eventually, they released him, and he led a quiet life on the outskirts of Kirkuk until recently."

"What happened to change that?"

"Our intelligence operatives in Iraq intercepted a phone call between him and his father. It was cryptic but eye-opening."

"What did you do about it?"

"We moved in and apprehended him. He has been forthcoming in our ..." he paused and considered his words, "conversations that have been ongoing."

"Where are you holding him?" Troy asked.

"As you and your team know, we don't have a big presence in Iraq anymore, but we do have resources in a FOB named McFly. It's a ..."

"We've been to McFly, Mr. Secretary, last fall. It's east of Kirkuk, and it's an absolute shi"—he saw the senior officers gathered around the table as they stared at him and thought better of his word choice—"dump, which is saying something considering the condition of most FOBs in Iraq."

"That's a fair assessment," the SecDef said.

"Do we know where Naseefa is now?"

The DNI spoke up. "Our asset indicated he moved to Accra and is staying in a house Ami owns. He's under the personal protection of Ami's security forces."

Charlie had stayed quiet but cleared her throat. "What do you need us to do, Mr. Secretary? Lots of details so far, but I'm not sure where this is going. Plenty of teams, such as Seals, CAG, and Force Recon, could get pulled into this. Why us?"

"The Omega Group and you, particularly Ms. Martin, have skills not always found in other teams. Ami is holding an arms auction at his compound in Ghana one week from today. He has these types of sales yearly but rarely done face-to-face. In this day and age, most transactions can be facilitated online. This one is different. Our intelligence indicates the nuclear weapon will be the crown jewel of the auction, but there will be lots of other weapons and commodities for sale. The whole affair is by invitation only. A who's who of international criminals and despotic leaders will be in attendance bidding for the items."

"Not many nations, let alone criminals, could afford to buy a nuke," the colonel said.

"Agreed," the SecDef replied. "But this gathering will have a lot of heavy hitters. People with deep pockets."

"And what do you expect us to do, Mr. Secretary?" Troy asked.

With a wide smile, the SecDef said, "You're going to attend the auction, Captain Evans."

"Me?"

"No, not just you. Charlie will go with you."

"I don't understand. How will Charlie and I get in? We're not exactly on the international criminal who's who list."

"You both speak French."

Troy looked at Charlie, and she looked right back at him. They both raised their eyebrows, acknowledging that it was an accurate statement. In unison, they both said, "Oui."

"Two of the invited guests are from Montreal. They are a married couple and the largest arms dealers in all of Canada."

"And?" Charlie asked.

The SecDef raised his eyebrows. "You're gonna take their place at the auction."

"I'm pretty sure Ami will know Charlie and I are not this couple," Troy said. "Surely he knows what they look like?"

SecDef shook his head. "No, he doesn't. They've never met. This couple are ghosts and always remain in the shadows. There's no known image of them in any government database. We have already confirmed Ami has never met them."

"Why did Ami invite them?"

"They are Ami's ticket into Canada, and he has done sporadic business with the couple over the years. He rewards his most faithful buyers with this once-in-a-lifetime invitation to meet face-to-face. Plus, they are looking for a dirty bomb, and Ami is offering one at this sale."

Troy looked skeptical. "Okay, say you are right, and nobody knows what they look like. I'm sure Ami will have some sort of way to verify everyone's identity. They won't be checking passports at the front door."

"Correct. There will be biometric verifications."

"That could create a problem," Troy said. "And if Ami has never met them and nobody knows what they look like, how will a biometric confirmation be possible?"

"We have it covered," the SecDef said.

"Ami can use DNA, fingerprints, or facial recognition devices to verify identities. And this couple were both fingerprinted at a young age. Ami has that data."

"I take it you have a way to bypass those checks for Charlie and myself?" Troy asked.

The SecDef nodded. "Captain, we wouldn't be having this conversation if we did not."

"And the couple? Where are they now?" Charlie asked.

"Their private jet left Montreal yesterday headed east. We placed an agent on the flight crew. Smoke filled the cabin, which forced the plane to make an emergency landing in Newfoundland."

"And when it landed?" Troy asked.

"Let's just say regular customs officials did not meet the plane. We detained the couple, and they are now in a secure facility we maintain outside St. Johns."

"Hold up," Troy said. "We take on these people's identities, go to this arms sale at Ami's compound in Ghana, and then what? If the nukes aren't there, what do you expect us to do?"

"Besides not get caught," Charlie added.

"Ami is paranoid about being spied on. So much so that he has no internet at the compound. He doesn't even allow cell phones on-site. Even for himself."

"I sense a but coming," Troy said.

"A big fat one," Charlie looked at Troy and made an obvious eye roll.

"But he runs one of the largest illegal arms business in the world. You can't keep track of all that with a pencil and paper. He has a computer system, a high-tech one at that. It's just not connected to anything outside the compound. It's a fully enclosed network but completely off the grid."

"We're supposed to get in and steal files from this enclosed network?" Troy asked. "Files that may help us find the nukes?"

"Essentially, yes," SecDef said. "But there's a little more to it than that."

"There is always more to it than that," Digger replied.

"Listen up, Omegas and Charlie. Here's our plan ..." The SecDef began.

7

CRYSTAL CITY

Two hours later, SecDef Wastradowski paused, then cleared his throat. He looked at those sitting on the table's right side, across from The Omega Group, and gestured with his left hand. "I'll need everyone to step out for this next part, excluding you, of course, Charlie."

The Secretary of Homeland Security, Director of National Intelligence, Chairman of Joint Chiefs of Staff, National Security Advisor, Attorney General, and Director of the Central Intelligence Agency got up and left the room one by one.

Once the others were gone, he turned toward the Omegas. "We have one more thing to discuss before formally wrapping up." He put his pointer finger in the air to indicate, *one minute*, picked up the receiver from the Cisco digital phone to his right and, a moment later, spoke into the receiver, "Send him in."

A minute later, a man in a dark suit entered from a door hidden from view built into the side of the conference room wall. The man carried himself differently from someone at the agency or bureau. But he had the look of a Secret Service agent. At least, that's what the team surmised later when they discussed the exchange.

Nobody around the table, except the SecDef, knew the person's identity.

The man in the dark suit came around to the head of the table and stood beside SecDef Wastradowski, who continued to sit in his chair.

With the briefest eye contact, the man looked at everyone, including Charlie, before speaking. "When your team recovers the nukes, and before they are delivered via the method described by the SecDef, we need something removed from each device and given personally to me."

"And you are?" Troy asked, speaking for the entire group.

The man in the suit displayed a prominent scowl at the question. "Someone who is requesting two items at the bequest of the President of the United States."

Troy's gaze narrowed. "That didn't answer the question, my man."

The SecDef raised his hand. "Who he is doesn't matter, Captain Evans, but your team can be certain his request comes straight from the president.

"Okay, so you work for, or at least speak for, POTUS, but what do we call you?" Troy pressed the issue.

"Nothing. I don't need to be called anything. All you need to know is I am here on behalf of the president."

"How mysterious," the Jackal replied, something the entire team thought, but only he uttered.

"Just listen to what he has to say," the SecDef said. "And this is not a request, Omegas. It's an order from your Commander-In-Chief."

The man in the dark suit looked back at the SecDef and nodded, then spoke for three minutes uninterrupted to The Omega Group members and Charlie.

When he stopped speaking, the colonel, who had remained quiet for a while, spoke up. "We appreciate the succinct and direct instructions."

"Why does POTUS want it back?" Troy asked. "Reagan has been dead for a long time. What does it matter if it got out?"

"The president is concerned that if those two items were to see the light of day, it could reflect negatively on the office of the presidency. Regardless of who occupies the office."

"And?"

"My job is to protect the office of the presidency at all costs. If the president feels the item needs to remain out of the public eye, then that is all any of us need to know. The directive is clear: retrieve the nukes and call in the team as instructed by the SecDef. However, your team is to remove the items the president requested and bring them back to me personally. If, for some unforeseen reason, they can't be retrieved, they must be destroyed."

"Copy that," Troy replied.

"You and your team can assure me that will occur?" the man in the suit asked.

"Well, there's no guarantees in life, my man. But we weren't brought into this situation because we have a reputation for failure."

"Good." The mysterious man turned and left the room through the same doorway built into the wall.

Once the man in the suit was gone, the SecDef spoke again. "Now we are done. Get after it, and don't let us down."

"We won't," Troy replied in a confident tone.

8

CRYSTAL CITY

It was after midnight on the East Coast, and exhaustion set in. However, the colonel and the rest of the team, including their newest member, Charlie, stayed another hour after the SecDef left the secure conference room. A decision on where to go first resulted in an intense discussion among all the team members. As always, they had full operational authority. After much back-and-forth, Troy recommended the course of action. The colonel agreed with Troy's fact-finding detour since they needed more intel.

As they left the conference room and made their way down the hall, Colonel Marshall, Troy, and Charlie led the way. Directly behind them, the Jackal nudged Harry, a wide grin on his face. He crouched slightly, his hand held low like he was about to catch a football, his gaze squarely on Charlie's pert derrière.

"Now that's nice," the Jackal said.

Harry nodded and chuckled.

The kick came at him lightning quick, and the next thing the Jackal knew, he was on the floor. Stunned, with his head spinning, he never saw her pivot or the roundhouse kick that struck him in the solar plexus. As he gasped for breath, Charlie was on top of him with her left foot on his throat.

In a stern but direct tone, she said, "If you ever disrespect me like that again, I'll kick you directly in the fucking balls. That is if you have any." She let the words sink in for a moment. "Nod, if you get my drift."

The Jackal, still dazed by the severity and speed she possessed, nodded after a few seconds.

Charlie pulled her foot off his throat, stood fully upright, and offered her hand to help pull him up. It took a moment, but he reached up and felt the smooth hand within his own as she yanked him to his feet. The strangest part occurred when she leaned in close, kissed his cheek, turned, and walked away.

Harry stood near his teammate and patted him on the back. "Dude!" he exclaimed. "You just got your ass handed to you by a chick!"

The Jackal grimaced slightly. "Sweet fancy Moses, I think I may be in love," he mumbled.

Charlie heard the comment and smirked ever so slightly but kept her gaze straight ahead.

Troy, who walked next to her, leaned closer. "You're gonna fit in fine with the boys, Charlie," he said before adding, "Yup, you'll be just fine."

9

— · —

RONALD REAGAN NATIONAL AIRPORT

GULFSTREAM G450

The Omega Group climbed the air stairs of the same Gulfstream G450 that had brought them to Virginia earlier in the day. They would have to sleep on the flight east, as it was 6,215 miles to their destination, including one stop to refuel. Flight time alone would be close to thirteen hours.

As they settled into the plush leather seats, the stewardess came by and took their drink orders.

"What will you have, Cap?" the outgoing woman in the blue skirt and matching blouse asked as she reached the row where Troy and Jesús sat.

Troy grinned. "Thanks for taking care of us, Megan. You don't have Bushmills Black Bush, do you?" It was Troy's favorite Irish whiskey but not a standard drink you would find on most private jets.

The woman smiled warmly. "I do," she said with a subtle wink. "Just for you, Cap. Courtesy of our pilot."

With a broad smile, Troy replied, "Thank Captain Messick for me. I should have known he would hook a brother up. And better make mine a double."

"I'll do just that," Megan replied. "And you?" she asked Jesús.

Jesús smiled. "My usual, Megan. Please and thank you."

"Of course. Glad to oblige."

A few minutes later, Megan returned with two drinks.

"That looks almost like a screwdriver, Jesús," Troy said as he saw the glass his friend held.

"It is Cap," Jesús replied with a grin. "She just held the vodka."

The two men clanged their glasses together. "Bottoms up," Troy said.

"Back to Iraq yet again," Jesús replied.

Troy shook his head. "Oye. Not a place I ever long to return to."

As the two men spoke, Charlie took the open seat across from them.

"Did you put in your drink order?" Troy asked.

Charlie smiled. "Yes, I told her already. Just water for me. I don't need alcohol clogging my judgment as we head east."

Jesús raised his glass with one hand, and with the other free hand, he tapped his chest. "Respect. I'm in the same way, ma'am."

"Ma'am?" Charlie asked. "Aren't we about the same age?"

Jesús smirked. "Sure, but I watched you kick the Jackal's ass, so I don't want to get on your bad side."

"Calling me ma'am ain't the way to do that."

"Duly noted," Jesús quipped.

Troy took another sip of his Bushmills. "Well, you're both doing better than me. This will help take the edge off and hopefully allow me to get a little shuteye in an hour or so."

"I get it, Cap. Trust me, I drank a bunch in college. But once I watched my roommate Chloe's flight hit the second tower. Well. My drinking days were done."

With a nod, Troy responded. "I get that. Those events shaped a lot of our lives in ways we didn't really comprehend at the time of the 9/11 attacks. Some folks drink to remember, while others drink to forget."

"I read your file, Cap, and fully understand how what took place in NYC altered your path."

Troy pursed his lips. "Absolutely. One thing those extremist pricks didn't calculate in their equation was that flying the planes into the towers, the Pentagon, and whatever Flight 93's target happened to be, well, it turned out to be one of the greatest recruitment opportunities of the modern era for the Department of Defense." Troy paused. "I know many more people who joined up after the terrorist attacks, then joined for any other reason. Me being one of those."

"Copy that," Charlie said. "I've experienced the same sentiments during my years in the military."

"I take it Division S comprises female soldiers with similar reasons for joining?" Jesús asked.

Charlie shrugged. "Yes, and no. There's certainly a few who came in after 9/11, but most of the team is a lot younger. Many were only a few years old during the attacks and subsequent wars that took place in Afghanistan and Iraq."

Troy and Jesús nodded but said nothing in response.

"I did have a question for you, though." Charlie said.

"Yeah, what's that?" Troy asked.

"Something I saw in your file."

Troy raised an eyebrow. "What about it?"

"Several redacted pages regarding your youth are in there," Charlie said.

"That's true." Troy nodded and shifted slightly in his chair.

"Care to elaborate on what the big secret is?"

"Huh." Troy glanced at the floor and then back up. "That's a story for another time, another place. Let's just say that the government redacts some things for legitimate national security reasons. In contrast, other things get redacted because the government can be weird about events even if they are public knowledge."

"And your redactions are for the former or the latter?"

Troy shrugged. "Let's just say sometimes I drink to forget. The details that the government redacted are memories I prefer not to have."

Charlie pursed her lips. "Roger that, Cap. I have a few of those myself."

10

KIRKUK, IRAQ

FORWARD OPERATING BASE MCFLY

Almost twenty-four hours later and seven time zones ahead of Washington D.C., the team was reminded why they all despised the "sandbox."

As they unloaded their gear at Forward Operating Base (FOB) McFly just east of Kirkuk, Troy saw a familiar face walking his way from another part of the compound.

"Radar!" Troy yelled.

Shannon "Radar" Roberts smiled widely as he turned and scurried over to his old friend. "Troy, how have you been? Haven't seen you in this part of the shit-hole for at least a year."

Troy laughed. "Kickin' it, my friend. They keep us on our toes, and we don't stay in the same place for very long."

"Still doing some of that secret squirrel stuff?" Radar asked.

Troy shrugged, rolled his eyes, and smiled but said nothing.

"Hear no evil, see no evil, speak no evil," Radar replied.

"Something like that," Troy answered. "How's Stacy and Chase?"

"Family is good. The boy is growing like a weed. Don't get to see them enough, but you know the drill."

"True that. Seen any action?" Troy asked.

"Me?" A sinister smirk formed at the corner of Radar's lips. "Maybe a little. You know I'm not some fobbit who is just riding out his time in this godforsaken country. I like to shoot at stuff when the opportunity arises." He offered a big grin. "You here for a little bit? Maybe grab some chow later?"

"Just passing through, my friend, but I'll try to track you down before we scoot. Maybe we can grab a coffee."

"Deal, be safe out there." Radar reached out and shook his friend's hand. "The unfriendly locals seem to think we might be target practice when we leave the FOB."

"Yes, sir, and always," Troy replied. He continued on to the Tactical Operations Center (TOC) and didn't encounter anyone he knew.

━━◄O►━━

The Omega Group left FOB McFly and traveled toward Bazain several hours after they arrived. Jalal al-Majid, the son of Naseefa, was in the middle of another interrogation session when the team met with the commanding officer, and it would be many hours before they could question Jalal. Troy utilized the downtime by driving out to Lake Dukan and checking out the abandoned facility that held the nuclear weapons when Saddam was in power. Surprisingly, the colonel decided to tag along. Commanding officers rarely join their team on missions, but Colonel Marshall wasn't your typical officer. He got sick of sitting behind a desk which came with the territory when you commanded a team.

The drive was uneventful—actually, it was boring as hell—and loud music filled the void. Since leaving the base, the Omegas saw more camels than humans. Violence in that region of Iraq died out over the years, and most of the flare-ups shifted to the west.

Just past Chamchamal, the two vehicles turned north. Their destination was the secret facility on the southern tip of Lake Dukan, which, until 2001, contained the two nukes.

The road toward the lake was smooth since it was newly paved courtesy of the United States taxpayers, who had pretty much rebuilt parts of Iraq for two decades with not much to show for the cash infusion. The drive imagery consisted of mountains in the distance and rolling hills on either side of the road. It was a desolate landscape with little to see besides the frequent reminders of constant warfare, which littered much of the Iraqi countryside.

⚊⚊⚊◆⚊⚊⚊

The music stopped pumping from the vehicle's speakers, and Troy's ears were immediately grateful. An hour straight of Rage Against the Machine was a bit much, even for someone who worked out to their songs on his Spotify playlist.

Troy turned around in the driver's seat. "What's next? My ears are about to bleed, so maybe we can get somewhat lighter. We still have forty minutes till Lake Dukan."

"You want some sissy music, a little Elton John maybe?" the Jackal asked from the back seat.

"No, Sarge is in the other vehicle," Troy retorted with a wide grin. "He'd likely cry if he missed "Daniel" playing at insane decibels."

"Let the mademoiselle decide." The Jackal turned toward Charlie.

"Whoa!" Troy exclaimed. "You're letting the newbie pick songs already?"

"Hey!" Charlie sat next to Troy and turned her head sharply at the comment. "Why shouldn't I get a say?" Her eyes narrowed as she glared at him. "Is it 'cause I'm a chick?"

"Of course not!" Troy shook his head as his face displayed a faux surprised expression and an imperceptible roll of his eyes. "We believe in a military that enforces equality, diversity, and whatever other PC nonsense I'm told to say as the commanding officer of this team." Troy chuckled. "Besides, I don't make the rules. I just enforce them, and it's not my fault. The Jackal has the hots for you. He's only letting you pick the songs because he's trying to make it downtown at some point." Troy adjusted his rearview mirror, and the Jackal's reflection was square in view. As the two men locked eyes, Troy said, "He must feel he has a real shot at rounding the bases."

"Man, I'm still standing next to home plate facing an 0-2 count with Charlie!" The Jackal shook his head.

"With a corked bat, from what I can tell." Harry sat next to the Jackal and poked him in the arm.

"No way, dude, you got to first already," Troy said. "Don't you remember when you got your ass kicked in the hallway before she planted a kiss on your cheek?"

"Oh, yeah, that." The Jackal threw his head back. "How can I forget? I'll never wash that cheek."

"First is as far as you're getting, playboy." Charlie glanced back at the Jackal and gave him a not-too-subtle wink. "You won't be rounding any bases, and no third base coach will wave you home."

To say that line put the biggest shit-eating grin on the Jackal's face would be the understatement of the year.

The Jackal reached into his rucksack on the floorboard of the vehicle. He fished around inside before pulling out a non-labeled plastic pill bottle. He held it up. "Anyone want one?"

"Dare I ask what that is?" Troy said.

"Please tell me that's some leftover herbal remedy the voodoo witch doctor concocted?" Harry asked.

The reference was a loaded question and had to do with one of the Jackal's many exes. This one spent an inordinate amount of money seeing a naturalist in the world of non-licensed holistic health. Often, references came up about this *Voodoo Witch Doctor*, and they always ended with lots of laughter and a fair amount of cursing.

"Heeeell, no," the Jackal replied in a drawn-out tone. "I bought this shit at GNC."

"Then where's the label? And why did you take it off?" Troy asked.

The Jackal shrugged and smirked at the same time. "Cause not everything I bring is kosher in all the countries we travel to."

Troy and Harry exchanged glances and said, "Don't ask, don't tell."

Everyone but Charlie laughed. "I'm clearly behind on the inside jokes between you chuckleheads."

Jesús's voice interrupted the back-and-forth banter. He and the other members followed behind Troy in an identical black armored Mercedes SUV.

"We've got company Cap, and they're approaching fast," Jesús said on the comms.

Troy looked into the rearview mirror of the expensive German vehicle they borrowed from the spooks. He then glanced toward the side mirror but didn't see anything.

"Roger that. How far back?"

Jesús, who was behind the wheel, consulted with Digger, who sat behind him and had his optics trained on vehicles approaching from the south.

"At least five miles. They appear to be in a four-truck convoy," Digger replied.

"Any chance they're friendlies?" Troy asked. "Iraqi army possibly?"

"Negative Cap, two of the pickups appear to have .50 cals mounted to the beds. It's hard to see clearly, but at least one of them has an insurgency flag waving above the cab."

"Copy that." Troy frowned. The senior officer at FOB McFly offered to send a small contingent of soldiers with them for support. Troy passed on the offer and immediately wondered if it was the right call. Unfortunately for the Omegas, returning to McFly wasn't an option, and the threat would need to be neutralized.

"Might I suggest we jump on it and get this baby up to eighty-eight miles per hour?" the Jackal said. "I, for one, don't want to see any serious shit. After all, we borrowed this ride from FOB McFly."

Troy rolled his eyes. "Only you could work in a *Back To The Future* crack at a time like this!"

11

IRAQ

Troy looked ahead and saw the road remained flat for many miles. They were driving through a wide valley. He knew the Omegas needed cover if these four trucks were coming for them, so he dropped the pedal to the floor. The powerful SUV responded immediately, and the RPMs jumped as they sped up. Jesús mirrored the increase in speed as he followed several car lengths behind.

"Let's put some distance between us and them," Troy said over his comms as he got the SUV to almost one hundred and forty kilometers per hour.

"You gonna try to outrun them?" Jesús asked.

"No, I'm just trying to buy us time as we look for our opportunity to strike where we can level the playing field."

Troy glanced at Charlie. "Welcome to Iraq," he said in a sarcastic tone. "I really hate this hell hole."

"Me too." She nodded. "For some reason, jihad isn't big in the South Pacific, so the Middle East is where we earn our stripes."

"True that," Troy said. He looked at the floorboard near Charlie's feet. "Grab the optics down there and see if you can find us some cover up ahead."

The voice of Jesús came over the comms. "They have increased their speed, Cap, to match ours. Clearly, they have hostile intentions."

"Copy that," Troy said.

"Can we call in air support?" the Jackal asked from the backseat. "Get a Reaper to drop a few hellfire's on their ass and take out the convoy?"

"Negative, it's all on us," Troy said as he shook his head. "The president issued a drawdown, and not many drones are tasked with this region. Before we could get air support, they would likely engage us."

Seconds later, Charlie found what Troy requested. "I got a structure on the side of the road about seven clicks ahead. It may be an old roadside checkpoint. It's pretty rundown but appears to be concrete. One building looks to be about ten meters long."

"Perfect cover," Troy said. He paused, and the plan came together in his mind within seconds. He activated the push-to-talk (PTT) switch on the left side of his chest and spoke to the whole team at the same time. "We'll pull off the road's edge near the structure ahead. Follow my lead, spin the SUVs around, and place them in a V-formation. I want Sarge's bravo on one hood and Digger on the other with his long rifle. The rest of us will scatter amongst the structure and the vehicles for cover. Let them take the first shot so their intentions are clear. Then we unleash hell on them. Understood?"

12

IRAQ

Troy received seven affirmative responses, which indicated everyone acknowledged the command. Even the colonel, who rode in the vehicle with Jesús, ceded tactical command to Troy while on an operation. He had hired the best and trusted Troy knew the course of action needed when the proverbial shit hit the fan.

"How many grenade launchers do we have?" Troy asked.

"Two," the Jackal responded. "I have one always on my HK, and Jesús has one he can attach to his."

"Okay, be ready to use them when the convoy gets close and opens fire," Troy said.

"Roger that," both men said in unison.

"Zero in, shoot straight, show no mercy," Troy said. "And remember the three F's!"

The other five Omega Group members responded with a "Hooah!"

Charlie looked at Troy with a puzzled expression but didn't say anything.

Everyone fell silent as they geared up mentally, each in their own way, for the coming assault. Time slowed down for each of them, and visualization was a common tool utilized by the team. They might see the events play out in different ways internally, but the end result never varied.

Several minutes later, they approached the dilapidated structure. Charlie was right. It looked like an old, abandoned military checkpoint. Several walls remained upright, and enough rubble provided excellent cover for an entire squad.

There was enough room for the eight soldiers comprising The Omega Group at that moment to spread out and cover all the angles.

Troy waited for the last second before he slowed down fast and cut the wheel hard to turn the Mercedes back toward the approaching convoy. Jesús made a similar move and abruptly stopped just off the side of the road with the front corner of his vehicle next to Troy's. Everyone bailed and grabbed the gear and ammo needed. The Omega Group had learned from constant overseas missions to always roll heavy and expect the unexpected when their boots hit the ground.

The team was in position less than a ninety seconds after the two vehicles stopped.

Within seconds, Digger had the bipod down on his Barrett Mk22 MRAD sniper rifle. He leaned against the side of the Mercedes and sighted in his optics at the approaching vehicles. The first thing to slow down was his breathing. He took measured, deliberate breaths. Next, he focused on lowering his racing heartbeat. As was his normal custom, he flexed his right index finger several times to get it ready.

Next to him on the opposite hood, Sarge had the M240 Bravo setup. The belt-fed automatic rifle air-cooled could unleash around seven hundred and fifty rounds per minute. If necessary, the ammo can deliver the 7.62 belt-fed rounds with a second can in reserve. However, if Sarge needed all fifteen hundred rounds, the Omegas were more than likely screwed.

The four Toyota Tundra pickups were less than a mile away.

Charlie naturally assimilated into the team. She was at the far left side of the structure and had her weapon ready to fire, the butt of the rifle snug against her shoulder. In her left hand, she held the optics. As the vehicles moved closer, she relayed what she saw on comms.

"The lead vehicle has two in the cab, one in the rear. The passenger looks like he has an RPG. The second vehicle has a mounted .50 cal, while the last truck does as well. I count a total of thirteen ... no, wait, possibly fourteen hajis between all four vehicles."

"Like shooting fish in a barrel," the Jackal said as he racked his weapon.

Harry reached into his T-shirt, removed his silver cross, kissed it, and then made the sign of the cross with the fingertips of his right hand.

Jesús bowed his head and prayed for safety before raising his weapon to usher the hostiles into the afterlife. The irony of both actions not lost on him or the others who comprised the team.

"Everyone ready?" Troy asked. "Let's do this by the book. Take the shot once they engage us, Digger."

Digger focused on the second vehicle, particularly the head of the man behind the vehicle-mounted machine gun. He waited patiently until the man fired his first burst. The shots were erratic and high. They hit nowhere near The Omega Group. The poorly trained man knew little about firing a heavy machine gun from a moving vehicle. His loss. Digger exhaled and squeezed off a round at the end of the breath. The bullet went just to the left. Considering the speed of the approaching vehicle, it was not unlikely. Few could make that shot.

The man on the truck heard the bullet whiz by his head and felt the velocity of the lead pierce the sky mere inches from him as he looked to his left, which was purely instinctual.

Digger recovered from the missed shot, adjusted, and fired a second round. They were too far away to hear the loud *thwack* as the bullet struck the side of the man's head. It sounded like a baseball bat striking a watermelon to those within the truck. Through his optics, Digger did see the red mist of blood as the hostile fighter's head exploded into the dry air. Pieces of the dead man's skull littered the desert landscape.

The force of the round pulled the jihadist from the truck bed and flung the corpse off the back. His body landed on the hood of the Tundra that followed. The driver of the vehicle, startled by the body that landed on his windshield, jerked the wheel and over-corrected. This sent the truck careening to the right, off the pavement, and into the desert landscape. When it hit the ditch, the Tundra lurched to the side and then rolled over. The driver's compartment crumpled and crushed to death all four men inside.

A helluva shot.

One bullet, five kills.

One bullet, five kills.

13

IRAQ

Sarge held his weapon tight as sweat dripped down the side of his head from the hairline. The lead vehicle was now close enough for him to open up the fully automatic weapon. As he pulled back on the trigger, the five-pound, eight-ounce trigger pull shook the gun, and bullets flew out of the barrel faster than his eyes could see them. Spent shell casings made a metallic clang as they came in contact with the hood of the Mercedes. Trails of smoke snuck out from the empty brass as the smell of cordite filled the air. Bullets shredded the front of the Tundra within seconds as round after round pierced the thin sheet metal and slammed into the engine block.

Somehow, two occupants dove out of the vehicle, including the man with the RPG. A third man leaped from the truck's rear and landed on the dusty ground. Troy, who stood toward the back-quarter panel of the Mercedes closest to the road, stepped out and unloaded a hail of bullets.

The first round struck the driver in the throat. As he involuntarily reached up to the gaping hole that opened in his windpipe, the next round struck him in the forehead, and he dropped to the ground.

The passenger hit the ground hard and rolled while still holding onto his RPG. No small feat. He appeared startled but raised the grenade launcher toward the two black Mercedes vehicles one hundred yards before him. Harry had him sighted in and before the hostile could depress the trigger, Harry sent a three-round burst into his face. The RPG fell to the ground without being fired.

Troy swung back behind the SUV for cover as a fury of bullets from the third man bounced off the side panel where he had just stood. As he moved to his left, he saw his team in full battle mode. It was a cacophony for the ears and a sight of beauty to behold with the eyes.

Each person fulfilled their role and worked together as a well-oiled machine. Troy believed his team's movements were like music, with the crescendo being death to whoever attempted to bring the fight to the Omegas.

About twenty feet away from Troy, Charlie stood fast at her position and unloaded a volley of bullets at the last man from the lead truck. Her arms, while certainly feminine, displayed distinct, toned muscles as she flexed and fired off three-round bursts from her rifle. The man collapsed as Charlie's bullets found their mark. Her technique perfect, her poise something to behold. It didn't hurt she had a body that made it hard for a man to divert his eyes.

Troy watched as the sun cast her silhouette across the structure. The provocative shadow moved and swayed in an intoxicating fashion. The look of an angel but a hardened warrior's grim, efficient marksmanship. Just like her namesake Sekhmet, Charlie moved like a lioness and pounced upon her prey with lethal force.

The two remaining Tundras came to a screeching halt on the pavement side-by-side. Digger easily dispatched the man who stood behind the second machine gun. In unison, Jesús and the Jackal stepped away from the structure that shielded them, and each shot a 40 mike-mike into the front end of the two vehicles. The engine blocks exploded as the two high-explosive rounds hit their intended targets. The fighters dove for cover out the truck doors. Several of them survived the explosions, but their luck proved fleeting. The Omega Group picked off the remaining fighters one by one. They stood no chance against the clearly superior fighting force.

Even the colonel, who rarely saw action anymore, raised his weapon and fired off a deadly burst that neutralized one attacker. Each of the members scored a kill in the firefight. The fourteen Iraqis never had a chance against The Omega Group. Their fate sealed the moment they engaged the team.

After surveying the battle scene, Troy gave the all-clear signal. The team came out from behind their cover, searched the vehicles, and checked each body to make sure everyone was dead.

Troy was near the two vehicles struck by the grenades when Harry called out to him. "Cap! You better come take a look at this."

Troy hustled over to the vehicle, which was farthest away.

Harry pulled the bodies out and made a startling discovery.

As Troy approached, Harry handed him a packet.

"Found this in the center console. It's not good, Cap. It's not good at all." Harry displayed a concerned look.

Troy took what Harry had given him and looked it over. His face contorted as he flipped through the eight glossy pieces of paper and shook his head, part in disgust, part in anger.

"How's this possible?" Harry asked.

Troy shook his head but didn't answer for a moment. "Finish your sweep."

Troy walked straight to the Mercedes, closest to the road, where the colonel hung up his phone.

"I called in the attack to the command center at McFly." The colonel noticed the upset look on Troy's face. "CO dispatched a cleanup crew to gather the bodies and see if they can ID any of them." He paused. "What is it?"

Troy held the eight black and white photos and pushed them into the colonel's chest. "The DOD has a leak, Colonel, and it could have gotten us all killed today."

Colonel Marshall reached up to his chest and pulled down the photos. As he flipped through each one, his mind raced. There was a photo of each operator, including himself and even Charlie. At the top of each image, it said in Arabic, *The Omega Group, Kill On Sight*. He heard what Troy said, but his mind went in a different direction. He nodded but said nothing.

"I don't like being hunted," Troy replied. "Especially when we have such a critical mission. It's awfully hard to keep up an effective fight on two fronts."

The colonel ignored the statement. "Others besides the DOD know we're in country."

Troy stared into his eyes. "So, what are you going to do about it?"

The colonel frowned. "I'm not sure yet."

"And what do we do in the meantime?"

Colonel Marshall rubbed his chin. "We continue on to Lake Dukan as you planned. Then, when we head back to the FOB, you will personally question Jalal. This incident changes nothing. Stick to the plan."

"Our team being hunted changes everything!" Troy exclaimed. There was no hiding his emotions. A pissed-off Troy meant trouble for anyone who stood in his way.

"Leave that to me." The colonel put both hands firmly on Troy's broad shoulders. "Keep on mission. Stay on task. Let me take care of what occurred today." He held up the photos and did not hide the look of disgust on his face.

Troy had reservations, but he also implicitly trusted Colonel Marshall. He reluctantly nodded. "As you wish, sir," he said as he turned away.

The colonel grabbed his arm.

Troy turned back.

"And son ... watch your six."

"I sleep with one eye open, sir," Troy said as he walked to the nearest vehicle to see what their firepower had done.

14

— • —

IRAQ

Troy walked toward the structure where Jesús and Sarge huddled deep in conversation. Troy joined them, and they all bowed their heads for a moment.

Charlie watched from a distance, unsure of what the men said.

When the discussion ended, Troy walked back to the vehicles, and Charlie approached. He smiled as he saw her. "You did well out there. Division S has some skills!"

"Expect otherwise?" Charlie asked.

"No, not really. I knew you could hold your own."

"Can I ask you a question?"

"Sure," Troy replied.

"Before the firefight, you said to remember the three F's. What's that all about?"

"Faith, Family, Freedom. The reason we do what we do."

She had a quizzical look on her face. "Freedom I get since most soldiers proclaim that one in spades. Family is a little more curious. I thought all of you guys were single except the colonel?"

"Sure, but we still have family, even if none of us are married. It's always good to remind oneself why you stay in the fight. And besides, the six of us are like family. In some ways, our bond is tighter, and the brotherhood is stronger. Blood isn't always thicker than water."

"Okay, I'll give you that. And faith?"

Troy shrugged. "What about it?"

"Um, well," Charlie paused for a moment. "No offense, but you guys don't strike me as very religious. That is except for Jesús."

A smile formed at the corner of Troy's mouth. "I tend to think of religion as the antithesis of faith. Over the years, I've made it a point not to confuse the two. Faith is the substance of things hoped for, the evidence of things not seen. Religion is man's attempt to explain God, and I honestly think man gets it wrong more than he gets it right. God cares about the inside, not so much the external."

"Sheesh. That's kinda deep, Cap." Charlie raised her eyebrows. "You a pastor somewhere when you are not kicking in doors?"

"Um, no on the pastor question. Now, I can't speak for everyone, but the guys all have faith in some measure. Not to say we all believe the same way, but that's not for me to judge."

"Even the Jackal?" Charlie asked with a wide smile.

"The Jackal is a complicated guy, and his faith might be buried a little deeper than some of us. He can be a hard nut to crack, but there's much more than his crass, immature exterior. Inside, his heart is true, his motives just."

"Interesting," Charlie said.

"Let's load up. We'll have countless hours to discuss philosophy, religion, or you name it while in Ghana."

They climbed into the vehicle. The Jackal and Harry were already waiting for them.

"So fellas, when do we discuss your love lives?" Charlie asked with a laugh as she looked around at the guys.

"I nominate Cap to start that chat," Harry said. "All in favor?"

Troy shook his head and glared at Charlie. "You like brief, boring conversations, huh?"

Charlie's eyes narrowed. "I'm sure you have one or more stories to share when it comes to taking a lover, Troy."

The Jackal spoke up. "Better call him Cap. Only one woman calls him by his given name, and that's Cate."

"Ahh, so the plot thickens," Charlie said.

Troy turned around and pointed his finger. "Shut your pie-hole, Jackal!"

The Jackal winked. "Love you too, brother!"

15

LAKE DUKAN, IRAQ

The two black Mercedes SUVs pulled up to the chain-link fence. *No Trespassing* signs peppered the slightly rusty barrier every few feet in Arabic.

Charlie looked at Troy. "You sure we're in the right place?"

Troy nodded. "GPS, don't lie." He touched the digital screen on the dashboard with his index finger.

"But there's nothing of significance here," she said.

"You've just described most of this Godforsaken country," Troy replied with a smirk.

Charlie was right. It looked like little more than a mostly empty lot. A six-foot-tall fence with barbed wire atop surrounded what appeared to be a five-acre barren plot of earth. The scattered vegetation that littered the area consisted of red yucca, and Jericho rose plants. There was also a handful of Gum Arabic trees that dotted the land. In the distance, the emerald waters of Lake Dukan and the barren mountain-scape surrounding the largest lake in the Kurdistan region of Iraq served as a backdrop.

In the direct center of the fenced land, several trees partially obstructed a slab of concrete in the shape of a right triangle that jutted out eight feet high from the dry, parched earth. The drab tan-painted concrete peeled off after years of exposure to the brutal rays of the Mideast sun.

All eight of them climbed from the two SUVs. The area was desolate, with no dwelling or building within eyesight, but no one took any chances. As they slowly made their way forward, they scanned every direction for hidden threats. They all cradled HK416s as they moved away from the vehicles toward the perimeter fence.

Before them the only sign of civilization, besides the concrete triangle jutting out of the ground, was remnants of a decrepit guard shack. The weathered roof partially collapsed as time and nature displayed her awesome power. The chain-link fence surrounding the property was still closed, secured by a thick padlock.

Troy looked at Sarge. "Mind grabbing the bolt cutters from the vehicle, Sarge?"

"Sure thing," Sarge said as he walked back to the Mercedes.

"Grab a pry bar while you're at it," Troy added.

"You got it, Cap."

Sarge returned a minute later. He squeezed the cutter handles together in one fluid motion of his enormous forearms, and the heavy lock snapped easily as it fell to the ground.

Once through the gate, the team approached the ninety-degree vertical side of the concrete structure. A heavy steel door greeted them. The door was seven feet tall and five feet wide, and although they had no way of knowing it, its thickness was eighteen inches. It was essentially a blast door. To the right of the door was a metal panel twelve inches square. It was smooth except for a keyhole directly in the center.

"You got the first key?" Troy asked as he looked back at the colonel.

"I do." Colonel Marshall stepped forward with a single, oversized brass key in his right hand. He inserted the key and turned it clockwise until a distinct *click* sound occurred. The panel opened to reveal a twelve-digit electronic keypad. Next, he entered the eight-digit code followed by the pound key, the access code provided during the briefing by the SecDef.

1-1-0-7-1-9-7-6-#

As he entered the final digit and pressed the pound key, a hissing sound occurred on the right side of the door, followed by the unmistakable sound of three locking rods sliding out from inside the door. A dull thud occurred when the process concluded to indicate the door's locking mechanism disengaged.

Troy pulled on the handle, and slowly, with an elongated creaking sound, the heavy door gave way and opened. They could only see the first few steps down and nothing but utter darkness below that. On the left-hand wall above the top step, several switches were in the downward position. Troy flicked the switches up, and the fluorescent lights above the stairs turned on after several brief flickers.

"Let there be light," Jesús said.

"I can't believe there's power out here in the middle of nowhere," Harry said.

The light fixtures made a humming sound as they illuminated. Troy smiled and looked at Charlie. He gestured with his right hand at the descending stairs. "Ladies first."

"On no," she replied as she stuck her index finger up and waved it back and forth. "No need to be gallant, Cap. I'll stay back and let one of you upstanding gents go down the creepy stairs first into the mysterious abyss below."

"Wuss," Troy said as he took the first step downward and nudged her with his elbow as he passed. "Guess all that me too stuff was just for show."

"I'd rather be alive than progressively DOA, Cap," Charlie replied with a feminine laugh.

Everybody followed Troy as he descended the narrow concrete stairs while the Jackal took up the rear position. It was a steep descent down into the bowels of the facility. A steel I-beam used to transport the two nukes underground in 1984 lined the roof. As they reached the bottom of the stairs, it was another twenty feet through a dimly lit tunnel before they reached the second door. This one was the same size as the first and appeared to be blast-resistant as well. Again, the colonel used another key to reveal a keypad and entered the unique code, this time six digits followed by the pound key.

0-9-1-1-7-4-#

The door opened similarly to the one above ground. Another flight of stairs led them even farther underground.

As they descended, the air smelled stale, even musty, and the only sounds were the hum of the ballasts that regulated the lighting and their own footfalls on the smooth concrete. Troy guessed they were almost fifty feet underground before they reached the last step.

The stairway led to a vast, dark room. With most of the lights burned out, the team used their EDC Ultimate 60 flashlights to illuminate their way as they explored the bowels of the bunker. As they made their way deeper into the compound, they realized how vast the complex appeared to be versus what they saw topside. They walked for over a half dozen minutes before they located a heavy vault door which stood ajar.

Approaching the door cautiously, they found the vault only contained two empty cradles. The metal cradles were a stark reminder that, at one point, two American-made nuclear weapons lay inside the vault. As the team walked around the vault, they sensed an eerie feeling of the room being like a crypt, minus any bodies.

On the other side of the subterranean complex, a series of rooms served as living quarters for the staff tasked with guarding the facility. According to the schematics provided to them, several other rooms were used as offices.

The team scoured each room for the next thirty minutes, but no one was quite certain what they hoped to find. Down one hallway, they found the tunnel entrance the weapons abductors used to enter the facility. They shone flashlights down the narrow tunnel, but eventually, the light faded, and they could not see an ending to the immense tunnel.

Digger and the Jackal were with each other much of the time. About ten minutes into the search, the Jackal leaned over and whispered, "What exactly does Cap hope to find?"

Digger shrugged in response and shook his head.

"This place was long ago abandoned," the Jackal stated. "Seems like an awfully dangerous trip out here to Buttsville for nada if you ask me."

With a nod of his head, Digger didn't disagree. "Yeah, it seems like a waste to me."

16

Lake Dukan

The team scoured the long-ago abandoned facility and found nothing of value before they made their way to the offices on the eastern portion of the underground structure. One belonged to Naseefa al-Majid, an office Troy was interested in examining. Papers strewn across the floor indicated Naseefa left in a hurry back in 2003. An informant within the Iraqi military confirmed the nukes were on site four days before the American special operations force raided the facility.

Troy walked around the sparse office. He held a long piece of rebar he had found outside the vault door in his right hand. As he paced the office, he struck the wooden floor with the four-foot piece of steel as he thought. Naseefa's office had wood flooring installed on top of the concrete. The steel striking the wood made a dull *thud* sound each time Troy repeated the motion.

After searching the office for several minutes, Troy examined every drawer and crevice. Doubt crept into his mind since they found nothing of interest throughout the facility.

What did I expect to find? Troy asked himself.

As he turned to leave, he saw a photo in the far corner of the room that caught his eye. He approached the photo and saw it was a personalized picture of Naseefa with his cousin, Saddam Hussein. Troy picked up the photo with his left hand and stared at it. He decided it would serve as an interesting memento of this trip. His right hand once again struck the rebar onto the wooden floor as it had countless times, but a curious thing happened.

There was no dull *thud* sound like every other time. What greeted his motion was a hollow *echo* sound. His ears perked up, and he slammed the rebar down again. The same hollow *echo* reverberated. He stepped a few feet away from the corner toward the center of the room, slammed down the rebar, and the dull *thud* sound occurred again. His mind raced, his heartbeat increased, and he believed at that moment his trip had not been in vain.

"Sarge," Troy yelled.

A moment passed before Sarge appeared at the door. "What is it, Cap?"

"Where's that pry bar?"

"Near the bottom of the stairs. Why?"

"Grab it for me, please," Troy said.

"You got it." Sarge exited the office and returned several minutes later with the angled piece of steel.

Troy went to the corner of the room and pried at the boards that ran horizontally across the floor. It took a couple of minutes, but once he pulled up enough of them, he saw the hidden chamber. By now, the entire team had crammed into the room, curious to see what Cap had found.

With a wide grin plastered across his weary face, Troy shined his flashlight down the dark hole, and something shiny glared back from the bottom. He crouched on the ground on all fours and reached into the black hole. Troy pulled out a dusty, silver box about the length and width of a legal file with a depth of about eight inches.

"You clever dog, you." The colonel patted Troy on his broad shoulder.

"Or just plain lucky," Digger said.

"As Seneca said, *Luck is what happens when preparation meets opportunity*," Troy said as he winked.

All eyes were on the box. Troy walked it over to the desk, delicately placed it down, and slowly opened the lid.

The Jackal stepped back. "Just in case it blows," he quipped. "I'm too pretty to get disfigured."

"Grow a set." Charlie glanced back at the Jackal.

"Oh, I have a pair, and I intend to keep um' right where they are. In one piece and fully functional!"

------⧫------

Inside the box, Troy found an assortment of items. Several stacks of Iraqi Dinar in various denominations lined the top of the container. As Troy removed them, he found several passports. When he opened each one, he noticed all the pictures were Naseefa al-Majid, yet the names differed on each document. There was even a United States passport within the stack. A small caliber handgun was also among the contents. Troy removed all the items and found several documents at the bottom. He flipped through each one and handed them off to various team members so they could inspect each page.

Then he found it—the most curious piece of paper in the collection. He looked it over with a keen eye and even spun it around several ways. His mind wondered what it could be at first.

Troy handed it to Digger. "What do you think this is?"

Digger took the piece of paper and looked at it. "Looks like a blueprint of some sort, Cap."

"I concur. But it's clearly not this facility."

Digger shook his head. "No chance, the dimensions are all wrong."

Troy pointed to the item in the center of the diagram. "And what does that look like?"

Digger scrutinized the drawing. His eyebrows raised as he looked up at Troy, and they made eye contact. "It looks like a cradle that would hold a nuclear warhead, Cap," he said with a concerned look on his face. "Two side-by-side, which leads me to believe it's for the pair of nukes we gave them."

"Exactly," Troy stated.

"Maybe it's where Naseefa planned to keep the weapons after he removed them from this facility," Harry said as he held the diagram.

"It's very possible," Troy replied.

"We have no way of knowing how many facilities the Iraqis designed to house the weapons." Sarge's baritone voice echoed around the small space. "I'm sure moving them from this place was no last-minute decision. Plans must have been in the works for a while. Think how long it took to dig the tunnel they used to sneak the two weapons out. That took lots of foresight and planning."

Troy nodded. "Very true."

"Why would Naseefa leave this box behind?" Harry asked. "Especially if he's the one who orchestrated the nukes being removed from the facility?"

Troy shrugged. "Good question. Maybe he intended to come back, or he simply forgot. Who knows? If we can get him, we can ask."

"Not sure it matters at this point," Harry replied. "Just seems an odd thing to leave if you're going to steal two nukes."

"Agreed," Troy said. "Sometimes people just screw up. Could be nothing more than that."

The team huddled around and discussed the diagram for a few minutes before the colonel interrupted. He looked down at his watch. "Great find, Cap. We can analyze it all we want, but it's about time we head topside. It's almost nightfall, and I don't want to be stuck coming out of here in the pitch dark. Anyway, our ride to McFly should have arrived by now."

"Not taking the Mercedes back?" Digger asked.

"No, not after the attack earlier. I arranged for two Blackhawks to escort us back to Kirkuk."

"And the vehicles?"

"That's the agency's problem," the colonel replied with a raised eyebrow.

Troy carefully put the items back into the box and left the diagram on top as he closed the lid. He headed toward the door with the box tucked under his left arm. The team followed behind as Troy led the way. Ten minutes later, with the facility doors sealed shut, the eight members were safe aboard the chopper heading southwest toward Kirkuk.

17

KIRKUK

FOB MCFLY

Two hours later, Troy's surroundings were remarkably different, yet in other ways, eerily the same. He scanned the sparse room with dull gray walls, off-white floors, and ceiling. A stainless-steel table adorned the center of the room with two metal chairs on either side. An overhead, round light swayed back and forth above the table, moved by an invisible breeze. Security cameras in each corner pointed toward the center of the space. A two-way mirror on the far wall displayed two men's reflections as they glared at each other.

After several minutes of complete silence, the olive-skinned man spoke. "I guess you want me to speak first." The indirect question was met with more silence. "You must be with the Central Intelligence Agency. Am I right?"

Troy shook his head but said nothing.

A curious expression formed on the olive-skinned man's face. "If you're not with the agency, who are you? What do you want?" The man sounded tired. Sleep eluded him for quite a while, courtesy of the people in the facility determined to derive valuable intel.

Troy cleared his throat. "I'm not with the agency. I'm a captain in the United States Army. Part of the US Special Forces operations."

Some consider interrogation to be an art form. The training can vary, and the techniques are not always consistent. The job is to extract information, while the approach to how that occurs enters a gray area from time to time. Everyone receives similar training and puts their own unique spin on what methods they administer to detainees. Certain methods work while others don't. During his stint with the Army, Troy only received basic classes on the art of interrogation. He experienced more advanced training at The Farm in Virginia, including The Omega Group men being on the receiving end of the interrogation process so they could know what detainees would undergo. It was not pleasant, but they needed to know what to expect. Troy experienced many interrogations while in the field and occasionally conducted his own. Sometimes, they occurred in facilities like where he sat, but most took place during missions where rules and procedures vary immensely. The situation determines the lines needed and when those lines become blurred and must be crossed.

———◦———

Troy needed intel before the next phase of the operation began. He wanted to connect the dots and discover information the interrogators had not retrieved. It was not always the case, but he decided before stepping into the room with Jalal that an honest discourse would be the best approach.

Jalal al-Majid looked surprised. "Special Ops? You're not a trained interrogator?"

"No, I'm not."

"Then what do you want from me?" A curious expression spread across Jalal's face.

"Answers," Troy said.

"I'm just a businessman, no more, no less."

"So your hosts have told me."

"These animals are not my hosts. I've told these barbarians who've held me against my will for weeks. I've told these monsters everything I know, which is not much."

Troy grew silent for a moment and considered his approach before he spoke once more. "That may be the case, but I have other questions they may not have asked."

"I doubt that. The sadistic people who run this facility are detail-oriented. They've asked everything."

"We'll see," Troy said.

"Do you have a name?" Jalal asked. "The other before you called themselves various things like Mr. Brown, Q, and even Star-Lord. All clearly pseudonyms. I've watched enough Hollywood movies, and I know for a fact Chris Pratt was not here in this room with me."

Most interrogators lie. Standard procedure dictates that real names shouldn't be used when questioning foreign detainees. But Troy couldn't give two squirts of piss for the standard procedure. He answered honestly and directly. "My name is Captain Troy Evans."

Jalal stared at him with an icy glare, full of contempt. After several tense seconds passed, Jalal said, "Can I ask you a couple questions, Captain Evans?" He paused before he added, "Before you question me."

It started as an unorthodox interrogation, and Troy let it continue in that manner. "Go for it." He nodded. "I'll be straight up with you. I just ask you to do the same for me."

"Do you think the Iraqi people want your military here?"

"Like right now or in general?" Troy asked.

"Period. Do they want you and your people here in their country?"

"It's a little too late for that. The war is officially over, and there are not many soldiers left in your country."

"The rest of you could leave. Most of your army has already tucked tail and left."

Jalal was clearly attempting to get under his skin, but Troy saw through the question and played along.

"You want the insurgency to tear apart what's left of your tattered nation?" Troy asked.

"They will anyway." Jalal threw his head back. "I highly doubt your government, especially your weak president, will do much to stop them. He wants to wash his hands of what the previous administrations have done to my country."

"We have a quote in my country. 'The only thing necessary for evil to triumph is for good men to do nothing,'" Troy said.

"Edmund Burke," Jalal replied. "I know the quote well, although there is no proof he actually said it."

"True but I still like the statement." Troy paused. "You were educated in some very prestigious schools around the world, Jalal."

"Correct. We're not all uneducated haji in my country, Captain Evans." Jalal punctured the words in a tone bathed with scorn and he balled his fist and thumped it against his chest. "No matter what you Americans believe about us."

"You had an education most of your fellow citizens could only dream of, but you really don't have a clue what I know or think about the average Iraqi, Jalal."

Jalal said nothing.

"I've spent years of my life here." Troy continued. "Along the way, I've met brave men and women and witnessed heroic acts as average citizens stood up for what's right. I believe your people are survivors and wish for a better future. Not unlike what Americans want. To answer your question, some want us here, but I'm sure most don't. But everyone wants the US dollars in their nations. If you recall, Saddam had billions of our currency hidden away here in your country."

"Be that as it may. My people don't want a 'little America' here in Iraq," Jalal countered with a scornful retort.

"I never said you did. What I'm saying is we are not so different, your people and mine. Deep down, humanity has the same innate desires, no matter what plot of earth they call home."

"We were safer under Saddam. All of us."

"All of you may be a bit of a stretch. Some may have been, but certainly not all. Members of the Ba'ath party were absolutely better off. I'm sure the al-Majid family did quite well under Saddam, you being family and all. Then again, he cut off the tongue of his own family members and threw people off rooftops for sport."

Jalal shook his head vigorously. "Saddam provided stability. Something the United States stole from my country."

"Saddam was a lunatic and mentally unstable. He was nothing more than a two-bit dictator who led his people through fear. And besides, Saddam is fucking dead. Hung by Iraqis in 2006."

If Troy was trying to win Jalal over, his approach sucked. But, there was a method to his madness, even if the others on the opposite side of the glass who observed his interrogation couldn't tell.

"Correct. And yet your nation supported him during the 1980s, no? Many say you even put him in power in 1963."

"The enemy of my enemy is my friend," Troy replied.

"Ahh, Pyreglide," Jalal said. "See, Saddam served his purpose, and America discarded him when they no longer needed him. You people have a history of doing that to various leaders worldwide."

"I'm pretty sure we won't see eye to eye on politics or the Hussein family," Troy said in a slightly perturbed tone. "Any more questions, Jalal?"

Jalal's eyes narrowed. "Do you believe Iraqis are better off now than they were under Saddam before your country's invasion?" He paused. "That is what I really want to know, Captain Evans. Answer me that question, please."

Troy had to admit that it was a good question, and the answer was likely no. But he wouldn't admit that, not to Jalal. He also knew no answer would suffice. The question was a trap.

After pausing, he said, "I'm not an Iraqi, so I can't answer that. But I do know the Iraqi citizens can now choose their own destiny. That wasn't an option under Saddam's rule. If your people want to be led by another tyrant, go ahead and take a step backward. But, if you want a relatively free and open society to move past the infighting and violence that has engulfed your nation. We've provided an amazing gift, and it's up to your people what they choose to do with it."

"You know nothing of my people," Jalal hissed. "Also, not all mankind wants the Western version of freedom. There are many who are alive that prefer to follow and not lead."

"I've bled with your people. Cared for them and wept with them. They are a remarkable people. But I've also seen firsthand some are hell-bent on killing each other and have been for over millennia. The Kurds, Sunni, and Shia tolerate each other, but deep down, hatred and animosity boil below the surface."

"And Saddam kept the internal destruction from occurring," Jalal interrupted. "He brought peace and stability to the nation."

"Through fear and terror," Troy said. "Do you think most Iraqis want to go back to that?"

A sudden smile formed at the corner of Jalal's lips. "Our conversation is getting nowhere, Captain Evans."

"You're right."

"And like I told you before, and the thugs who have interrogated me. I know nothing. Your visit was a waste, I'm afraid."

Troy wondered for a moment if Jalal was right. *Did he risk the lives of his team for nothing? Was his gut wrong?* The questions washed over him like a towering wave.

"My father didn't tell me where he hid the weapon," Jalal said. "I've told your interrogators that in countless ways, and it's the truth. Look into my eyes. I'm not trying to deceive you."

Troy looked into the features of the man across from him. Jalal's eyes convinced him of the truth. His father had not provided the location. *But maybe he told him something that would help.*

"I found something at the Lake Dukan site. A box hidden inside your father's office under the floor. For the life of me, I can't figure out why your father would have left it behind."

Jalal looked down at the desk. When he looked back up, his features changed. Troy perceived the look to be best described as shame.

"I believe I know what you are referring to." Jalal replied.

"How so?"

"My father fled the facility the day before the weapons were retrieved. He intended to go back for the items in the box. But…"

"But what?" Troy asked.

"I told him it was too dangerous to return on account of the invasion of your forces. So, I told him I would go and retrieve the items."

Troy's gaze narrowed. "And based on your facial expressions, and the fact we retrieved the box today, I know you never did what you said you would do."

Jalal nodded. "I didn't even try. I lied to my father and told him I retrieved the box and destroyed the contents. My story placated him."

"Why did you deceive him?"

Jalal shrugged. "I was afraid to go back there. Thought I would get caught. Based on where he told me he hid the items, I believed they would never be found."

"They stayed secret for a long time, but not anymore."

"I'm not sure it matters anymore. Nothing in the box reveled the location of the devises where he moved them according to my father." Jalal said.

"There's a schematic in the box." Troy replied.

"Ok, but I can assure you I have no idea where the place in the drawing is located. Like I said, my father never told me the location where he hid the weapons. I can't reveal a place if I know nothing about it."

— ◦ —

"Do you love your father?" Troy asked as he changed tactics.

The question threw Jalal off. He scrunched his bow. "Excuse me?"

"It's a simple question. Do you love your father?"

Without hesitation, Jalal replied, "Of course."

"You would do anything to protect him?"

"Yes," Jalal answered. "Even die for him if Allah wills it."

"My mission is to find and secure the weapons your father removed from the facility years ago. I've also been informed we are to leave no living witnesses." Troy paused for a moment before he continued. "Get my drift? My directive is to kill your father after I recover the nukes."

Jalal glared at Troy while the revelation took hold. His face displayed his intentions. However, the shackles upon his wrists and ankles kept him at bay.

Troy understood that passion. It was something he held within himself for many, many years.

"But I can show him mercy," Troy said. "I can do my best to protect your father."

Jalal, filled with rage, hissed, "And why would you do that? You lie, and your men here, they lie."

"Everything I've told you is the truth, Jalal. I'm well versed in loss and understand all too well how it feels to lose those you hold most dear."

Jalal controlled his anger and took a moment before he responded. "You can't guarantee his safety. If the United States government wants my father eliminated, then he's a dead man."

"I'm not sure of my own survival," Troy said. "But I can promise you I'll do everything in my power to protect your father and reunite the two of you."

"Why? Why would you do such a thing? Especially if it contradicts your orders."

Troy held out his hand and extended it toward Jalal, who looked at it like a foreign object. Jalal doubted his gesture.

"Why would you think I could trust you?" Jalal asked.

With his arm hanging mid-air, Troy said, "Because my word is my bond. And I have never, ever broken that bond my entire life." As he spoke the words, Troy looked directly at Jalal. "If I say I'll do my best to spare your father, you can be assured that come hell or high water, I'll do just that."

Jalal stared into Troy's deep blue eyes. If the eyes are truly the window to the soul, Jalal could see the man before him was being honest.

A fierceness burned within Troy's eyes, but compassion was also close to the surface.

Not fully realizing at the time why he did so, Jalal reached across the table and firmly grasped Troy's hand. The men shook hands for a moment before Jalal withdrew his hand. "So you do your best to spare my father. What's next?"

"He comes back to Iraq."

Jalal immediately shook his head. "No! The Iraqi High Tribunal will put him on trial for his ties to the Ba'ath Party. Do you think they will treat him fairly? There's zero chance he'll be provided a legitimate and impartial form of justice here in Iraq. Corruption is rife in the United States, but fraud is almost second nature in Iraq, Captain Evans. I don't have the financial means to ensure his trial is not a sham."

"Like I told you, the United States government wants your father dead. So your choice is quite simple. If you tell me nothing, your father dies once we track him down, or you can trust me and tell me what I need to know, and your father may live to stand trial in Iraq. But make no mistake, the choice is yours to make. His life is in your hands."

"I told you, Captain Evans. He never told me where he took them after they left the Lake Dukan facility," Jalal said. "My father didn't wish for that burden or target to be upon my brow."

"But he told you something." Troy spoke in a softer tone. "He gave you some clue, Jalal. I feel it in my bones. Whatever that is, it will allow me to find the weapons. I know it to be true."

<hr>

Jalal let out a long breath. It almost sounded like the last exhale of air as a person perishes. He looked down, then up once more, and locked eyes with Troy.

"This is all I know. My father's last words to me, Captain Evans, before he fled Iraq were *Babylon Will Rise!*"

<hr>

The phrase sunk in, and it clicked almost immediately. It was the clue Troy hoped to receive.

Bingo, he thought.

PART II

18

KIRKUK, IRAQ TO PARIS, FRANCE

Once they left FOB McFly in Iraq, The Omega Group boarded the same private jet that ushered them into the country, with a destination in Paris, France. The six-hour flight allowed the team ample opportunity to discuss the next steps for the mission. They examined every detail and created contingencies where needed. The Omega Group achieved a high level of success directly due to their meticulous preparation. Few operators planned or anticipated complications like their team. It's what kept them alive when so many others faltered.

As the plane landed at Charles de Gaulle, it taxied to an unmarked private hangar far from prying eyes. The large hangar doors closed, and the plane was safely inside the structure. Only then did the agency staff approach the plane.

Two hours later, with the transformations completed, the agency staff departed. Their attention to detail impressed The Omega Group. Over a dozen people worked tirelessly to assist Troy, Charlie, and the other members in getting everything just right. Digger checked and then double-checked all the specialized electronic equipment needed to complete the mission, and only when he signed off was the team ready to depart.

While one plane pulled into the oversized hangar, three departed.

Troy and Charlie were the first to leave in the Falcon 900. The five remaining members of The Omega Group were not happy to see Troy leave without them. Each man took great pride in doing whatever it took to keep Troy safe while on a mission, even if that meant risking their own life. They all knew Troy and Charlie would largely be on their own in Ghana, especially the night of the auction, and none of them liked the uncertainty of the mission.

Thirty minutes after the Falcon left, the G450, which carried Sarge, Digger, the Jackal, Jesús, and Harry, accelerated down the runway and sliced through the dark night sky. Their final destination was also Ghana, but they were entering the country via a less direct route.

Last, a Citation X, which carried Colonel Marshall, departed. The events in Iraq outside of Lake Dukan created a quandary. Fully aware someone was targeting his team, the colonel decided it prudent he head to Washington, D.C., and conduct an off-the-books meeting. If everything went according to the plan, he expected to join the team in Ghana within two days.

19

AT CRUISING ALTITUDE

DASSAULT FALCON 900

The smooth leather seats sucked Troy in, and after wiggling around for a few seconds, he found his sweet spot. Over the past several years, Troy found himself on countless private jets. More than a farm boy from Idaho could have dreamed, but he had to admit the Italian leather seats on the Dassault Falcon 900 exceeded all others. The owners of the plane clearly spared no expense. Even the smell that emanated from the seats reminded Troy of Florence.

If only I had a piping hot cappuccino and a generous slice of tiramisu. Troy thought.

"I thought most SF guys roughed it?" Charlie asked as she sat across from Troy and watched him get comfortable in the plush leather seat.

"Most guys ain't me." Troy smirked as he rubbed the arm of the chair. "It pays to be one of the cool kids."

Charlie rolled her eyes. "Whatever."

"I'm kidding. Trust me, I rough it ninety-five percent of the time, but now and then, I get to splurge and act like I'm a big deal. Which I'm clearly not."

"According to what I hear around the community, you are kind of a big deal."

"Don't believe everything you hear. Those guys lie like the devil."

"I agree." Charlie nodded. "And I tend to think you might be a bigger deal than some let on, including yourself."

"Nah." Troy shrugged. "I have a job to do and try my best to do it. Besides, the rest of the Omegas are really the ones that make us all look good."

"I'm serious, Cap. The missions you have led are legendary. Operations Retribution, Scribe, Raptor, Silver Dragon, Devil-Dog, Pope, Arrowhead, and the list goes on and on. Hell, those are only the ones I've even heard about. Only God knows how many missions exist where nobody has ever even heard of the names."

Troy smirked. "Some of those are top secret, above both of our pay grades to discuss."

Charlie shrugged. "A girl hears things. Plus, my clearance is on par with yours, Mr. Big Deal."

Troy shook his head back and forth. "No doubt. Besides, lots of teamwork went on for all those ops you mentioned, Charlie. There's no such thing as a one-man show. One only finds lone action heroes in fiction novels, which are mere figments of the author's imagination. Trust me, Jack Ryan, James Reece, Elle Anderson, and Mitch Rapp only exist on paper."

"Mitch, who?" she asked.

Troy's face scrunched together. "You telling me you don't know about author Vince Flynn's main protagonist? You live under a rock or something? He's a real badass."

Charlie let out a laugh. "Just playing with you, Cap. Of course, I've read the entire series with Transfer Of Power being my fave. We both know it's pretty much required reading in the SF world. Although I'm kinda partial to the Jason Bourne character Ludlum crafted if you ask my opinion."

"Ludlum, le Carré, Forsyth, Stoker, Fleming, Tolkien, Lewis ... the list goes on. Books are the greatest form of escapism man ever created."

"And here you are, being modest and deflecting my compliments away from you. Trying to switch the subject to badass authors."

Troy blushed. "Really, I'm just a guy on a fancy plane with a job to do," he answered with a wide smile.

"Yeah ... to possibly save the world."

"Trust me, my actions alone won't save the world."

"If you say so."

"Just another flight, another mission." Troy spoke in a subdued tone.

"And it may be your last flight." Charlie gave a quick wink.

"If I die before I wake ..."

"I pray the Lord my soul to take." Charlie finished the bedtime prayer.

"Well, if Ami finds out who we really are ..." Troy paused as he pondered what would happen. "Let's just say his reputation is not for showing mercy. It will be both of our last flights."

"I've read the stories about what happens to anyone who crosses him," Charlie nodded. "They don't exactly meet pleasant ends. Wood chippers, filleting victims alive, guillotines, and many other gruesome techniques he employs."

"He seems to like blunt objects to exact his revenge. I read in the intel brief he claimed shooting a person was, and I quote, *Too impersonal, almost inhumane. If you're going to go to the trouble of killing someone, they may as well suffer.* Kind of ironic since this guy has sold more firearms and bullets to more dictators and terrorist organizations than we can even fathom."

Charlie stared hard at Troy, a little too hard, as he said the last few words.

"What?" he asked. A puzzled expression showed on his face. His tongue immediately moved around inside his mouth. "Do I have something in my teeth?"

She smiled warmly. "No, I think the disguise makes you appear much older, distinguished even."

"More mature?" Troy asked with a smirk.

"On the surface," she retorted. "The speckled gray they added to the goatee makes you look twenty years older. Although I'm not sure, I like you with black hair and glasses."

———— ◦◦◦ ————

Troy turned his hands over with his palms facing up and examined his skin. The agency staff had done a remarkable job adhering the fake fingerprints to his own. With the naked eye, you couldn't tell where the fabricated skin stopped and his own began. They had assured him the prosthetic skin was fully waterproof and would not break down for at least seventy-two hours.

"How about me?" Charlie asked as Troy looked up from his hands. "Did they alter my appearance that much? I haven't dared to look in the mirror yet. Seeing someone else looking back at me might creep me out."

Troy nodded. "The changes are remarkable. It's amazing how a few subtle changes transformed your features so dramatically. The brown contact lenses might be necessary, but I like your green eyes better. But you look good as a redhead. If the Jackal was around ... well, let's just say I'd have to beat him off you with a stick. He really digs redheads. I mean, it almost borders on an obsession."

"Think I can do just fine in that arena. I kicked his ass once already." Charlie smiled as she balled her fist and pounded it into the open palm of her other hand. It made a distinct smacking sound. "But thanks for having my six, Cap."

"You're an outstanding soldier, Charlie. Pound for pound, you stack up against anyone I have ever served with. I'm honored to have you on the team for this mission."

"Thanks, and I'll try to not let you down."

"You won't," Troy replied.

Charlie's face contorted from a wide smile to a concerned expression within seconds.

"What is it?" Troy asked.

"How about if the intel is wrong? And they know we're not Mr. and Mrs. Lapointe? What if the biometrics fail or they test something that we're not equipped to handle?"

"Then our first trip to Ghana will suck big time, and it'll be our last trip to the dark continent."

"I'm serious," Charlie replied.

"So am I." Troy answered with a nod. "We'll be as good as dead if we're caught."

"But how can the agency be sure neither Ami nor one of his associates know what Phillipe and Madeline look like? Do you really believe there's no image of them on any database somewhere?"

"Don't forget one of the other guests as well. There's always a chance they have met the Lapointes over the years and may see right through our flimsy disguises." Troy laughed as he rolled his eyes.

"Come on now, Cap, I'm not playing! Aren't you at all worried for your own safety?"

<hr />

Troy stopped ribbing Charlie since he could see it bothered her. He got serious. "The way I see it, your life is like a novel. There's a first page, and there's a last. Nobody ever knows how many pages lie between the covers. If I'm closer to the last page than I am to the first, so be it. I made peace with my maker a long time ago, and I'm ready for the journey to end whenever He sees fit."

"How poetic." Charlie rolled her eyes.

"And you?" Troy asked.

"I'm not much of a poet. I'm more of a cynic."

"But are you ready for it all to end if this is our last mission?"

"You asking if I believe in God or an afterlife?"

"Both, I guess." Troy squinted as he stared at her.

Her expression changed from perplexed to stoic. "What if I said neither?"

"Really? I wouldn't take you for an atheist."

Charlie shook her head and seemed to ponder the question for a moment before she replied. "I wouldn't call myself an atheist per se. A piece of me still believes in a higher power. What form that takes, I'm not sure I can say with any certainty. What I do know is I've witnessed a lot of horrors in my life, even though my upbringing would suggest otherwise. Because of what I've seen and the depravity mankind is capable of, I'm not sure what I believe most of the time …" Her voice trailed off, and she grew quiet for a few moments. "Faith is something I've still not discovered."

"Fair enough," Troy said. "And please don't think I'm judging you. I was just curious. I think knowing where we go when this ride we call life ends is a far easier way to enjoy the journey. If you ever wanna dig into the whole afterlife convo after the mission is over, hit me up. I can chat about whatever you want."

"Fair enough and thanks for the offer. Why don't you just keep us both safe so I don't have to find out if there's a heaven or a hell in the next few days."

"I'll do my best," Troy said. "But I can't make any promises."

"If anyone can keep both of our asses safe, it's the famous Troy Evans."

Troy sighed and lowered his head. "Famous and infamous are only separated by an *i-n* you know?"

Charlie smiled.

A few awkward moments of silence passed.

———⋅◆⋅———

Charlie raised the thick manila folder. "Better get back to my homework. By the time this bird lands, I need to be Mrs. Madeline Lapointe."

"Don't forget the French accent. Be sure to lay it on real thick. Especially when we need to speak English at the auction."

"Ouais," Charlie answered in perfect French.

For the next two hours, they did their best to read and memorize every morsel of information contained in the folders since their lives would depend on not being discovered as frauds. Also, the fate of the world may be in the balance based on whoever purchased the rogue nuke at the auction.

Nothing like a slight bit of pressure. Troy thought as he went over the packet another time.

The flight attendant interrupted their research when she brought them dinner. Served on pastel-colored china with a 24-karat gold ring around the outside of the plates, the meal included braised short ribs, roasted root vegetables, sautéed mushrooms, and arugula salad.

"You pick the menu tonight?" Charlie asked, her voice contained a hint of sarcasm.

"Me?" Troy said in mock surprise. "No way. After a few days back in the sandbox, I only crave a pepperoni and jalapeño pizza. Throw in some wings and a few bottles of Hefeweizen, and I'm good to go. But this fancy grub looks pretty good, so I'm not complaining. The Lapointes obviously have exquisite tastes."

For a little while, they engaged in mainly small talk, favorite movies, best concerts, and the stupidest things they had done while in the military. Standard dinner conversation soldiers engage in while passing time on missions. After twenty minutes, Charlie steered the conversation toward a serious topic.

"You think you're right about where Naseefa stashed the nukes?"

"Makes sense." Troy tilted his head upward. "At least my gut says that's where the one that will be auctioned off is. I don't think I could have devised a better location myself. As for the one Ami bought, I suspect he moved it already."

"But how could Naseefa get the weapon there without raising suspicion?"

"A location like that would not be difficult if you pay off government officials. The hard part is us proving that's where it is now. It's not like we can go in there and dig the place up."

"Yes, you're right," Charlie said.

Troy took his last bite of food and placed his fork down. "Anyway, the agency is sending a few folks to poke around down there. We gave them a copy of the blueprint discovered at Lake Dukan. Maybe they'll get lucky and find something. They just can't draw any unwanted attention. I suspect someone who works for Ami or Naseefa watches the area. Actually, I'm sure the entire region is under surveillance. How could it not be?"

"True."

"Hopefully, when we recover the data at the auction, my suspicions will be confirmed. Then we can get the nuke before the highest bidder retrieves the device."

"Maybe it's already at Ami's compound?"

Troy shook his head. "No, the intel is clear. The asset said Ami would never bring either nuke to where he lived. He has some paranoia about it going off, supposedly."

Charlie eyed him intently for several moments as he spoke. There was a fierceness in her gaze.

Troy looked down at the intel packet and ignored her movements.

Charlie pushed aside her tray, stood, and walked over to his seat. She wore a tan pair of capris with a light blue blouse. The pants hugged her firm legs snugly, and the blouse was loose, with the top two buttons unfastened, which did little to hide her desirable assets as she leaned forward. The outfit came straight from Madeline Lapointe's luggage. Without saying a word, she got close. Close enough that her legs touched his, and her left hand rested on his leg just above his knee. She leaned over, put her head against the base of his neck, and gently kissed his skin. Her wet lips caused his skin to react.

20

— · —

At Cruising Altitude

Dassault Falcon 900

"Charlie!" Troy exclaimed as his body tensed. "What the hell are you doing?"

At first, he thought she was getting close to look at something he was reading, but instinctually, Troy put his arms out to rebuff the advance as her lips touched his skin.

She pulled back and looked him square in the eyes. A disapproving expression plastered across her face. "That was a test," she proclaimed as she turned, returned to her seat, and sat down in a huff. Her arms crossed under her chest.

"Huh?" Troy asked. "What do you mean a test?"

"You failed." She stared straight ahead, a deadpan expression on her face.

"I'm lost." His head was spinning. *What game is she playing? Is she coming on to me? Did I lead her on somehow?*

"We're supposed to be husband and wife, Cap. If you react that way when we are in Ghana, it will get us both killed."

Troy considered her words. Still confused as hell, he finally got it. It took only a second to realize she was right. He knew now what she meant by a test. Troy nodded. "Okay, good point. That's not the way I need to react once we land. But next time, just tell me we need to pretend to be husband and wife, and I'll gladly play the part, okay?"

"Fair enough. But mainly, I wanted to see how you would react."

Troy chuckled. "You really are a ball buster, you know that, right?"

"Most men would be turned on if an attractive woman kissed their neck …"

"Hold up, Charlie!" Troy thought he may have offended her. "I didn't mean to act like you're not attractive ... or ... I mean ..." His cheeks warmed. "Any guy would admit that you're hot as hell and would be a fool to say otherwise. It's just that ..." He paused for a moment before continuing. "I make it a point to never mix business with pleasure. It's a surefire way to get killed or, at the very least, in some serious trouble. In public, I'll play whatever part we need, but here on the plane, this is business."

There was an awkward pause. Charlie studied his features and examined his body language. "Whoever she is. You still love her, don't you?"

Troy was quiet for a moment. His mind raced. There was no way that conversation could get started. Not now. Too much on the line. "I tell you what, Charlie," he finally replied. "If we complete this mission without being chopped up into fertilizer and fed to the sharks in the Gulf of Guinea, I'll answer that question."

Charlie smiled. "Seriously?"

"Scout's honor." Troy raised three fingers on his right hand. "In the meantime, you gonna try and kiss me again?"

Charlie laughed. "You bet, Cap, and when you least expect it."

"If you mess with the bull, you get the horns," Troy replied with a wide smile.

"Ha. Don't worry. I know what to squeeze really damn hard in order to control a bull."

21

ACCRA, GHANA

The Dassault Falcon 900 touched down at the Kotoka International Airport and taxied to the private jet terminal at the far end of the runway. Several minutes later, the door opened, and the airstairs lowered. The humid night air punctured the coolness inside the plane's fuselage.

Troy had to admit he hated the heat of the Middle East, but at least it was a dry heat. He couldn't stand the humidity. In Accra, the humidity hovered at around ninety-five percent. Thick enough to cut the air with a Yarborough knife.

A minute later, a customs official entered the plane and asked for passports from everyone on board. He paid conspicuous attention to the two belonging to Phillipe and Madeline Lapointe.

Troy didn't like the man's facial expressions. When the customs official replied, "Stay here please," and left the plane, Troy decided he needed a gun cradled in his hand just to be safe. He reached under the seat, removed the weapon from the hidden holster, and wrapped his fingers around the grip of the Kimber 1911. Just the touch of the cold steel against his warm skin calmed his nerves in an instant. He disengaged the thumb safety and tucked the weapon under his right thigh. He moved the manila folder on his lap, which helped cover the weapon's grip, just as a different man with a fierce expression stepped inside the plane.

The man wore an expensive gray suit. Beneath it, a four-buttoned vest, a white dress shirt, and a matching gray silk tie. His gold-rimmed glasses and oversized wristwatch stood out as Troy sized him up. He looked like a native of Africa but was dressed to the nines. Clearly, he was not employed by any government agency and certainly not associated with the airport. Behind him followed two heavily armed men.

Troy's body tensed as he looked at the three targets. His mind imagined reaching for the Kimber. If the need arose, in what order would he shoot the three men? The stern look on the man's face mellowed as he raised a charcoal-colored briefcase.

"Sorry for the delay, Mr. and Mrs. Lapointe, but Mr. Sulzer requires biometric verification before you can enter the Republic of Ghana." With that, the man opened the briefcase, which contained an imprint of a hand on the center of the glass's surface. "Right hand, please," he said, followed by, "Ladies first."

"I wasn't aware our fingerprints were on file?" Troy asked in English, his words uttered with a heavy French accent.

"Mr. Sulzer has unlimited resources." The man in the gray suit replied as he turned to Charlie. "Mrs. Lapointe, your hand, please."

Charlie smiled outwardly, while on the inside, her heart raced. The time arrived to see how good the spooks really were at their jobs. She held her hand on the glass for a few seconds before an electronic beep emitted from the device, followed by a green light flashing in the far-right corner. "Welcome to Accra, Mrs. Lapointe," he said. She let herself relax, albeit slightly.

Troy was next, and he achieved the same result. "Thank you, Mr. Lapointe," the man replied before he asked, "So I'm told you came from Paris today?"

"Yes," Troy said.

"Well, since you departed from the city of light, I hope you enjoy your stay in the jewel of Ghana." The man spoke the words with the utmost sincerity in his voice. "A car is waiting to take you to your accommodations." The man gestured to the open airplane door with his left hand. "Mr. Sulzer has procured the finest resort for the enjoyment of his most honored guests. I believe you will find it will far outshine what you experienced while in Paris."

Troy nodded. "We look forward to our stay."

The man in the gray suit and the other two men moved closer to the plane door as Troy stashed the gun and manilla folder in a secure lockbox under the seat across from him.

Two minutes later, he and Charlie followed the man in the gray suit off the plane.

A sense of foreboding overtook Troy as he walked down the airstairs and planted his feet firmly on African soil. It was a feeling he rarely experienced. At first, he didn't even recognize what was happening. Outwardly, he didn't let the concern show its ugly face, but inside, he struggled. It was almost as if a heavy burden weighed on him soon after they landed in Ghana. Not knowing what may have caused such a reaction, he pushed the emotions deep down to a place where he could compartmentalize and stick to the mission.

22

LOMÉ, TOGO

About thirty minutes after Troy and Charlie touched down in Accra, the rest of The Omega Group, minus the colonel, landed in Lomé, Togo. A tiny sliver of a country in West Africa, the agency chose Togo in the early eighties as an ideal location for a classified facility. The compound west of Lomé contained its own airfield and served as a central hub for the agency's ever-growing presence in Sub-Sahara Africa. Its proximity to Accra made it the perfect location to ferry the team into neighboring Ghana since there were no assurances the team could land in Ghana undetected.

Two agency members rode in the vehicle's cab as it left Lomé. Inside the back of the vehicle, the team made themselves as comfortable as possible for the three-hour drive to Accra.

As the white Isuzu NPS box truck waited at the border crossing, its diesel engine drowned out much of the noise from the other vehicles that idled nearby. Forty-five minutes after arriving, the Isuzu finally pulled up to the security checkpoint. The sign to the left instructed them to shut off the engine, which the agency driver did reluctantly.

A young man emerged from the rickety shack and approached the vehicle. He looked to be in his early twenties and very much wet behind the ears. The young border official eyed the two white men in front of the Isuzu suspiciously as he got close to the driver's side door. He was not one of the normal border guards who understood not to ask questions and simply accepted the white envelope before letting the vehicle go without a second glance.

"Purpose of your visit," he asked in broken English with a deep frown.

The two men were ready for this contingency, but the senior agent who drove didn't like the young man's attitude. He handed him a piece of paper that contained a false shipping manifest. "Electric components for the parliamentary building in Accra," he said as he pointed to the back of the van.

The border officer's eyes narrowed as he pointed to the rear of the vehicle. "Step out of the vehicle and show me."

"I just told you what's in there," the driver replied forcefully.

The tone clearly provoked the young man, who put his right hand on the butt of his holstered pistol. "Get out of the vehicle now and step to the back of your vehicle!"

With years of experience, the agent played it cool, knowing he needed to diffuse the situation pronto. He stepped out of the driver's door, walked to the back of the vehicle, and pointed to the large brass lock on the rear door.

"Open it," the young man ordered.

"I don't have the key. Nobody may open those doors by authority of the Ghana government."

The young man pointed to the badge on his uniform just above his heart. "I am the only authority that matters right here."

It appeared the situation might spin out of control.

"Fine." The young man turned to walk back to the guard shack. "I'll get bolt cutters."

"Hold up," the driver said. "I've got something for you."

The young border agent watched as the man reached into his jacket. He quickly withdrew his holstered sidearm, shaking his right hand, and pointed it at the driver.

"Whoa! Whoa!" The driver exclaimed as he raised his left hand in the air while his right hand withdrew a thick white envelope from the inside pocket of his light jacket. "Hold up now. You don't need to pull that thing out."

"What is that?" The young man asked.

Ignoring the question, the agent asked, "How much money do you make in a month?"

With a sneer, the man replied, "Not enough."

"Let me change that." The driver handed the envelope to the young man.

With his gun still pointing at the man before him, the tremor in his right subsided as he reached out with his left hand and snatched the thick white envelope from the man's hand. As he kept his glance still at the man, he looked down as his left hand pulled open the flap with his thumb. He had never seen so much money in his whole life. All new crisp C-Notes, as the people in his country called the American one-hundred-dollar bills.

"We good now?" the driver asked.

For a few seconds, the young boy ignored the question. Then, in a broken voice, he replied, "Yes, we're good. You may pass."

"Thought so," the man said.

In the back of the vehicle, the members of The Omega Group breathed a collective sigh of relief. They heard the exchange from the vent in the top corner of the cab that separated the front and rear of the Isuzu. Each member gripped their weapons as the first sign of trouble, not knowing if the incident would escalate into a full-blown gun battle. Luckily, it didn't, and they relaxed as the engine roared to life. The vehicle passed through the checkpoint without further incident.

The young man walked back to the guard shack as the white Isuzu drove off. He dropped his ID badge on the uncomfortable wooden seat he so despised. A broad smile was clearly visible on his face, not a common sight from border agents from any country. He walked away from his post, heading toward the parking lot where his old, worn-out vehicle waited. The next vehicle that pulled up to the checkpoint beeped furiously as he walked away. The young man ignored the sound of the blaring horn. His boss watched from the far checkpoint booth and yelled at him. But the young man heard nothing. He climbed into his car, started the old engine, and disappeared. Never to return to his border job again.

A few minutes down the road, the driver sighed as he drove down the N1 toward Accra. "That was close," he admitted to the man to his right.

"Too close," the passenger replied.

"What would you have done if the bribe didn't work and the boy had tried to open the rear door?"

The passenger raised his Glock 19, which had been tucked away by the side of his seat, and coldly replied, "I would have stepped outside, shot both of you, and then drove like a bat out of hell for Accra."

Frowning, the driver said, "Nice to know where I rank."

"Sorry, dude. But during an active operation, we all are expendable. You would do the same to me if the roles were reversed and I had climbed into the driver's seat."

The driver nodded. "I would now, after what you just said."

23

McLean, Virginia

Colonel Marshall knew better than to show up unannounced. After all, it was after midnight on the East Coast, and the man he had flown seven hours and thirty-three minutes to see did not appreciate uninvited guests. While on the plane, he placed a call to let the correct people know when he would arrive.

The black Chevy suburban pulled up in front of the colonial-style house in the Potomac Hills neighborhood in McLean, VA. It parked behind an identical color and styled vehicle. As the colonel stepped out, a lone lamppost illuminated the sidewalk before him. He carried at his side a small black duffel bag. Two stone-faced men stood at the foot of the steps as he proceeded down the brick walkway.

"He's expecting me." The colonel spoke with authority.

"We're aware, sir," one of the two men said.

"Or we wouldn't have allowed you to get this close to the residence," the other added.

The guard on the right pointed at the colonel's hip. "We need your sidearm, Colonel Marshall."

Colonel Marshall knew the drill. As he withdrew his weapon, the distinct sound of metal rubbing against Kydex occurred. He handed the weapon barrel pointed downward to the younger man.

"Go right in." The agent gestured to the front door. "He's waiting for you in the study, second room on the right."

"I've been here before." Colonel Marshall nodded, walked past the two men, and proceeded up the ten red brick stairs.

A fire was roaring in the study, even though it was hardly cold outside. Its flames cracked and hissed as they danced up toward the flue. The man who sat cross-legged in the leather chair with a glass of brandy in his hand didn't bother to stand as William entered the room.

"Drink?" he asked.

"Scotch if you have it," the colonel said.

"Does the pope have holy water?" Came the sarcastic reply. "It's over on the bar." The man motioned toward the exquisite mahogany bar that covered one entire wall.

The colonel poured himself a stiff drink, a double, and sat in the chair across from the Secretary of Defense. An ornate marble table separated the two men.

"Well," the SecDef said. "Your message said it was urgent. And the fact you wouldn't say anything over the phone makes me believe it could be dire. Shouldn't you be in Africa right now with your team?" He arched his eyebrows.

"I should be," Colonel Marshall said in a gruff tone.

"But?"

"This happened." William removed from the black bag and laid down a series of photos showing the carnage on the roadside as the team made their way to Lake Dukan.

With a meticulous examination, the SecDef looked over the photos. A few moments passed before he asked, "I take it there have been no casualties for your men?"

"Not even a scratch."

"Why didn't you call it in?"

"I'm here now," the colonel answered in a curt tone.

"And the men that attacked you?" SecDef asked.

"All dead."

"Clearly." The SecDef held up one photo that showed a man with half his head blown off. "But who were they?"

"Not sure yet." Colonel Marshall removed a gallon-sized Ziploc plastic bag from the duffel bag and dropped its contents on the wooden table. "But maybe these will give us a few answers."

"Jesus H. Christ!" The SecDef recoiled from the sight of the severed index fingers. The bottom of the bag was coated in thick, coagulated blood. "What the hell is that?"

"A finger from each of the fourteen haji that tried to kill me and my men."

"Why in God's name did you cut off their fingers?"

"To identify them," he replied in a matter-of-fact tone.

"Did you really need to bring them here?"

"I think sometimes the folks in Washington get too cozy in their nice, isolated offices. It's good to bring a taste of the fieldwork to the powers that be." Next, Colonel Marshall slapped another batch of photos on top of the first. They were the photos they had retrieved from the truck that showed each member of The Omega Group.

"Dammit." Clearly stunned, the SecDef flipped through the photos. "You recovered these from the men you killed?"

"Roger that."

"We've got a big problem."

William nodded. "Something like that."

"Clearly, they knew you would be there and targeted you and the Omegas."

"Correct. My team is being hunted. Look at the pictures, one for each of us, including Charlie. Someone has it out for us."

"But who would want to do that?"

"That's what I'm going to find out."

"You'll have the full cooperation of the DOD and any other intelligence agencies you need. The Omega Group's mission is too valuable to have them fighting a two-pronged battle. They must succeed in Africa, or we might have a nuclear attack on the United States or one of our allies."

"I already have plenty of resources at my discretion."

"Then what do you want from me if not my assistance?"

"I want carte blanche."

For a minute, the SecDef said nothing. He considered what was being requested and thought about the consequences of consenting to the colonel's request. The Omega Group operated outside the normal chain of command under the purview of Section Seven, but there were still rules in place. There were assurances that they must follow a specific framework when they operated outside American soil. The colonel now asked that all that be discarded.

The SecDef considered the request and realized that if The Omega Group, one of the nation's most elite teams, was targeted, he really had no choice but to acquiesce.

"You have it. Take the gloves off…" The SecDef paused for a second. "With one caveat."

"Which is?"

"If you find the mole is someone inside the government, I must be consulted before you act."

The colonel had a sneaking suspicion who might be behind the attack, but he could never express his concerns out loud. If he were wrong, it would certainly cost him his career.

"Deal," Colonel Marshall said.

With his own glass of amber-colored liquid raised in the air, the SecDef replied, "Happy hunting, and woe to any person who merits the attention of The Omega Group."

William smiled, then threw back the rest of the liquid in one quick motion. It warmed his throat on its way down the hatch. He placed the emptied glass on the table, making a distinct *clunk* sound before standing up and then turning to leave.

The SecDef said nothing.

As the colonel reached the doorway, he paused and looked back at the man who had sat before the fire. "Fire and brimstone will reign down on anyone that attempts to harm my men, Mr. Secretary. Make no mistake."

With pursed lips, the SecDef nodded and raised his thick glass again. "Amen!" he exclaimed.

24

ACCRA

PALM BAY RESORT

Troy and Charlie walked out the front door of the luxurious Palm Bay Resort with their hands firmly clasped and smiles plastered across their faces. She leaned in close to Troy. Her head touched his broad shoulders as they stopped at the circular driveway steps from the others gathered outside. The two of them were the embodiment of a couple very much in love.

❖

From the moment they stepped off the plane in Ghana, Troy and Charlie took on the personas of Phillipe and Madeline Lapointe, and for thirty-six hours, they played the parts perfectly. While at the resort, they interacted with very few guests or staff members, figuring the less they saw or spoke to others, the better for their cover.

They adhered to strict radio silence during their stay at the Palm Bay Resort. There were no electronic communications with the rest of The Omega Group under any circumstances. The agency provided them with something that resembled a pop-up tent, which they assembled in the shower anytime they needed to talk freely. Both Troy and Charlie knew the suite contained listening devices and surveillance cameras. Only after Troy verified the bathroom checked out clean did they roll in the suitcase and set it up. Once sealed, the tent blocked all electronic communication, meaning it was safe to talk without fear of eavesdropping devices intercepting their conversations.

A rock under a hammock at the far end of the secluded, private beach served as a drop location to exchange information with the rest of the team. The brief phrases left on the slips of paper would be meaningless to anyone who may have stumbled across them, but they allowed them to relay valuable intel back and forth. Sarge and Harry checked the drop site every four hours while the other three members stayed at the safe house six miles away on the outskirts of Accra.

Halfway through the second day in Accra, the colonel arrived. During the flight from the United States to Ghana, he garnered valuable intel. Only a few hours before they left for the auction, he passed the information along to Troy and Charlie via the drop location.

•••

Forty people gathered outside the Palm Bay Resort around the circular drive lined with crushed seashells. Before them, wrapped around and down the driveway, idled twenty Land Rover Sentinels. At around $250,000 USD, each armored vehicle could withstand 7.62-millimeter high-velocity armored piercing bullets, DM51 grenades, and even a thirty-three-pound charge of TNT underneath or on the roof. In layman's terms, they were badass vehicles that served as a drivable fortress built around client comfort and protection. Ami wanted to send a message to those attending his auction; their safety was paramount to him. None of the guests refused his offer to shuttle them to his compound inside the Sentinels.

Troy leaned in close to Charlie as they made their way to the line of vehicles.

"You know how much those bad boys cost?" he whispered into her ear. He then gave her ear lobe a little bite to keep up appearances.

Charlie smiled and nodded. "No clue," she replied in French. "More than my Honda Civic?"

"A quarter of a rock each."

Her facial expressions revealed she didn't have a clue what the phrase *a quarter of a rock* meant.

"That's five million bucks total for all of them," Troy said.

"Guess crime pays after all," she retorted.

As they moved forward, an attendant checked them for weapons and gave her purse a cursory peek through before he smiled wide, said *thank you*, handed back her purse, and opened the rear passenger door of the next Sentinel to pull forward.

"Lucky number seven," Troy said in heavily accented English as they climbed inside.

"Is that good?" Charlie asked.

"My favorite number. I always throw a few chips down on red number seven when I'm in Sin City and see a roulette wheel. We may live through tonight, after all." He quickly added, "Maybe."

The drive from the resort to Ami's compound bordering the Shai Hills Resource Reserve took about thirty-five minutes. From the second they left the resort, they immediately realized the Sentinel driver loved to talk. He regaled Troy and Charlie with countless stories about Ami and the high regard the people of Ghana felt for him. They wondered if Ami instructed him to say what he did or if the man simply believed the praise he exuded. Either way, they listened, nodded, and occasionally added a few comments as they appeared to enjoy the scenic drive.

25

— · —

ACCRA

SULZER COMPOUND

Finally, the twenty vehicles pulled off the main road and drove along the private driveway for almost a mile. Darkness engulfed the region as the sun finally dipped its crimson brow below the horizon. The winding road passed through a thick grove of trees as the luxurious vehicles hugged the last curve and emerged at the base of a sloping hillside.

An eight-foot-tall perimeter fence encircled the property, while an imposing steel gate blocked the entrance to Ami Sulzer's vast compound. The magnificent house, which contained almost 30,000 square feet, sat at the top of the hill. To the right of the main house, a large pond and horse stable were visible with help from the moonlight.

The heavy steel gate opened before the first vehicle got within a hundred feet of the guard house, and each Sentinel maintained a constant speed as the 5.0-liter V8 easily climbed up the hillside. A carefully orchestrated welcome occurred once all the vehicles arrived at the top.

Ami stood just off the driveway in a black tailored Italian suit and met each person as they climbed from the vehicles. At five foot seven inches, Ami always let his slight stature work to his advantage. People looked down on him when growing up, but he never let that bother him. In fact, he let them think less of him as he studied them, learned their weaknesses, and then exploited them for personal gain. As he became more powerful and ruthless, he witnessed firsthand as condescension toward him turned to fear. He savored every sweet morsel of fright his persona elicited as he became one of the largest arms dealers the world had ever seen.

As the seventh vehicle arrived, it pulled up and came to a slow stop. Charlie stepped out first, followed by Troy. Although they had never met, Ami treated Phillipe and Madeline Lapointe as long-lost friends. He raised Charlie's hand and kissed the top of it gently.

"Welcome to my humble abode, Phillipe and Madeline. I take it the trip from Montreal went well?"

"It was a wonderful trip." Troy answered in heavily accented English. "We are grateful for the hospitality you have shown us since we arrived and honored to finally meet you face to face."

"The resort is heavenly," Charlie added.

"I'm glad you've enjoyed it, Mademoiselle." Ami stared into her eyes. "You look exquisite, by the way. More lovely than I could have imagined." He spoke in such a way as to draw her in, not make her feel uneasy. Ami had a suave way about him. He chose his words carefully and spoke in an alluring tone. Women found him tantalizing, and men envied his way with the opposite sex.

Charlie blushed slightly, and she perceived Ami was impressed with what he saw. The form-fitting black strapless cocktail dress accentuated her curves, which was the point of wearing it.

Ami then looked at Troy. "I apologize our paths have only crossed via invoices, manifests, and electronic correspondence so far."

"You've remedied that by inviting my wife and me to your home, oui?"

"True." Ami turned and gestured to the magnificent wooden front door. "Please make yourself comfortable. Dinner will be served in forty-five minutes in the great hall. Feel free to enjoy all the amenities my humble home has to offer."

Troy and Charlie moved away from the host so he could see to his next guest. As they entered the foyer, four security guards greeted them. The big, burly men displayed smiles on their faces, but they meant business.

As the two of them stood in the ornate room, one of the security guards turned and said to the guy next to him, "She sure has a lot of makeup." He tried to whisper, but his voice carried, and it was loud enough for her to hear what the man said.

Her smile shifted, and her brow tightened. "A girl has to look her best for such debonair and handsome men like yourselves." She remarked before her facial expression shifted to a warm smile.

The man blushed, realizing he could have offended one of the guests. Ami would not approve of such a thing. "I'm so sorry, ma'am. I didn't mean to—" The man spoke in broken English.

"Nonsense." Troy cut him off mid-phrase with a wave of his hand. "No offense taken, right dear?"

"Of course not," Charlie responded.

In full Phillipe Lapointe act, Troy walked over to the man who made the makeup comment and leaned in close. "I'll keep this as our little secret, my friend."

"I appreciate that, Mr. Lapointe." The security guard had blanched. "If you need anything tonight, ask for me. My name is Saul."

"Better Call Saul. I can do that if the need arises," Troy replied.

Saul smiled but clearly didn't get the television reference.

26

ACCRA

With very little time before dinner in the great hall, Troy and Charlie knew they must move with haste. Memorizing the layout of the complex beforehand, the two operators entered the house with a defined purpose. The agency asset provided the detailed schematic so The Omega Group, CIA, and several other alphabet agencies used that information to concoct a plan that allowed them access to the data source needed to complete the mission.

First, they needed to bypass the security system, which was no simple process. Any number of things could go wrong, but Troy and Charlie had to trust the plan. If it went all to hell, they would have to improvise or likely die.

As they walked down the east hallway, a couple walked toward them. The woman smiled warmly at Troy and Charlie. She and her partner slowed as they approached. The woman wore a red strapless gown, her arms and legs adorned with numerous tattoos in various shapes and sizes. Most of them had musical references or connotations. Troy could read one phrase on her left arm, which read *Will Never Be Voiceless*. Her leg had a symbol Troy knew to be the *Planet Zero* album design from the band Shinedown, one of his favorite musical acts. On a chance encounter years before, Troy had dinner with Barry Kerch, the drummer for the band, and their director of security at an Italian restaurant named Giovannis in Cardiff, Wales. The memory brough a smile to his face.

The woman extended her hand and introduced herself as Anke Dul-van Dooren. Her partner was named Han. They were from The Netherlands and made small talk about the opulence of Ami's palace. Troy and Charlie only had a few precious minutes, and he didn't want to come across as rude, so he used the excuse they needed to visit the lavatory, and that they would be glad to catch up with Anke and Han later when they were all back in the banquet hall.

After the run-in with the couple, several workers passed them and made friendly nods. Troy and Charlie returned their smiles and acted like they observed the works of art that adorned the walls and studied the countless rare artifacts on countless pedestals and shelves.

⚊⚊⚊◆⚊⚊⚊

After about five minutes meandering the hallway, they reached the door that looked like many others they passed. Troy glanced both ways, and with the coast clear, he nodded, and Charlie slid into the room. Troy stayed outside and made it appear like he took great interest in an exquisite mural on the opposite wall. There were no surveillance cameras pointed at or near the door Charlie entered. Used for storage, the room contained nothing of interest, but what lay inside the walls mattered. She went to the far corner of the room and, using the width of her hand, measured the approximate distance and made a mark three feet and eight inches over from the southern wall.

Next, she took out the black lipstick tube, popped off the top, and removed the red lipstick. Beneath the lipstick, an X-ACTO knife remained hidden. Charlie took the knife and made a rectangular incision on the wall, four inches high and six inches wide. Within a minute, she had the sheetrock removed. Using her LED flashlight, she illuminated the space and confirmed a batch of wires hidden behind the wall.

Charlie removed two oversized pressed powder cases from her purse, laid them on the floor, and quickly removed the tops. Under the actual powder were four small devices. Two from each case. The tiny electronic pieces of equipment were no larger than a Tylenol pill each. Smooth on one side, they contained razor-sharp prongs on the other. Charlie took each device and firmly pressed them into the four coaxial cables bundled together. The end of the devices had tiny LED lights that each turned green as soon as they pierced the skin of the cables and connected with the wires inside. Finally, Charlie took a tube of lip primer, unscrewed the bottom, and removed an item shaped like an AAA battery. She clicked a button on the bottom of this additional device and, once the light turned green, stuffed it into the battery of cables. A marvel of technology, the device transmitted data for up to ten miles. Its signal could pierce earth and stone. She replaced the sheetrock and covered the hole, even moving boxes from the other side of the room to conceal the damaged wall.

Seven minutes after walking into the room, she stepped back out, her task completed.

Troy looked at his watch and smiled. "Under ten minutes, that's pretty damn good time."

"What can I say," Charlie said with a devilish glance. "I'm awfully good with my hands."

"I bet," Troy replied.

"You missed your chance on the plane to find out Mr. Knight in shining armor."

"Story of my life. A day late and a dollar short."

"I'm sure a strapping guy like you will get the girl one day," she said with a laugh.

Troy nodded and brought his left arm to his hip, forming a loop. "My lady," he said with one last dig. "I guess I'm stuck with you for now."

"How gallant of you." Charlie brought her right arm into his, and with her left arm, she patted his shoulder. "And might I add, you're pretty damn lucky to have a gal like me on your side."

"Yeah, you're probably right." Troy swung his right hip into her. "I bet the Jackal is wishing we could switch places tonight."

"In his wet dreams maybe," Charlie said with a laugh. "And Cap. Let's try to not die tonight."

"That's the plan."

They made their way to the great hall without incident, grateful the first part of their mission went off without a hitch but knowing the rest of the evening wouldn't be so straightforward.

27

— • —

ACCRA

Five miles away, in a white box van pulled off the side of the road, the monitors in front of Digger came alive.

"We own video," Digger said a moment later.

Sarge turned around in the driver's seat and tapped furiously on the steering wheel. "I told you they'd be able to do it."

Digger silently watched the video feeds for several minutes.

"Do you see them?" Sarge asked.

"No, not yet," Digger replied.

"Start recording the hall and office when it's empty so we can have the playback video loop ready."

"Yeah, I'm already on it, Sarge." Another minute passed in silence as images flickered across the multiple screens. "I see them. They just entered the great hall."

"They look okay?" Sarge asked.

"Yes, fine. Both appear to be smiling."

Sarge smirked. "Next part will wipe that grin off their faces.

"No doubt."

Sarge dialed the colonel. "We have eyes inside the compound, sir."

"Roger that." The colonel answered the phone from a safe house outside Accra. They had a vehicle ready in case they needed to rush toward the compound. It would take less than six minutes to arrive. But if that contingency became necessary, the likelihood that Cap and Charlie would make it out alive was virtually nil. He put the call on speaker so the Jackal and Harry, who were in the room with him, could hear what was being said as well. "How's Cap and Charlie?"

"They both just walked arm-in-arm in front of the several surveillance cameras, sir."

"Everything look okay?" the colonel asked.

"Yes, sir. Cap and Charlie appear to be fine, but it sure looks weird seeing him dressed up in that monkey suit. And with that disguise, well, he just doesn't look himself."

"That's the point. Besides, I'm sure he feels weird wearing it." Colonel Marshall let out an audible grunt.

"What about Charlie?" The Jackal now stood next to the colonel. "She looks hot as hell in her cocktail dress, doesn't she?"

Sarge didn't acknowledge the question. He knew better. And also knew the reaction that would come next.

The colonel's head snapped to his right, and his eyes burned. "Shut it, Jackal, and keep your mind on the mission."

"Yes, sir."

"Anyway, Charlie would eat you for dinner if she knew you were ogling her in that little black dress."

"Well, douse me in barbecue sauce and stick a cornbread muffin in my mouth, Colonel. I'm ready to be her main course any day of the week."

The colonel rolled his eyes. "You're incorrigible and a dumbass, all at the same time."

"Grab me a screenshot, fellas," the Jackal said in a quieter voice as he ignored the comment.

"No chance in hell, creeper," Sarge replied.

28

ACCRA

The meal Ami served in the great hall exceeded even his guests' wildest expectations. Undeterred by cost and determined to offer the very best, Ami flew in two world-renowned chefs from three-star Michelin restaurants to prepare the evening's meal. The menu had something for every guest. For Troy and Charlie, it was like nothing they had ever experienced, nor would they likely ever experience again.

Troy looked several tables over and saw Naseefa al-Majid sitting in a place of honor near the host. He looked identical to the photos provided. Without making it obvious, Troy watched him for several moments and wondered if he could keep his promise to Jalal. After the auction, the plan to snag Naseefa seemed tenuous at best, and lots could go wrong. Even though Naseefa's survival was not guaranteed, Troy had to try. He gave his word, after all, and his word was his bond.

Once dinner ended it was time for the first part of the auction to begin. Guests moved from the great hall to the banquet hall in the northwest portion of the main floor, a room twice the size of the great hall, where the auction would begin. All those in attendance knew the evening comprised three bidding sessions, with brief receptions filling the gaps. Ami asked everyone to stay until the end. In fact, he planned a special presentation when the auction ended. Forty leather chairs were placed in a semi-circle and were four rows deep. In the front of the room, the auctioneer stood at his podium with the items presented behind him when the bidding began.

The real Lapointes planned to attend the auction for one reason: to purchase a dirty bomb, not for themselves, but for a client. As the intermediaries, their clients would pay them handsomely to do so. Ami knew why they came, and he expected the bidding to be competitive. Troy and Charlie were aware that to not blow cover, they needed to be all-in when the bidding started. The agency cracked into Lapointe's bank accounts and provided the necessary access for both Troy and Charlie. The account had a balance of close to thirty million dollars, more than enough money to buy the dirty bomb and then some.

Thirty-three minutes into the auction, the item came up for bid. The interest and bidding became intense. Multiple well-funded terrorist groups got into the action. Two of the groups ran up the bids. For a few minutes, Troy wasn't sure if the Lapointes pockets were deep enough to win. But in the end, they topped a group with ties to a Syrian terror organization.

Troy leaned close to Charlie as they won the bid. "Damn Shabiha's almost snagged it from us!"

She nodded but said nothing in response to the derogatory term used to describe certain groups in Syria.

Twenty minutes later, someone purchased the last item, and the first session came to a close. A brief interlude took place, which included a champagne toast and an assortment of desserts. Several times, Troy felt eyes upon him. One time, he glanced over to see Ami look, then nodded his direction. Troy returned the gesture with a warm smile.

The second session began with fanfare as the first item presented started an intense bidding war and almost a physical altercation. Ami stood off to the side of the room and smiled. He had enough security to ensure order prevailed but couldn't help taking a sick pleasure in the commotion and watching grown men squabble.

When the auctioneer introduced the fourth item, Ami made a sweeping movement with his hand and walked out the rear door. Eight of the people in attendance followed his lead. These were the heavy hitters, the men with deep pockets. Troy smiled as the intel appeared once again to be accurate. The nuclear weapon auction would not occur during the main auction but in a private room to the right of the banquet hall with only those in attendance who had the financial resources to purchase the weapon of mass destruction. This ruled out eighty-five percent of those in the room, including the Lapointes.

Ami's departure served as the cue for Troy and Charlie. The time arrived for the most treacherous part of the evening. With Ami and the others meeting in the other room, the focus of security would be on that part of the home.

Charlie whispered something in Troy's ear. He nodded and stood as she did. As they walked to the door on the west side of the room, he told the attendant his wife needed a restroom. The man nodded and gestured down the hall. Troy thanked him, and they proceeded in that direction.

29

ACCRA

"Eyes on Cap and Charlie," Digger said as he watched on the video feed as they left the banquet hall and proceeded toward the bathroom.

"Which way they headed?" Sarge asked.

"Southeast hallway," Digger replied.

"Toward the basement?"

"Appears so, Sarge."

"Is it clear to start the video loop?"

Digger nodded. "Copy that."

"This better work." Jesús sat just to the right of Digger. Unable to watch, he used his outstretched hands and coupled the crown of his head.

"It will," Digger replied.

"But how can you be so sure?" Jesús asked.

Digger cleared his throat twice in a loud tone. "Because if it doesn't, they're as good as dead."

Sarge spoke in a firm tone. "Put your prayer cap on for them, Jesús."

With a nod, Jesús replied, "My brother, it never comes off!"

After a few clicks on his keyboard, Digger said, "Looped tape is running."

"We'll know pretty quickly if it's working," Sarge said as he looked at both men. "Both the tape and the prayers."

A man stood at the door leading to the lower level, where Ami kept his office and, more importantly, his laptop. The intel from the informant allowed them to know about the security presence, so they factored it into their plan. Just past that door was the ladies' bathroom. On the wall were several display cases containing various rare and extremely valuable firearms. The hallway was completely empty except for the lone sentry.

Charlie passed by the man guarding the door and gave him a warm smile. "Restroom?" she asked as she gently touched his exposed skin between his wrist and rolled up collared shirt.

The man blushed, pointed to the next door, and said, "Right there, ma'am." Most guests rarely acknowledged him, and suddenly, this attractive woman looked in his direction and smiled as her skin touched his.

Troy stopped at the cases and appeared to examine the contents with great care.

Two minutes later, he gestured to the man as he pointed to an item in the case. "Is this really one of the gold-plated Tabuk AK-47s owned by Saddam Hussein?"

The sentry smiled, broke protocol, and walked over to the case. "It is. A gift from the former Iraqi President to Mr. Sulzer personally."

"You don't say?" Troy asked.

"He has many remarkable items, even more valuable than this one." The man pointed to the left of the AK-47. "This is the actual Walther PPK Adolph Hitler used to commit suicide."

"Oui? Not possible." Troy used his thick French accent, feigning surprise. "I read that weapon was lost to history."

"That's simply not true." The man began a lengthy explanation of how Ami not only located the weapon but also verified the authenticity of its infamous past.

As Troy distracted the sentry, Charlie edged out of the ladies' room, quietly opened the door that led to the basement, and slipped downstairs undetected. At the bottom of the stairs, she saw several objects near the bottom step, discounted them, and made her way with haste thirty feet down the hall to the office at the end. Before she turned the door handle, she looked up to see the two security cameras mounted just above the door looking directly at her. *God, I hope this is working, and Ami's security team isn't watching*, she thought before she turned the door handle. If Digger didn't own the video feed, her foray into Ami's office would be brief, extremely painful, and almost certainly deadly.

With her eyes fixed on the camera, a devilish idea crossed her mind. She made a slightly graphic gesture directed at the boys on the other end of the fiber optic cable, hoping it would give them a little lift and bring smiles to their faces.

It did. She just had no way of knowing.

Charlie entered the pitch-black room and had no choice but to turn on the lights. Smaller than she expected, it measured only twelve by twelve. A solid cherry desk sat in the middle of the room while a loveseat, several small tables, and a flat-screen television completed it. The features and décor were sparse compared to the opulence found elsewhere throughout the house. She wondered if the rest of the house simply acted as show and if the true Ami lived a more simplistic life.

She breathed a sigh of relief when her eyes locked on the MacBook Pro, which sat on the leather desk pad. Quickly, she stepped over to the laptop and removed from her purse the pink lipstick tube. Within seconds, she unscrewed the bottom and removed the flash drive. Not a normal piece of hardware, the prototype drive provided by the NSA could hold up to 12TB of data and copy any files regardless of the encryption or security protocols on the device. Charlie took the flash drive and stuck it into the USB port. The laptop, which appeared to be off when she inserted the drive, came to life a couple of seconds later. A progress box appeared at the center of the screen, indicating that the data transfer had begun. The genius programmers at the NSA had included a countdown clock to let her know how long it would take to copy the encrypted MacBook's contents to the flash drive. The display read twelve minutes to completion, indicating that 1.6TB of data had to be transferred from the laptop to the drive.

It would be the longest twelve minutes of her life. She also wondered if Troy needed to improvise upstairs while she was away for so long.

30

— · —

ACCRA

Looking down at Phillipe Lapointe's Omega Seamaster watch that adorned his right wrist, Troy realized it had only been seven minutes since Charlie slipped downstairs. He continued to discuss the impressive array of firearms with the guard when Ami Sulzer walked toward him. Troy's muscles involuntarily tightened.

Was Ami headed for his office?

If so, the results could be disastrous for Charlie and, by default, himself. His mind raced but he did not let that show on his features. A warm smile slid across his face as the host approached. Troy couldn't believe the auction for the nuke finished so quickly.

Had something gone wrong?

"Ahh, Phillipe, I see you have located my collection of unique firearms," Ami said as he approached.

"I have. My hunch is your full collection is much larger than this."

"That's true, it is. I have a vault that holds the vast majority."

"Now that sounds impressive." Troy smiled. "Any chance I can get a peek?"

Ami nodded. "Maybe once the auction ends, I can open it and give those interested a private tour."

"I'd like that very much."

Ami looked around. "Where's your bride?"

Troy tilted his head away from them. "In the restroom."

"Is she okay?" Ami looked genuinely concerned.

Movies portray villains as people who lack humanity or care for others. However, Troy found that some of the truly despicable people he encountered were often quite kind in certain situations—another paradox of life.

"I believe so. I'll check on her in a few. Her stomach gave her fits during the second part of the auction."

"Oh my! Was it something she ate? I was assured by the chefs …"

Troy put up a hand and cut him off. "The food was sublime. It's nothing like that. She picked up a nasty stomach bacteria while we traveled to Indonesia a few months ago, and ever since then, her stomach has had occasional issues regardless of what she eats. Trust me, it had nothing to do with what you served."

"Would it help if we got Madeline ginger ale or something to calm her stomach?" Ami asked.

With a warm smile, Troy replied, "Yes, I'm sure my wife would very much appreciate that gesture."

Ami looked at the guard, who returned to standing near the door and nodded. The man immediately left his post and headed toward the kitchen.

A voice down the hall beckoned. They needed Ami in the banquet hall with a question about one of the items. "Care to join me?" Ami asked as he looked at Troy.

"I should probably wait for Madeline," he answered.

"Nonsense." Ami's eyes narrowed, and with a fierce gaze, he said, "My associate will check on her and bring the tonic to aid in her discomfort."

Refusing could raise an alarm with his host. "Of course, as you wish. I'd be honored to join you."

"Very well, follow me."

As they walked down the hall and took a left, two men passed by them, headed in the direction they had just left. Ami whispered something in one of the men's ears as he got close, but Troy could not make out what he said.

The man nodded, and Ami continued on his way to the banquet hall.

31

ACCRA

Charlie felt beads of perspiration on her forehead as the data download was completed. Almost thirteen minutes had passed from when she sneaked downstairs to when she removed the flash drive. It was too long but she had no control over how long the technology took to complete the vital task. Charlie slipped out the door, leaving the room exactly as she found it, and walked as fast as possible toward the stairs.

Then she heard something, making her freeze. Voices trailed down the stairs. She had no time to retreat.

They caught her.

Charlie came face to face with the two men at the foot of the stairs. They appeared to be two of the security men she saw during dinner, but she had not spoken with either. She recalled seeing one of them stare in her general direction several times.

Both men had enormous smiles and appeared to be carrying on, but as soon as they saw her, the smiles disappeared.

"What are you doing down here?" the larger of the two men asked in a grave tone.

Charlie did her best to act confused. "Wrong turn, I believe," she replied in her thick French accent. "I thought this was the way toward the women's bathroom. I guess I should have known it wasn't for guests when I encountered the stairs. No worries, I ended up finding a bathroom at the end of the hall and used it since I had to go really, really bad." She had a sheepish look as she said all this.

The man on the left, who was much smaller, eyed her suspiciously. "I'll need to let Ami know you were down here," he said, pointing to her. "Wait right there until I make a call."

"That won't be necessary," she replied, moving toward the stairs and pushing past both men.

The man to her right reached out as she tried to slip by and pulled her toward him with a violent tug while at the same time, he spun her around, and his left arm came across her neck which encircled her throat tight. Her windpipe rested in the elbow pit of his muscled arm. Charlie's mind raced. She wasn't sure what to do at the moment.

Should I fight? Surely, I can take these two assholes without much effort. "Look bitch." The man growled. "You're not going anywhere until we say you can leave."

"What are you doing?" The smaller man pleaded. "Ami will have us killed if we harm one of his guests."

"Go upstairs, get Ami. He must know what's going on. This woman is up to something down here. I know she is lying to us."

"You don't want to do that." Charlie hissed through clenched teeth as she gasped for breath, and her face turned a shade of red.

"And why not?" the larger man behind her asked.

"Because I'll kill both of you with my own hands before Shorty makes it up the stairs." She spoke with full sincerity in gasps of breaths. As she spoke, Charlie's eyes darted to her right at the end of the stairs, the object she searched for just within reach. She could feel his breath on her neck but knew the larger man doubted her, so she added. "Listen to me, shit for brains, I'm not someone to be trifled with."

Both men laughed at her comment.

The smaller man scoffed as he replied with a derisive tone, "What's that phrase? Oh, right! Sticks and stones may break my bones, but words will never hurt me ..."

Using all the strength she could muster, Charlie bent her left arm, raised it, and then brought it down and back with tremendous force into the man's solar plexus. It literally knocked the breath out of the man, causing him to double over. His death grip loosened, and she reached out with her right hand and grabbed the broom handle, which leaned against the wall at the base of the last step. At the same time, she pushed away from him with her left hand. The larger man saw the motion but could do nothing to stop her. His body frame, while quite large, moved lethargically.

The shorter man seemed perplexed and frozen in place as all this occurred in a fraction of a second.

With lightning-quick reflexes, Charlie gripped the handle and swung it upward, striking the jaw bone of the larger man with enough force to snap off the last six inches of the broom handle, leaving a jagged pointed end instead of a rounded tip. The intensity of the strike stunned the man momentarily as blood began to flow from the wound on his neck and onto his white dress shirt. Charlie took the remaining handle and snapped it over her leg, breaking it into two pieces. She now had two pointed ends on the stick measuring three feet long.

Charlie dropped one of the sharpened sticks to the ground while she clenched the other one with her right hand. Her next motion entailed a knife hand chop with her now free left hand to the throat of the shorter man. The strike to his throat almost knocked him out, but not quite. Charlie then turned back to the larger man. She knew what she had to do. He staggered from the blow, but she knew he would come at her with everything he had. Charlie could see the rage within him grow as each drop of blood flowed out of the fresh wound.

With tremendous force, she took the jagged broom handle in her right hand and plunged it deep into the man's chest. Death came instantly as she thrust it between the two ribs in the thoracic cage and completely pierced his heart through the middle. The large man fell backward and slowly slid down the gray faux-painted wall until he lay flat against the ground, the broom handle sticking out of his chest, seemingly suspended in midair. A stunned expression plastered across his face as his eyes turned glassy and the last bit of air expelled from his mouth.

Without wasting a second, Charlie grabbed the smaller man by the shoulders, who held his injured throat, and threw him upon the larger man. The broom handle impaled him, and even though it missed his heart by a few inches' death would embrace him with its icy fingers. She kicked his body, driving the wooden stick through his torso. The smaller man gasped for breath. A shocked expression covered his face as he reached for his chest and the wooden object that now protruded through it. Charlie leaned over him from behind and, with her arms, grabbed his neck and twisted violently. A distinct snapping sound, like a wishbone being cracked, told her the spinal cord was severed. His body shuddered, then stopped moving as his limbs dropped toward the ground.

The scene was gruesome, even for someone like Charlie, who had witnessed death up close and personal on numerous occasions.

⚬

She opened the first door to her right. It appeared to be a storage closet. The weight of the two men impaled together like a shish kabob made her grunt as she dragged their bodies across the carpeted floor. After a minute of straining, she had the two bodies inside the small space.

Several rags were on a shelf, as were some cleaning supplies; she took the rags and did her best to clean up the blood that pooled on the carpet in the hallway. Fortunately, the carpet was dark in color, and the blood didn't stand out terribly much. Plus, she hoped to be long gone before anyone discovered the bodies. Before closing the closet door, Charlie looked at the bodies one more time and surveyed the death her hands caused.

Rage still pulsated from within as Charlie spit on the bodies of the two men. "Watch who you call a bitch next time."

Charlie felt no guilt, knowing if the smaller man had made it up the stairs alive, she and Troy would have met a much more horrific end.

Reaching the top of the stairs, she looked out the peephole built into the door and saw the hall upstairs appeared to be empty. Sliding out the door, she closed it slowly, unaware she left a streak of blood on the left side of the door frame as she departed.

32

ACCRA

Digger watched the monitor with a look of disbelief plastered across his face as Charlie struggled and then overpowered the two men. He reached out to the colonel via comms as soon as the larger man grabbed her around the neck.

"What's wrong?" the colonel, who was on his cell phone, asked.

"Charlie's in trouble, sir."

I'll have to call you back, the colonel said as he disconnected the call. "What's the issue?"

Digger recounted what happened to Charlie and the two men.

The colonel said nothing. He only listened.

When Charlie impaled the two men, Digger's eyes widened. "Damn! She just jacked both those guys up with a broom handle," he exclaimed in shock.

"That was brutal," Sarge said as he looked on and watched the scene unfold in real-time.

"Charlie just turned the two security dudes into human skewers," Digger said as he shook his head.

They all breathed a collective sigh of relief that she survived, but the immediate problem became what would happen to Charlie and Troy now that there were two dead security guards stuffed into a closet in the basement.

"Leaving the safe house within the next three minutes in one of the armored Mercedes," the colonel said.

"Destination?" Digger asked.

"I'm coming to you," the colonel replied. "Troy and Charlie will likely need to make like a bat out of hell from that compound, and they'll need any support we can give them."

"Agreed, sir."

"She got the data from Ami's laptop, right?" the colonel asked.

"Yes, sir. The download completed, and she has the flash drive."

"Good! Keep an eye on the surveillance cameras and make sure you, Sarge, and Jesús are ready for a firefight. The Jackal, Harry, and I are outbound."

"Copy that, Colonel. We'll be ready to smoke whoever we have to ..."

33

ACCRA

Troy stood at the rear of the banquet hall and looked at his watch once more. *Charlie should be back by now.* In the front of the ornately decorated room, Ami engaged in an intense discussion with two men. The apparent disagreement centered on a particular item being bid upon as the two men questioned its authenticity.

Just then, the man who had gone to get Charlie a drink walked through the back door and approached Troy. "Mr. Lapointe," the man said. "I knocked on the bathroom door and tried to give your wife the drink. She did not reply after several attempts, so I went to check and see that she was okay. But, she was not there?" The man had a concerned look on his face.

Troy lied with ease. "Thank you for the concern, my friend. You must have just missed her. She stopped by here a minute ago and said she would step outside and get a breath of fresh air. Maybe you could bring it to her outside?"

"Of course," the man replied. "It would be my pleasure." He slipped back out the door.

Knowing it only bought him a few minutes, Troy, seeing Ami occupied, left the room. Walking down the hall, he came face-to-face with Charlie as she rounded a corner.

Charlie looked terrible. Clearly, something went wrong.

"Are you okay? What the hell happened?"

"Umm, not really. It was kinda intense." She rubbed her cheek. A streak of crimson blood lined her face as she removed her hand.

"My God, you're bleeding!" Troy exclaimed.

She shook her head. "It's not my blood."

"What the hell happened?"

"I got the files. All of them. It took longer than I expected. When I was at the base of the stairs and headed back up, I ran into two men."

"Who?"

"I don't know, two of Ami's security goons I guess. But one of them tried to stop me from coming back upstairs. They were going to call Ami since I was downstairs where I shouldn't have been."

"So it got physical?"

"Yeah, it got intense fast. One of them grabbed me, and I had to fight for my life."

"And?"

"I won, they lost." She spoke in an exacerbated tone. "We need to get the hell out of here, and I mean now! As soon as someone finds the bodies, they will lock this place down, and we will be goners."

"Bodies?" Troy asked.

"Yeah, I stuffed both of them in a closet near Ami's office."

Troy thought for a second. With the restroom a few doors down, he motioned her to it. "We need to clean this blood off you ASAP, then high-tail it to the front door, get a car, and get the hell out of Dodge. Ami thinks you don't feel well since I spoke with him when you were downstairs copying the files."

"Will he let us leave?"

"I'll say you feel worse, and I need to bring you back to the resort. But if he or his security staff see you with blood on your face, the gig is up. We must move fast, Charlie. You sure you're okay?"

Her eyes narrowed. "Yeah, I'm good. Sadly, it's not the first time I've impaled a human being!"

"You're just a treasure trove of rainbows, unicorns, and sparkles, aren't yah?"

"Hooah!" Charlie exclaimed. "You have no idea."

Three minutes later, with Charlie cleaned up as much as possible, they walked through the maze of halls to the front door. Before they reached it, though, they ran into the last person they wanted to see.

"Phillipe! How are you, Madeline?" Ami asked.

Charlie did her best to act like she felt terrible.

"She feels worse, Ami, much worse," Troy replied.

"I'm so sorry to hear this. What can I do for her?"

"Think it's best that I bring her back to the resort. She has medicine there that should be able to help. She needs rest."

"Of course!" Ami snapped his fingers and spoke to one of the men near the front door. "Have a car readied for the Lapointes. They need to be brought back to the resort with great haste."

"Thanks for understanding," Troy said. "Once she gets settled in the room, I'll have the driver bring me back."

"No," Ami replied. "You should stay with your bride. You purchased what you came for, after all, no?"

"Yes, I did," Troy said. "But I must insist. We did not come all the way here to disregard your hospitality by not staying until the end of the evening. Besides, you owe me that tour of the armory."

"Are you sure?" Ami stared into Troy's eyes and then over at Charlie, who appeared quite weak.

"I'll be fine once I take my pills and rest," she replied in a fragile voice. "Phillipe needs to return."

"As you wish," Ami replied. "Please feel better, Madeline. I'm sorry your visit had to end on such a sour note, but I'll come by tomorrow and check on you at the resort."

A voice behind them said, "I'll walk them out to the vehicle, Ami." Neither Troy nor Charlie turned to see who spoke.

Ami replied, "I appreciate that."

"Thank you again for your generosity," Charlie said as she turned away and walked with her husband outside the front door.

Ami watched the two guests depart.

34

ACCRA

The guard couldn't find Madeline Lapointe, no matter where he looked outside. Finally, he put the glass on a railing and returned to his post. As he approached the door, he noticed the streak of blood along the doorframe. His heart raced as he opened the door and descended the stairs, taking three at a time. He stopped at the base of the steps and looked down the hall. There, he saw evidence of more blood on the carpet and the walls. As he opened the second door, he found the bodies. The mangled corpses lay side by side, a wooden stick connecting them.

The beleaguered man ran down the hall and flipped up a hidden panel located behind a landscape painting depicting the city of Jerusalem. Never before had he pushed the red button, but today, he pressed it firmly. A voice came over the speaker, and the guard explained what he had found.

The silent alarm triggered security protocols. Large metal shutters would roll down over every window and door in seconds. The house that looked so welcoming would convert into a fortress-style bunker in less than two minutes.

◆

As they stepped outside into the sticky, humid night air, Troy felt a firm grip take hold of his shoulder. Before he could turn, the same voice that said he would walk them out spoke. "So, did you get it?"

Troy turned and came face to face with a man he didn't recognize. A fire burned deep within the man's eyes, that much he could tell.

"Get what?" Troy asked. "Do I know you?"

"I know why you came," the man replied.

"Really?"

"They sent you."

"Excuse me?" Troy wondered what game he was playing and, more importantly, who the hell was this man?

As he leaned in closer, the man said, "I'm the one who provided intel to the agency. I know what you came for."

With those words, Troy realized the man standing before him was the asset they believed had been killed. But clearly, he survived.

"You're still alive? We thought Ami killed you."

"Almost, but I made it. Did you copy the data?"

"Yes, we have it. Will it tell us what I need to know?"

"It should."

"Do you know where the nukes are?"

The man shook his head, knowing he only had a few seconds to speak since the Land Rover was pulling up the driveway. "I know one is in the United States. The other one sold tonight. Only Ami and Naseefa know the location."

"Will the info we recovered tell us both locations?"

"Yes, I believe so, but it will be buried deep within the encrypted files."

"We believe the one sold tonight is still in Iraq and have a good hunch where they hid it."

The man nodded. "Keeping it in Iraq makes sense."

The Land Rover pulled up next to the three of them. Their time had expired. "Come with us," Troy pleaded. "For your own safety."

"I can't."

"Ami will kill you if he finds out what you did for us."

The man smiled. "My friend, I'm already dead, and my fate was sealed the day I agreed to work for this monster."

Troy shook his head. "Our fate is not written in stone. We can choose our future."

"Maybe for you, but it's too late for me." The man gestured to the Land Rover. "Get in the damn vehicle before you both die with me here at the hands of a ruthless arms dealer."

Troy nodded. "Thank you for what you did."

"Don't thank me yet. Just recover those nukes."

Troy and Charlie climbed into the Land Rover.

As the door closed, a commotion started behind them as several men burst out the front door. "We need to go," he told the driver. "My wife is ill, and we must return to the resort immediately."

The driver put the vehicle in gear and accelerated, but the radio in the center console came to life. "Do not leave, I repeat, do not leave!" a voice commanded.

Troy looked behind and saw the heavy metal shutters lower. The compound transformed into a hardened bunker. The gig was up, and someone must have found the bodies. He knew Ami gave the order since Troy recognized the voice from the radio. "Ignore that order and drive," Troy demanded, even though he knew it would be a waste of breath. He prepared himself for what would happen in the next fraction of a second.

The man slammed hard on the brakes, slowing the vehicle as it descended the hill leading away from the compound. After hitting the brakes, the driver reached for the Glock on his right hip but didn't move fast enough. Troy grabbed the driver's right hand firmly while, at the same time, his left elbow crashed into the side of the man's temple, knocking the man out cold. After removing the gun, Troy climbed over the gearshift to take control of the vehicle, which continued to roll down the driveway and pick up speed.

A second later, the first volley of bullets sprayed the back of the Sentinel. The bulletproof glass absorbed the rounds, but they still made a hell of a cracking noise.

Time was up.

Troy threw open the driver's side door and pushed the unconscious driver out, then slammed the door shut. "Climb up front." Troy dropped the pedal to the floor. The Land Rover sped up with tremendous speed for a vehicle of its size.

As they careened down the driveway, Charlie pointed and yelled, "The guard has an RPG!"

Two hundred feet ahead, the man at the guard house emerged. With his left hand, he pushed the button to close the heavy steel gate while his right hand held a shoulder-mounted RPG-7 launcher. Troy considered lowering the driver's side window, but there wasn't a chance in hell that he could make the shot from a speeding vehicle at that distance.

The distinctive red burst of flames shot out the back of the weapon in the evening's darkness, and a puff of white, billowing smoke encompassed the guard. The warhead careened through space at over 250 meters per second.

"Brace for impact!" Troy screamed as he gripped the wheel harder. His knuckles turned white as he jerked the wheel sharply to the right.

35

ACCRA

"Where are you?" Sarge asked.

"Three minutes away. We're trying to get there as fast as this vehicle will scoot. The Jackal is driving this thing like a bat out of hell." The colonel answered Sarge's call on the first ring. "Did they make it out of the compound?"

"No, not before a shitstorm erupted," Sarge replied, followed by a long pause.

"And?"

"What do you think? It's Cap we're talking about here. If anyone can make it out of hell and back, it's our fearless leader."

"I pray you're right," the colonel said.

"It's guaranteed that Jesús is praying overtime right now."

"Roger that," the colonel replied. "We need whatever miracles he can summon."

The RPG warhead landed fifteen feet to the left of the Sentinel with a deadly concussive blast. Pieces of the driveway, chunks of soil, and shards of shrapnel careened in every direction.

Built to withstand a direct hit, the Land Rover shuddered violently as the shock wave pushed the 5,000-pound vehicle to the right and almost lifted it off the ground. No small feat. The impact jostled Troy and Charlie around the cab like rag dolls, but miraculously, Troy kept his hands firmly wrapped around the leather steering wheel. With the two right wheels slipping off the edge of the driveway, he struggled and pulled the wheel sharply to the left, aligning all four wheels back on solid footing.

Troy wasn't about to discover what damage a direct hit might inflict on the armored vehicle as he saw the guard re-load another warhead. He knew what must be done.

Aware it would be close, Troy felt sure that if they didn't get out before the gate shut, neither he nor Charlie would stand a chance of surviving.

Straightening out the vehicle, he accelerated while his left hand reached over and hit the automatic window button, which lowered the driver's side window. Next, he removed the Glock 22 wedged between his right thigh and the smooth leather seat. In one fluid motion, he racked the weapon. Without question, the shot would be virtually impossible, and he would have to do it with his left hand. That made little difference since Troy trained extensively and was an expert marksman with both hands. Plus, when the pressure boiled over to a point where most people faltered, Troy didn't.

The speedometer on the Sentinel registered 85 MPH as Troy rested his left hand on the driver's side mirror. It took all of his strength to hold the weapon steady as the resistance from the wind fought his attempt to keep his hand in place. Fortunately, the smooth pavement of the driveway and the high-end suspension of the vehicle didn't add to the difficulty.

They were less than fifty feet from the guardhouse, and the second warhead clicked in place as the man who held it took deadly aim at the vehicle barreling down on him.

Troy's first two shots went far to the left as they ricocheted off the side of the building. Moving his hand ever so slightly, Troy let the next volley fly as he rapidly unloaded the magazine. The fifth and sixth rounds struck the man's forehead. As the back of his head exploded, the signal from his brain to his fingertips registered, and he depressed the trigger on the RPG-7 launcher. While falling backward, the warhead launched with a burst of crimson against the blackness of the night sky.

Fortunately, the ordnance shot up in the air with no real threat to Troy or Charlie as it came down in the middle of the lawn away from everybody.

With the gate closed more than halfway, the Land Rover approached and continued to gain speed. The speedometer registered triple digits as it approached the gate. It would be close, too close for comfort. With a metallic screech, the three-inch cylinder-shaped tips of the gate scraped viciously against the side of the Sentinel as it passed between the guard house and the gate.

Once through, Charlie looked at Troy. Her eyes were wide as saucers.

"Dammit, that was close," she yelled.

"You think?" He stared forward and pressed hard on the brake pedal to keep from losing control. They almost reached the spot where the driveway turned sharp and entered the thick woods. As he handed Charlie the Glock, he said, "I'm out. See if you can find any more mags."

Her eyes darted around the interior cab as she searched for ammo. Then she saw it. "Phone, I got a phone," she said, holding up the smartphone that the driver wedged between the seat and center console.

"Does it have a passcode?"

"Negative," Charlie replied. "It opened right to the home screen."

"Call Digger," Troy said.

36

_— • —_

ACCRA

Next to the keyboard, turned with the screen facing downward, a cell phone vibrated. Four quick bursts, followed by four more. Digger flipped over the phone but didn't recognize the number.

The caller ID said, _Unknown, Accra, Ghana._

"You gonna answer that?" Jesús asked with a curious expression displayed on his face.

Digger shrugged. "It's not one of our numbers."

"Answer it," Sarge said from the front seat.

With a heavy sigh, Digger clicked the speakerphone button. "Who is this?"

"Where the hell are you guys?"

"Charlie?" Digger sat up straighter and gripped the armrests on his chair.

"No, it's Beyonce. Who do you think would be calling right now, dickhead?"

Digger couldn't help but laugh out loud. Charlie might be the most sarcastic woman he had ever met. She could dish it out and take it with the best of them. "We're five miles south of Ami's compound, parked alongside the N2. Where are you?"

"Coming your way and coming in hot. Be ready for us."

"Roger that. The colonel just arrived with the others. We are in a white box truck and black Mercedes. You can't miss us."

Charlie handed Troy the phone, who spoke in an overtly irritated tone. "We need to ditch this Land Rover and move to the next phase, pronto."

"Copy that, Cap," Digger replied. "As soon as you give me that flash drive, I can upload its content to the shared server, and the analysts can get to work on breaking the encryption and start poring over the contents."

"We'll be at your location in two minutes." The line disconnected.

The colonel, Harry, and the Jackal climbed into the white box van halfway through the call.

"Thoughts?" the colonel asked the team.

Digger shrugged. "I'd say leave the Land Rover here. Chances are, it might have a tracker. We can't risk them following us. Plus, Ami will send a team after them, and you can be sure they will be rolling heavy. I'd prefer to keep the gunfights to a minimum if we can."

With pursed lips, Colonel Marshall nodded. "Agreed."

⸺◆⸺

Five minutes later, a five-pound block of M112 exploded inside the Land Rover, rendering the fortress-like vehicle into a heaping mess of flames and debris scattered across the roadway and onto the grass embankment.

Charlie handed Digger the flash drive as the van sped away from the immobilized Land Rover.

Digger put it into his USB drive and uploaded it to the server. "It's go time," he said.

Several minutes passed in relative silence as Sarge tried to put as much distance between them as possible from where Troy and Charlie had ditched the vehicle.

"You getting a good upload signal from a moving van?" Troy asked.

"Roger that, Cap. We are using Starlink. Elon Musk makes the best shit. Dudes weird for sure, but who cares when you're brilliant and create amazing companies. The upload is moving fast. Won't take long," Digger said.

Sarge remained focused on the road as he increased the speed. He tilted his head back toward the rear of the van. "Good job, you two."

Troy and Charlie looked at each other and smiled. "It was a close call," Charlie replied. "Thought we were goners once or twice, but Cap really got us out of there in the nick of time."

"It was a team effort," Troy said.

"Remind me to keep broomsticks away from you," the Jackal said, the comment directed at Charlie.

She laughed. "You should see where I can stick one when I get really pissed. The chest is quick, other places, not so quick."

The four men inside the box van exchanged apprehensive glances, and no one wanted to say what they all thought.

Hard pass.

Both vehicles carrying The Omega Group barreled their way down the N2 to a compound just outside Accra, where Ami had kept Naseefa for the past several months. They would hit the vehicle he traveled in before it pulled into the gated home.

37

ACCRA

Ami's fist slammed hard onto the top of the cherry desk. "What the hell did they get?"

Nobody in the room said a word. A deadly silence permeated the office as soon as they all stepped inside.

"The Lapointes. What the hell did they steal from me?" Ami asked once more. Everybody present knew he wouldn't ask a third time.

His chief of security, Dan Coates, originally from the United Kingdom and a retired member of the British SAS, stood across from the desk with his arms crossed. He could stand up to most men at six foot two and close to two-hundred and forty pounds. But not now, not with Ami in this livid state. With the rage erupting from his boss, he lowered his head, hesitant to make eye contact. "We have no way of knowing, sir."

"Excuse me, Daniel?" Ami hissed as spittle formed at the corner of his stretched lips. "Did I just hear you correctly?"

"Ami, I apologize, but we don't have many facts at the moment since the Lapointes only fled a dozen or so minutes ago. Somehow, they got into our surveillance system and looped the video from the hallway and down here. With no surveillance footage, it's difficult to know what they did or why."

The anger stretched across Ami's face as he shook his head back and forth.

Dan continued. "It would be wise to assume they targeted your laptop and have everything ..."

As he spoke the last few words and before Dan could finish the sentence, Ami reached into the top center drawer, pulled out the .357 Magnum, cocked it, then pulled the trigger in one quick motion. He split Dan's head in two as he fired the hollow point round at his face from point-blank range. The sound was deafening inside the closed room, and it took a couple of minutes before anyone could hear a thing. Even when they could, the ringing sound overpowered all others.

Ami lowered his head and placed the gun at the side of his body while everyone recovered from the sound. He then raised the gun and pointed it at the man who stood just to the right of the lifeless, still-twitching corpse. "You just got promoted, Ishmael," he shouted as he clicked back the hammer with his thumb. "Don't fail me like your boss. Get me some damn answers as to what they took and why. Phillipe and Madeline Lapointe would not be capable of pulling off anything like this on their own. They must be working with someone to make it past my security protocols."

Sweat formed on Ishmael's brow, and he nodded feverishly as he picked up the laptop and left the room. "I'm on it," he replied over his shoulder in a broken voice.

Ami placed the steel weapon on the desk and looked at the person to his left.

A perplexed look covered the man's face. "Do you think the Lapointes were working with the Americans?" the man asked.

The rage within Ami seethed from his pores. "Obviously. CIA, most likely, but I wouldn't rule out MI6, FSB, ISI, or even Mossad. In fact, we must consider the possibility the man and woman who entered my home were not the Lapointes. It could have been imposters. They drove the Land Rover like operators, not arms dealers."

"But if it's the Americans, I thought you have an arrangement with the CIA?"

"Apparently not anymore if they orchestrated this breach," Ami replied.

"What do you want to do?" the man asked, flexing his jaw to try to stop the ringing in his ears.

"Call the airport. Get my plane ready. We need to complete the transaction for the nuke immediately."

"And what about the guests upstairs?"

"What about them?" Ami's eyes narrowed.

"It will look odd if their host suddenly disappears without explanation."

"I'll come up with something. I always do."

"As you wish," the man said.

"And I want to take the helo to the airport, not a convoy."

"Of course." The man reached for the phone on the desk to call for the helicopter and also instruct the plane to be ready to leave at a moment's notice.

38

ACCRA

Naseefa al-Majid made his way down to the basement. As he reached the bottom step, the sound of a large caliber weapon discharged at the end of the hall. The sound ricocheted through the hall even though the door at the end of the hall remained closed.

Naseefa froze as a sudden fear encompassed him. Afraid to move, his legs resisted the movement forward. His legs won out, and his mind relented as he didn't move for almost three minutes.

When the door opened, a man who carried a laptop moved down the hall toward him with a panicked look. Blood splatter and what appeared to be pieces of dark matted hair and gray matter permeated the man's white dress shirt, face, and neck. Naseefa tried to ask what happened, but the man never stopped his hurried pace. He simply shook his head and muttered, "You don't want to go in there." Before Naseefa could respond, the man took the stairs two steps at a time and disappeared.

A few minutes later, Ami emerged from the room, followed by two other men. A red crimson burned within his eyes. As if his very soul appeared on fire. He stopped as he reached Naseefa, who stood like a statue, paralyzed by fear.

"Do you have what you need?" Ami asked in a perturbed tone.

"For what?" Naseefa asked, unsure what the shorter man meant by the question.

"To retrieve the weapon, dammit."

Naseefa shook his head. "Like I told you, I need a bag from the house where I've been staying. I thought we would depart in the morning."

"The plans have changed." Ami's gaze narrowed. "Go get it."

"Now? What about the rest of the night and the remaining items you plan to auction?"

Ami ignored the question. "I'm sending two security teams with you. They will escort you to the house. Get what you need, and we will rendezvous at the airport. I'm going to inform the buyer right now of our altered plans. Do you understand?" It was a rhetorical question.

"Two security teams? Am I in some sort of danger? We heard commotion outdoors and the sound of gunfire and explosions."

Ami once again ignored the questions. "Get back to the house, retrieve what you need, and my men will bring you to the airport. I'll explain what is happening then, not now."

Naseefa didn't have a clue what was happening or why the gunshot occurred in the room Ami had just stepped out of, but he also knew not to question Ami again. He would prefer to see another dawn and knew the fastest way to keep that from occurring would be to piss off Ami.

With a nod, Naseefa said, "I'll leave right now."

Ami didn't wait for his response. He bounded up the stairs and left Naseefa alone, with only his thoughts and a slight ringing sound in his left ear.

39

ACCRA

"We've got movement." Digger watched as the red circular dot appeared on his monitor. He tracked the movement as the signal slowly headed toward the N2, away from Ami's compound. With two oversized screens mounted to the vehicle's rear side panel, a narrow shelf held his keyboard and mouse. Hardware for the computer system rested inside a crate on the floor, while a drum throne provided him something to sit on.

The entire team was crammed into the back of the white box van. With so many people in a small, enclosed space, the air felt thick. It would be a gross understatement to say they were like sardines in a tin can.

"And how, pray tell, did you get a tracker on the vehicle used by Naseefa?" Troy asked as he slapped Digger on the shoulder.

A wide grin spread across Digger's face. "Slid it on the undercarriage of his vehicle. Very dangerous mission, Cap. I could have been run over!"

"While it was moving?" Troy pursed his lips and slowly nodded. The expression suggested he was impressed.

"Please," the Jackal interjected. "You're talking about super nerd here." He pushed the back of Digger's head forward in a playful motion. "This is our techie geek, not Jason Bourne!"

Digger pushed the hand away. "Shut it, you twat." As soon as the words left his mouth, he noticed Charlie's gaze. "Shit, I mean, ohh, sorry about that. Not used to a woman present on our missions." Digger's cheeks grew a few shades of pink.

Charlie smiled and then looked at the Jackal. "All good, man. Besides, I'm pretty sure the Jackal knows he's a twat. The rest of us sure do, after all."

With a hearty laugh, the Jackal turned toward Charlie. "I know deep down you love me. It's okay to let it out by using demeaning words and belittling phrases. The truth will come out one day."

Charlie stuck a finger in her mouth and feigned vomiting.

Troy rolled his eyes. "So what really happened? How did your group of nincompoops get a tracking device on Naseefa's ride."

"We stuck it on the vehicle at a Starbucks in Accra," Jesús replied. "Can you believe that?"

"You're kidding?" Charlie asked.

"Dude ordered a white chocolate mocha," Sarge said. "What a sissy!"

"Hey! I like those," the Jackal added.

"Like I said ..." Sarge said.

"What's the security detail look like that transported Naseefa back and forth?" Troy needed them back on the objective.

"They're badasses," the Jackal said. "No push-overs, to be sure."

"Wouldn't expect Ami to employ a bunch of rent-a-cops," Troy said. "Ami has made a lot of enemies over the years, people with a unique skill set. And he's smart enough to realize skimping on security staff is a quick way to meet one's maker."

"You and Charlie evaded his security," Jesús said.

Troy rolled his eyes. "Yeah, barely."

"I took care of the team inside. Cap had the exterior guards," Charlie replied with a smirk.

The red circle on the screen moved onto the N2, heading southwest toward their position. The tracker could also pick up audio, which allowed it to run voice recognition software. Two minutes later, it confirmed Naseefa's presence in the vehicle. Digger clicked away on his keyboard and brought up the satellite feed.

"It's a two-vehicle convoy. Naseefa appears to be in the second vehicle," Digger said.

"How long do we have?" The colonel pointed to the screen.

"Eleven minutes," Digger replied.

"That gives us ten minutes to solidify the plan and get into position," Troy said as he looked at the colonel.

"It's your show, Cap," he replied.

<h1 style="text-align:center">40</h1>

<h2 style="text-align:center">ACCRA</h2>

Two dozen exquisite women moved through the banquet hall, serving drinks and hors d'oeuvres to those gathered in the room. They wore revealing dresses, displayed inviting smiles, and knew how to string along the guests and distract them. Ami was no fool. He knew that besides a man's god being his belly, another way to keep a man satiated occurred through the lust of his eyes. The women present served both functions nicely.

Before stepping outside the room and going downstairs, Ami addressed the concerned group after the events in front of his compound. Sounds of automatic gunfire and explosions just outside the front door reverberated inside as Troy and Charlie escaped. Based on the type of clientele at the auction, Ami knew the situation needed to be discussed to regain the confidence of those assembled. He explained to the guests it was nothing more than a minor security issue and that his team had dealt with the threat. No need for concern. And like that, the women emerged, as did the booze and food. Within a few minutes, the party began in earnest as Ami excused himself.

Most of them did not even notice when he returned. Ami slipped into the room with a purpose. He went straight to the back-right corner, where a man stood surrounded by four oversized, burly guards. The man had an olive complexion and an expertly styled black goatee. Unlike many men in his culture, this man wore no robe. The Ermenegildo Zegna suit he wore spoke of style and sophistication. That it cost over $22,000 USD, let others know the man had money to burn. Ami didn't ask why he wanted to buy the nuke. After all, it really wasn't any of his business. The man had deep pockets because of abundant family wealth and easily won the bid.

Ami approached the man and leaned in close. The bodyguards took a step back. "We need to leave shortly," he whispered.

"Tonight?" the dapper man asked.

Ami nodded. "Yes."

"That was not part of the agreement."

"Things changed," Ami said.

The man's brow furrowed. "Am I to think this security issue was more than you let on?"

Ami flat-out lied to the man with ease. "Not at all. Like I said, it was a minor incident. However, I leave nothing to chance, and out of an abundance of caution, I've decided we leave tonight to retrieve the device. We should be there by the time dawn breaks."

The man eyed Ami cautiously and said nothing for several seconds. "As you wish," he relented. "You have my money already, and I expect to receive exactly what I paid for."

"And you shall have just that. My jet will take us to the device." Ami smiled broadly. "Just as I promised."

"Do I have time for one more drink?"

With eyebrows raised and now a devious smile, Ami asked, "What would your father say about such vices?"

Ami motioned, and one of the attractive, scantily clad women brought over a tray containing an assortment of drinks. Ami grabbed one, as did the well-dressed man. The woman with jet-black hair had long legs and wore a black strapless cocktail dress with an extremely low neckline. Her ample cleavage left little to the imagination. Both men enjoyed the view.

"My father would say Allah allows the faithful to indulge from time to time." The man raised the glass in the air.

"I like how your father and Allah think, Rahman." Ami touched his glass to the one held by Rahman Salek.

"As do I," Rahman said as he pointed to the attractive waitress. "How about her? Does the money I gave you also cover a dalliance with her?"

Ami laughed, a deep heart sound from deep within. "I'm sure it can be arranged."

Rahman nodded. "Allah and my father don't need to know about that part of the deal."

"My lips are sealed." He tossed back the drink, and the warm burn of the alcohol felt good as it passed down Ami's dry throat. The liquid courage lowered his blood pressure, which had climbed dangerously high after the incident.

41

Accra

"One minute out," Digger said into his comms.

"Hit em'," Cap said from the other vehicle. "And hit em' hard. We get only one chance to take him alive."

The road that led to where Ami housed Naseefa veered off the N2 about two miles outside Accra. Warehouses primarily lined one side of the road, all owned by Ami to store his illicit trade. At the end of the road stood the house Naseefa called home for several months. Modest by most standards, the three-story home sat on ten acres, giving him plenty of space. After the sale went through, Naseefa could purchase any home he wanted around the world. Of course, it would need to be in a country that did not have an extradition agreement in place with the United States.

An eight-foot-high wooden fence bordered the side of the road from where it came off the N2 all the way to the home a quarter mile away. Fifty feet before the entrance to the gated home, a driveway on the right side led to the last warehouse. The two vehicles parked side by side in the driveway. With everything in place, The Omega Group needed to execute the plan flawlessly. Having a bit of luck on their side wouldn't hurt, either.

Digger intently watched the tracker and the surveillance camera he placed along the roadside. His pointer finger hovered over the detonator button as he waited for the right second to unleash hell at the convoy's lead vehicle. "Ten seconds," he said so that everyone could know the time had arrived.

The two-vehicle convoy pulled off the N2 and descended the narrow, dark road. Naseefa sat in the rear passenger seat. He had a sneaking suspicion once he handed over the second nuke, his usefulness to Ami would be no more. Death seemed likely. He questioned Ami, who assured him they had made a deal and he would uphold his end once the weapon found its way into the hands of the new owner. Naseefa doubted his sincerity, but the draw of untold millions clouded his judgment. His mind turned to his son and daughter. It had been a long time since he saw them. His prayer to Allah was that if the cold embrace of death came for him, his family would reap the rewards of all the hard work. His last will and testament directed his two children to inherit the vast fortune the two weapons of mass destruction brought. After all, he did it for them as the money meant very little to him.

The man to Naseefa's left watched keenly as the older man glanced out the window. He thought of the last words Ami spoke to him before they walked outside. Pulling one of his most trusted guards close, Ami whispered. *If something were to happen tonight and someone comes for Naseefa, he cannot be taken alive under any circumstances. His secrets must die with him.* The man assured Ami he understood. He didn't care for Naseefa. He believed men like him got rich by being in the right place at the right time, not because of any special skill set or particular intellectual superiority. *Yes. I hope someone does come for him. I would take great pleasure in spilling his filthy Iraqi blood.*

The lead vehicle was sixty feet from the gate and slowed just as the five tightly grouped claymore mines mounted on the wooden fence discharged simultaneously. The force of the explosion, less than five feet from the left side of the armored Land Rover, rocked the vehicle. Traveling at 1,200 meters per second, the 3,500 steel balls measuring 1/8 inch peppered the side of the vehicle. Fracturing the two driver-side windows, the force of the explosions blew both windows into the cab of the vehicle while the shock wave slammed the vehicle with tremendous force, causing it to lurch to the right and tip over onto its side, killing two of the four guards instantly.

Less than ten feet behind, the second vehicle's driver barely had time to reach for the brake pedal when the explosion occurred. This did no good since, at the same time, the armored Mercedes SUV driven by the Jackal slammed into the side of the Land Rover. The action jostled the three security guards and Naseefa as the force of the vehicle strike hit the passenger side door just ahead of where Naseefa sat.

The next few minutes were a blur for Naseefa. An intense gunfight erupted as The Omega Group surrounded the vehicle and lay down a tremendous amount of suppressing fire.

With the lead vehicle on its side, Sarge, Harry, the Jackal, and Charlie approached, ready to fire. There was only one way of escape for whoever survived the blast inside the Land Rover: through the two destroyed windows on the driver's side. The Omegas tossed four grenades into the open windows and took cover. Three seconds later, with four back-to-back explosions, no doubt remained that the inhabitants were all dead. The four teammates converged on the second Land Rover and joined the others.

The men tasked with guarding Naseefa in the second vehicle didn't stand much of a chance.

However, one of them almost took out Charlie. The passenger forced his crumpled door open, rolled out of the vehicle, and raised his weapon. He took dead aim at Charlie as she approached, but the Jackal saw his movements and shoved her out of the way just as the round whizzed past her head. The subsonic round traveled close enough to be felt as it nearly grazed her ear. With his rifle raised, the Jackal drilled the shooter with a three-round burst to the bridge of his nose.

Charlie knew what occurred and gave a subtle nod to the Jackal, who grinned and winked.

As the man who sat across from Naseefa stepped outside, he immediately realized his folly as the other two men from the front of the vehicle were dead within seconds. Still standing in the doorway, two rounds struck him in the back. Both slugs hit him between the shoulder blades, and the light in his eyes dimmed. Falling forward, he had one last conscious thought. Complete his mission and make Ami proud.

He raised the MP5, took aim at Naseefa's head, and squeezed the trigger just as a third round struck him in the back of the head and sent him into the pitch darkness of eternity.

The last bullet to the back of the head changed the trajectory of the weapon, and instead of the round spewing out and striking Naseefa in the temple, the round entered about seven inches lower into his neck.

With the last man down, Troy lurched open the rear passenger side door. That's when he saw the dilemma. Naseefa slumped forward as a steady stream of blood squirted out of his jugular in a stream and covered the seat back in front of him.

"Oh, shit!" Troy screamed. "Harry, get over here!"

Harry rushed to his side, pulled a cloth from his pocket, and applied pressure to the wound. "This ain't good, Cap. Not good at all!"

"Can you save him?" Troy asked.

Harry pulled the cloth off as blood once more squirted into the air as he examined the entrance and exit wound. As he reapplied pressure, he turned his head and looked at Troy. "No, I can only delay the inevitable. He can't be saved, not out here in the field, and he'll be dead before we can get to any facility that might be able to help."

Troy swore viciously out loud, a rarity for him, but then he thought for a moment. Next, he reached for the phone in his pocket. "Keep him alive and keep him conscious as long as you can. We need his intel, and only one person can help us get that now."

42

ACCRA

Troy placed a call and succinctly told the person who answered what to do.

"But he's asleep," the person replied.

"Then get in there and wake his ass up." Troy spoke in a gruff tone. "You have sixty seconds to have him on the phone. In fact, I want to see him on FaceTime!"

A lump formed in the person's throat. "Sir, yes, sir."

Harry did the best he could to keep Naseefa alive. Unfortunately, it would be a losing battle within several minutes. He pushed several doses of morphine to help with the debilitating pain but knew too much would simply kill Naseefa even faster.

As the drugs kicked in, Naseefa's eyes rolled back in his head. Harry couldn't let him pass. He smacked his cheek hard enough to bring him back to the present.

Naseefa's eyes focused straight ahead, and recognition showed on his face as the image from a pixilated source came into focus. "Jalal! My son!"

"Father!" Jalal exclaimed in a strong yet fading voice from the FaceTime app.

"He doesn't have long." Troy held the phone away from his body so Jalal could see him. "I did the best I could to live up to my end of the bargain, Jalal, but it appears Ami's men had a kill order for your father. They shot him when our team attempted to rescue him to keep him from spilling his secrets."

"I understand," Jalal said. At that moment, he realized there would be no happy ending for his family. His gaze darted from Troy back to his father. Jalal fought back tears as his voice cracked. "Father, these men need the location of the weapon you hid."

Naseefa shook his head slightly in protest. "I can't ..." he replied.

"You must," Jalal said. "My freedom and, very possibly, my life depend on it! I'm currently in their custody."

Tears flowed freely down Naseefa's face as he stared at his firstborn child. Troy's voice made him turn slightly away from the screen and into the blue eyes of the rough man who stood beside him and held the iPhone.

"Here's the deal," Troy said to Naseefa. "You give up the location of the remaining nuke, and Jalal goes free. Your family will be safe, including your daughter. You have my word on that."

"He is a man of honor," Jalal said from the screen before the fading visage of his father.

"Your son and daughter can keep the money from the weapon sale. All of it!" Troy said forcefully. "We don't want the money and only care about getting both nukes back."

Standing in the doorway from the opposite side of the vehicle, the colonel glared as Troy uttered the last few words.

The reply from Naseefa occurred instantly, without pause. "It's in Babylon. Under the ancient city of Babylon. Locked in a vault."

Based on Jalal's interrogation, Troy already suspected that to be the case, but he needed confirmation from Naseefa. Troy held the schematic in hand and pushed it before Naseefa. "Is it here?"

"Yes, how did you get that?" Naseefa asked. His voice became frail, his words drawn out and spoke in a whisper as his life force faded.

Ignoring the question, he asked, "Are there any booby traps or anything I need to be made aware of?"

"You'll need the combo for the safe vault. It's impenetrable without it."

"Give it to me," Troy demanded.

Naseefa rattled off the number he knew by heart, which Troy memorized. "There is also a biometric component. The system will only open with my handprint." Naseefa pointed at the schematic. "There's a secret entrance to the left of the Ishtar gate. From the end, the third stone block will reveal a hidden shaft." The last few words were difficult to make out as his strength failed.

"Understood," Troy said. "Does Ami have the code to enter the vault?"

Naseefa shook his head back and forth. With a voice that lost any of its forcefulness, he replied, "I think that is the only reason he let me live this long."

Harry, who had been standing to the side monitoring Naseefa's vitals all along, nudged Troy. "His pulse is dropping fast, Cap. He has seconds or a minute at most before he'll lose consciousness."

Troy nodded and put his hand on Naseefa's shoulder. "Talk with your son," he said. "Say your goodbyes."

As the father and son openly wept and expressed their love for one another a tear formed in the corner of Troy's eye as he stood there holding the phone. Troy would move heaven and earth to have one more conversation with his dad. The chance to say a last goodbye. Even if it only lasted a few seconds.

A minute later, Naseefa's speech slowed, his eyes rolled back, and his head slumped forward as his body finally gave up the fight.

Troy spoke a few words to Jalal and assured him the release he so desperately wanted would happen shortly. Jalal thanked him for trying to save his father and expressed gratitude for the chance to say goodbye.

⸻ ◆ ⸻

"Your mouth just cashed a check your bank account can't clear, soldier," the colonel said harshly as the call ended. "Just cause you have operational authority, Cap, does not mean you can promise millions of dollars to someone held in custody."

"I did what I had to do to get the necessary intel."

Colonel Marshall raised his eyebrows. "The IT team may have cracked Ami's system and got us the same info."

"Sorry, bossman, but that was not likely, and certainly, even if they hacked Ami's hard drive, it would not be in time." Troy's head forcefully shook back and forth. "This was the fastest way to ensure we located the nuke and retrieved it before Ami had the chance. And besides, I made a promise to Jalal."

"Just so we are on the same page. That's blood money you just promised to the son of our enemy."

"How so?"

"Naseefa sold two nuclear weapons. God only knows what will be done with them."

Troy looked hard at the colonel. "Sir, I'm not in any way justifying what Naseefa was willing to do. However, let's be honest with each other. The United States is the one responsible for providing Saddam with biological and nuclear weapons. So, to some degree, the blood is on us as to whatever happens to them. Naseefa might very well be a bad guy with selfish intentions, but that's not my problem now. That's for the man upstairs to deal with, and Naseefa's with him as we speak."

"We might have to agree to disagree this time, son."

"It is what it is." Troy shrugged.

"Very well," the colonel said. "What's next?"

"The airport. We need to get to Babylon before the sun rises. Ami may already be on his way. I'm pretty sure our paths are on a collision course, and we need to reach that weapon before he does."

"But he won't be able to access the vault without the access code and biometric identifier."

"Do you really want to take the chance that he doesn't have a workaround in place, sir? Anyway, I know from personal experience any vault can be opened with the right tools. Trust me on that. I have firsthand experience. And I damn well believe Ami will make sure he'll have whatever he needs to access that vault."

"And what do you need to access the vault?" The colonel's eyes went from Troy to Naseefa.

Troy looked down to the lifeless body of Naseefa. "We'll need that hand, sir."

"Someone grab a machete from the back of the Mercedes," the colonel demanded.

"Who wants to do the deed?" Troy asked.

He got no volunteers.

"Fine," Troy replied. "Hand it to me." He pointed to the razor-sharp blade.

"Literally," the Jackal said in a sarcastic tone.

"Double-time it," the colonel ordered in a harsh voice.

"You heard the man," Troy yelled to the rest of the team. "Let's move out, Omegas!"

Nobody watched as Troy raised the machete and brought it down with one quick motion.

Like a Damascus steel chef's knife through a Wagyu filet, Troy got what he needed.

***

"Helo is on the ground," the man said as he approached Ami.

"And the team with Naseefa?"

"Still no word. The tracker says the two vehicles are just outside the gate, but nobody is answering inside the two vehicles or at the house. We've sent a recovery team to check on their status."

Ami's face contorted into a snarl. "No need. That means the security force failed me. Naseefa has either been taken alive or killed."

"What now? Don't we need him to enter the vault?"

"It would make our task easier," Ami said. "But it's still possible without him."

"How do we get in?"

"Bring the Hilti drills," Ami instructed.

"Which one?"

"All of them! Also, the other equipment we discussed. We will get in one way or the other."

Rahman Salek watched the discussion between both men from the shadows. His face displayed a concerned curiosity. He approached Ami when the other man left. "Another problem?"

Ami replied with a warm smile. "I'm not a man who dwells on problems, Rahman. I'm the man who delivers solutions."

PART III

43

AT CRUISING ALTITUDE

GULFSTREAM G450

Troy climbed the Gulfstream's airstairs, but his feet felt like lead, as multiple days without solid sleep took its toll.

Standing at the top of the stairs, Harry blocked the entrance to the sleek jet.

"Move it, squirt." Troy had a playful grin plastered on his face as he gave his medical sergeant a forceful shove with his left hand, an alligator skin carry-on bag in his right. The bag a gift from a Saudi prince after a mission known to only a select few, Operation Sheikh. It looked flamboyant, which Troy was not. He carried it each trip more tongue in cheek than a representation of who he was as a person.

Troy certainly didn't tower over Harry, but he had him by a few inches and now and then would nudge him about the height difference. Harry would normally reply with his superior IQ, and they would both treat it like a draw.

Harry turned around. "Sorry, Cap. Sarge is yapping his trap and jamming the aisle."

"I heard that." Sarge bellowed from inside the plane. "Don't make me hurt you, Doc."

Troy put his arm around Harry's shoulder and pulled him closer. "You did good out there, Doc. You kept Naseefa alive long enough to get the intel we needed and might have saved countless lives by your actions."

"Thanks, Cap. I appreciate the support. We all play our part."

"You bet." Troy patted him firmly on the shoulder. "Now get going. We don't got all night."

"Yes, sir," Harry said as he stepped inside and slipped past Sarge.

Troy climbed into the plane, pulled the airstairs up, and locked the cabin door since he was the last one to enter. He peeked into the cockpit. "Door's closed and secure, Captain," Troy said.

"Appreciate it, Cap," Mickey Messick replied.

"Colonel told you we need to push it up a bit, right?" Troy asked.

"Yes, he sure did. I should have us wheels up in less than three minutes."

"Appreciate it."

"No worries." Mickey flicked the flight control panel screen with his right index finger, which caused a snapping sound. "Computer says flight time is seven hours and forty-six minutes, but I'll get her up to max cruise speed and shave off some time for you boys." Then, with a wink, he added, "And the pretty lady."

"Oh, by the way." Troy reached into his carry-on bag and removed a large glass bottle. "Got this for you."

Mickey turned back and extended his hand to receive the bottle of Woodford Reserve. His favorite bourbon. "Sweet and the maple wood finish to boot. Mighty kind of you, Cap. Means a lot that you remembered which one I like."

"Can't forget about my favorite pilot, now can I?"

"Better not," Mickey said, turning his attention back to the flight controls. "Let's get this bird airborne and to Al-Hillah."

Troy moved down the aisles toward the rear of the plane.

"Sit your asses down," the colonel said in an authoritarian voice. "And listen up."

Everyone took their seats quickly as the plane taxied to the active runway.

"We've got less than seven hours of flight time to Iraq," the colonel said. "I need you all to get some rack time before we land. It's been pretty crazy since we left the States, and I need everyone as fresh as possible when we arrive in Babylon. We don't know what obstacles we'll face recovering the nuke, and every one of you needs to be as sharp as a blade."

Troy nodded as he listened to the colonel. His body felt the effects of sleep deprivation. Over the years, he learned to deal with those times when sleep was a luxury. Troy and the rest of the team were adept at falling asleep almost on command between missions or when they could steal a few moments. Planes, helicopters, tanks, and even side-by-side, they could sleep just about anywhere under any condition. The Jackal fell asleep while riding a camel once in Saudi Arabia while on a night op. When he fell off and came close to getting stepped on by the next camel, the rest of the team ridiculed him unmercifully. He never lived that one down. They often call him "camel toe" to remind him of the experience.

"How much time do you realistically need to formulate a plan?" The colonel stared at Troy.

Troy looked at Digger, who gave an initial shrug. "What do you think? Ninety minutes should do it, right?"

Digger nodded. "Yeah, max ninety minutes, and we're good. With the blueprint in our possession, I need some satellite intel, which I can get in just a few minutes. Besides that, it should be pretty straightforward. After we left Iraq, I built a 3-D model on my laptop using the schematics you found, Cap. So, I think we're familiar with the layout already. Plus, we already know how to get in, thanks to what Naseefa told us. The bottom line is we have to recover that nuke. We'll need a plan for what to do if we arrive first and how to handle Ami when he arrives. Either way, we must be ready for a firefight."

"Anyone disagree?" the colonel asked as he looked around at the others.

The rest of the Omegas and Charlie shook their heads.

"Good, I like it when you all agree with me." The colonel looked at his watch. "Then I think ..."

The sound of the engines roared as the plane shuddered slightly. With the cockpit door ajar, Captain Messick said, "Take your seat, Colonel. I'm about to punch it."

The colonel, who stood in the aisle between the first row of seats, merely gripped the seats on either side of him tighter and replied, "Throttle her," over his shoulder. "I'll be just fine right here, son."

"Another bottle of bourbon to you if you make him fall flat on his ass," Troy hollered over the sound of the engine roar.

"Deal!" Mickey exclaimed as he pushed the thrust levers forward.

As the sleek jet barreled down the runway, the colonel stood fast, his feet planted on the floor like reinforced rebar. A smile formed on his mouth as the plane lifted off and cut through the blackened sky. "As I was saying," he continued. "Take thirty minutes or so and relax, even have a nip of something from the bar if need be. Do whatever you got to do to unwind ..."

"No karaoke?" the Jackal asked in mock surprise.

With a shake of his head, the colonel said, "No way. Not this flight. I said unwind, not get ramped up, and act like a bunch of lunatics."

Charlie looked around with a perplexed look on her face. "Am I missing something?"

"Oh," the colonel said, "The boys haven't filled you in on their musical talents?"

"Apparently not." Her eyes narrowed.

"Colonel!" Cap said as he put a finger to his mouth to silence his commanding officer.

Colonel Marshall ignored the gesture. "Pretty sure she needs to know the whole story about you boys." He laughed and looked directly at Charlie. "Your buddies here travel with their own karaoke machine. Just don't ask which one likes it the most, or you'll likely get into a fistfight."

"And ... another layer of the onion is revealed," Charlie said with a shake of her head.

"Aww, man, no Taylor Swift tonight?" Jesús asked.

Charlie rolled her eyes. "You gotta be kidding me, right?"

"Shake it off, baby." Sarge stood and gave an exaggerated shake of his hips.

"Jesus!" Charlie bit her lip.

"Present," Jesús replied. "You called?"

"Uggh. Not you." Charlie rolled her eyes. "The trinity one."

"Ouch, heathen" Jesús said. "That hurts."

Charlie ignored the comment. "It sounds like what you boys really need are some chicks."

"Know any available?" Digger asked with his eyebrows raised.

"I like blondes with big knockers," Harry replied. "But ain't picky."

"You boys are all the same. Pathetic 101. But ... I might know a few eligible young ladies who register on the desperate scale." Charlie winked, then brushed her tongue along the top of her lip in a smooth, sensual manner. "That is if you fellas could handle them."

"You're one hell of a tease." Troy pointed at her and shook his finger back and forth.

"As I was saying." The colonel slapped his hands together, which made a cracking sound that pierced the interior of the fuselage. "Thirty minutes to wind down, then lights out. Five and half hours of rack time with no exceptions. Then everyone gets up, and we concoct a plan. Got it?"

Everyone nodded.

"I've got a few calls to make to tie up some loose ends," the colonel said. "I'll use the back room to avoid disturbing everyone." With that, he moved down the center aisle and toward the plane's rear before stopping at Troy's seat. "Cap, a word, please."

"Yes, sir," Troy said as he stood and walked down the last few aisles behind his commanding officer.

⚫

Once inside the rear compartment, the colonel closed the door and lowered his voice. "When's the last time you talked to Pat?"

"On the drive to the airport after we intercepted Naseefa."

Colonel Marshall nodded. "Everything's in place?"

"He said it was, yes," Troy replied.

"Call and double-check. Then get some sleep. You look exhausted, and I need you fresh when we arrive in Babylon."

"Roger that, Colonel."

44

OAK RIDGE, TENNESSEE

Pat O'Shea sat in his cluttered office located in eastern Tennessee at the Y-12 National Security Complex. Stacks of papers and briefings adorned his desk. As usual, he was way behind on recreational reading since meetings and classified briefings filled most of his days. He glanced out the panoramic window and wished for nothing more than to steal a few minutes and step outside. It was a brisk day in the eastern Tennessee mountains, and he longed to feel the cool breeze against his cheeks. The sight of leaves falling just outside his window made him smile, which quickly passed as he looked back on his desk at the briefing about Iran's nuclear capabilities.

As Under Secretary for the National Nuclear Security Administration (NNSA), his superiors preferred him to be based in D.C., and, granted, he spent most of his time in the nation's capital, but as often as possible, he made his way back home to Tennessee, where his wife and kids lived. He didn't want his family to grow up in the rat race of northern Virginia, so he relocated them to Tennessee many years back when he started at the NNSA.

Troy's dad, Matt, was friends with Pat, and they met via their government jobs after the events of 9/11. If it wasn't for the events of the Zechariah Option, they may have become the best of friends.

As his phone rang, Pat's eyes diverted from the Iranian briefing and fixed on the digital display screen displaying the words "Unknown Caller." Few people had his direct line, so it was best to answer.

"Mr. Secretary," the slightly static-sounding voice said.

"That's Mr. Under Secretary to you."

Troy chuckled. "No doubt. With your title, I still think you should be pouring someone coffee somewhere. Not leading one of the most vital departments safeguarding our nation's nuclear stockpile."

"Smartass," Pat said with full sincerity. "Where are you?"

"I'm at 32,000 feet and climbing."

"Always living your life by the seat of your pants, huh, Evans? At least you're not jumping out at that altitude."

"Not today, at least, but don't get me started on that."

"Everything, okay?"

"Yeah, about to get some rack time," Troy said.

"What's your ETA?"

"Seven to eight hours, give or take."

"Perfect."

"Just confirming we are still good to go. Are the assets in place?"

"They'll be there shortly. I have a recovery team inbound as we speak. They're scheduled to land at the same airfield as your team in the next few hours. Once everything is in place, they'll be ready for the call to extract the weapon."

"Just what I wanted to hear," Troy said. "I'll call you back when we have boots on the ground."

"So, just about the time I'm fast asleep?"

"You old guys have to get up and piss half a dozen times a night. I'll be sure to call during one of those moments."

"Watch it, Troy. You just might live long enough to be in my shoes one day."

Troy chuckled. "Probably. Since only the good die young."

Pat genuinely cared for Troy in a paternal way and wanted to ensure things were fine under that tough guy façade. Troy could be a hard nut to crack, but they had bled and experienced great loss together. He had Troy's back and, more importantly, his implicit trust. After what happened in Drexel years ago, Pat made it a point to check in on Troy as often as possible. "I'm sure the past few days have been rough."

"The Department of Defense does not pay me to file reports into manila folders."

"Touché," Pat replied.

"But I'll survive, and we'll get the nuke. Don't worry about me, Pat. I've been in tighter spots."

"I know from firsthand experience, but I still worry. We also have the second nuke to find. My team, along with the NSA and CIA, are doing everything they can to pour over the data you and Charlie recovered from Ami's laptop. We'll track it down."

"I'm sure you will," Troy said in an even tone. "And in the meantime, we'll do what we must on this end to secure the nuke in Babylon."

"That's why the government assigned this mission to the Omegas. You guys never fail."

Troy ignored the compliment. "Any updates on the measure Ami might take if something were to happen to him?"

"Nothing concrete, but the agency has been leaning on some sources pretty hard and may have caught a slight break."

"How so?"

"More than one of the people they brought in for questioning said the same story. If Ami were to die, all hell would break loose on United States soil, according to the sources."

"Meaning he'd use the nuke somewhere in the lower forty-eight?"

"Correct. At least that is what they are reading between the lines."

"That makes me think the weapon might already be smuggled into the country."

"Agreed. That's what the agency suspects."

"So, the moral of the story is get the nuke in Babylon and keep Ami alive so he doesn't vaporize a major US city in retaliation."

"Pretty much, Captain Evans. That should be easy to do, right?"

"You know how many easy days we have on this job?"

"About as many as I have without meetings or conference calls."

"Aren't we both just slaves to the grind?"

"Tell me about it, and we both serve the same master. Just don't die in Babylon. After all, you still owe me a dinner," Pat said. "Getting shot or coming home in a pine box is no excuse to not pay up."

"Yeah, I remember," Troy said. "I should've never bet on the NCAA March Madness brackets."

"Don't be a sore loser. I'll be eating like a king on your dime."

"Working on that spare tire, are you?"

"Please, I bet I can outrun you in a mile-long race."

"You're an old man," Troy said with a laugh. "You can try, but never forget what second place really stands for." As he looked down the aisle the back door opened so he quickly added, "The colonel is giving me the stink eye. Time for rack time. I'll talk with you soon, Pat."

Pat didn't have a chance of outrunning Troy in any foot race, but he threw the dig out there to bust his friend's chops. "Godspeed, Troy. I can already taste that filet, lobster tail, and twice-baked mac and cheese I'll be ordering on your dime. Plus, that butterscotch crème brûlée with an espresso will be simply divine."

"Gonna milk everything you can out of the meal at Del Frisco's Double Eagle Steakhouse, huh, old man?"

"Damn straight, young punk." Pat replied. "I like spending a Captain's money."

45

At Cruising Altitude

Gulfstream G450

Charlie sat across from the Jackal near the rear of the plane in relative silence. Per the colonel's orders, everyone was supposed to get some shut-eye in less than fifteen minutes.

Their seats faced each other, and she reached across the space that separated them and grabbed his knee, giving it a firm squeeze. "Thanks," she said.

A perplexed look spread across his face. "For what?" the Jackal asked as he looked down at his knee. A tingle ran up his body as she let go of his knee and withdrew her hand slowly.

"For giving me that shove back there when we made a play for Naseefa."

"Oh, that! No problem, not a biggie."

"Well, it's a biggie to me. You saved my ass back there."

The wide smile moved across his face. "And a nice ass it is." He braced himself for what he figured would be a punch or two. But much to his surprise, it didn't come.

Instead, Charlie smiled and almost appeared to blush. "So, I've heard once or twice over the years."

"Yeah, it's not one of those frumpy, fat, and misshaped ones you normally see on military broads."

"Wow, what started as a compliment about my ass turned into a vicious insult to most of the other women who serve," Charlie said. Then she laughed. It was a girlish laugh that the Jackal had not recalled hearing since they met. "But I'm flattered ... I think."

"Anyway, that's what teammates do. They got each other's backsides."

"Well, I appreciate that," she said before quickly adding, "Maybe you're not such a jerk after all."

"Hey now!" exclaimed the Jackal in mock protest. "I got a rep to maintain."

Charlie leaned in close. With a nod, she indicated she wanted him to do likewise.

He did, unsure what she would do next.

Her voice lowered. "I think it's all for show, that sexist, immature reputation of yours. I suspect that at the core, you're really a sensitive guy who just hasn't found the right girl yet."

The Jackal's features softened for a moment. "Can I tell you something?" he asked in barely a whisper as his eyes gazed into hers.

"Sure," Charlie said in full sincerity.

"To be completely honest. I'm damaged goods."

Her face tightened as a perplexed expression formed on her brow. "Aren't we all?"

"Not like me." He clammed up. His body noticeably stiffened as he looked away toward the window.

"I'll keep whatever it is to myself," Charlie replied as her expression changed to compassionate concern. "I promise." She reached out and clasped his hands within hers.

Her smooth, soft skin felt like silk to his rough hands. "I got hurt once, and it turned out pretty bad."

"Most people get hurt," she replied, then quickly added, "Who was she?"

"My high school sweetheart."

"Dumped you for the star quarterback?"

He shook his head vigorously. "No. In fact, I was the quarterback, and she was the head cheerleader. Dated all four years of high school. The perfect couple, according to everyone. Her name was Jill, and we got married right out of school. Kind of what you did in the small town where I'm from. Then I enlisted a month after graduation."

"Military life can be difficult for relationships. What happened?"

"Things were going well, at least so I thought. Then, I came back from my first deployment to Iraq after six months away. Within four weeks of being home, she told me she was pregnant. I was on cloud nine, so excited to be a dad …" His voice trailed off.

"And?"

"At the first ultrasound, I found out the due date."

"Uh oh!" Charlie exclaimed.

"Now, I'm not the smartest bulb in the cardboard box, but I can do simple math. One and one make two. And I can figure out when forty weeks begins …"

"So, it wasn't yours."

"Nope."

"What did you do?"

"Well, after we got home, I confronted her about it not being my kid, and she blew up. Said I must be having PTSD."

"And?"

"I walked upstairs, grabbed my go bag and a few personal possessions, and walked out the front door. I never looked back and didn't respond to her yelling or frantic screams. Just climbed into my truck and drove away."

"Wow! Then what?"

"A week later, the other dude moved into the house. Our home. Some enlisted puke assigned to the support team."

"Divorce?"

"Oh yeah, she took me to the cleaners."

"But why if she was the one who cheated?"

"Didn't matter, I let her have it all. I didn't care. Plus, I walked out on a pregnant woman who swore I was the father. The judge didn't take too kindly to that."

"You could have demanded a DNA test."

"Yup. But I didn't care. I wanted out. So I paid up and never looked back."

"Ever see her again?"

The Jackal nodded. "Ran into both of them at the PX several months later."

"And?"

"She turned the other way and couldn't face me. He acted like a tough guy and got into my face. He shoved me, and I dropped him to the ground in a split second. I leaned over and told him how much of an ass-kicking I could give him with both hands tied behind my back ..."

"What did he do?"

"He tuck-tailed and ran. Never saw either one of them again. Course, I never stepped foot in the PX again after that. Within six months, I qualified for the Q course. The rest is history. After graduating, I was assigned to 10th Group and moved to Fort Carson, Colorado."

"That's crazy," Charlie said.

"Got a letter from her last year while we were on an extended mission at Bagram. It had been years since the divorce. I couldn't read the letter, so Sarge read it for me. I told him I just wanted to hear a synopsis."

"What did it say?"

"Basically, after all these years, she finally admitted the kid wasn't mine. No surprise there, but for many years, she insisted I was the father. She included a picture, and Sarge said he was a pretty cute kid. Apparently, the dude that knocked her up got killed in Iraq while on a deployment. She asked for forgiveness and wanted me back. You know how it goes ..."

"So, what did you do?"

"Pulled out my Zippo and burned the damn letter right then and there."

"Ashes to ashes, huh?"

"And dust to dust," the Jackal finished the phrase.

"Guess that answers the playboy, tough exterior."

"Once bitten, twice shy."

"You don't appear to be the shy type." She retorted as she reached over and squeezed his knee one more time.

46

AT CRUISING ALTITUDE

BOEING 757-200

The Boeing 757-200 reached cruising altitude as Ami sat in his chair and tapped nervously on his armrest. His mind considered the uncertain situation that awaited them in Iraq.

He purchased the plane several years back from British Airways when they retired their aging fleet. Ami made moderate renovations at great personal cost. Once they removed the passenger seats, Ami installed several sitting areas and four private bedrooms, including showers. Those in his inner circle balked at the money he spent, but Ami knew his line of work proved deadly for most involved. Considering the time he spent in the air, he figured comfort should trump cost.

One of his people walked up the aisle and took the empty seat across from him.

"What do you have for me?" Ami asked in a firm tone.

The man opened a folder with several photos. "Our contact at Kotoka International took these and emailed them to me."

Ami flipped through the dozen or so pictures. None of the men looked familiar in the first several photos. "Hmm," he said as he examined each photo.

"Our contact said they're American. The plane landed earlier today. It's a Gulfstream G450 with tail number N781MF registered with a charter company, Doc Wiseman Gulfstream, based out of McLean, VA."

"It's a front, a shell company," Ami said.

"Most likely."

"Probably owned by the agency or some other American government entity."

"Agreed."

"What's this?" Ami flipped to one of the photos. He leaned in closer and stared intently at the photo. "This man I know," he said, thrusting the photo back to the man across from him.

"Who is it?"

"Colonel William Marshall. One of the more decorated members of the Special Forces community. Rumors are he runs his own team, and now that's off the books. Mainly black ops missions. They even have some clever name they're called, although it isn't coming to me at the moment."

"Any chance him being in Accra was just a coincidence?"

Ami shook his head. "None." Then he got to the next photo, where a man and a woman looked exactly like Phillipe and Madeline Lapointe. "Bingo! It's them."

"This photo confirms they were not who they claimed to be?"

"Yes, especially if they are with Colonel Marshall," Ami replied sarcastically. "What did the IT guys figure out about the laptop?"

"They copied the entire hard drive, but since it's encrypted, it should take a while for anyone to crack into the data."

"No." Ami shook his head furiously. "The Americans have floors of staff at Fort Meade to handle this. We must assume they already have the hard drive's contents and are scouring the files for whatever they can use against me."

"What about your relationship with the agency? Won't they protect you?"

"We must work under the premise that they'll burn me. When you fail to be useful anymore or cause more harm than good, the Americans are famous for discarding their allies. Look what they did to Saddam. They had him hung like a traitor, which, of course, he was. I recall a quote from Nguyen Van Thieu, a former leader of South Vietnam during the 1970s. He said, *It is so easy to be an enemy of the United States, but so difficult to be a friend.* No truer words have been spoken about those backstabbing bastards in Washington."

"So, what do we do about this team headed by Colonel Marshall?"

"For now, we focus on retrieving the nuke in Iraq for our buyer before they do," Ami said. "Where's the colonel's plane headed?"

"They filed a flight plan for Paris."

"I doubt that is their destination. When did they take off?"

"Almost forty minutes before us."

Ami pulled up a few websites and calculated the max speed for the G450 versus his 757-200, then picked up the phone next to him. His pilot answered, "We need to increase speed. Push the engines as hard as you can. We need to arrive faster than we planned."

With that, he placed the phone back in its cradle. He figured the colonel would land at an airfield closer to Babylon than he could with his aircraft. There's no way he could get to Babylon before them. In fact, he had to consider they might track his movements somehow and could be waiting for him when he landed. His mind raced at the possibilities.

"What do you suggest ..." the man started to say, but Ami shut him up with one finger raised to his lips.

"Not now, I need a few minutes to think. I need to make a few calls. How many men do we have in Iraq?"

"Ten, including the ones with us now."

"Four men in Babylon are watching the site around the clock, correct?"

"Yes, we have them disguised in various official roles around Babylon."

"They'll be no match for Colonel Marshall's team, and they will most assuredly arrive before we do."

"I agree."

"We need more men. Make some calls and see who else you can round up. I need hardened fighters, men willing to die. See if you can get me zealots and tell them it's for the cause of Allah. You know what to do. Make sure they are fed the usual garbage about the need for martyrs to fulfill Allah's desires. The seventy-two virgins lie normally works in situations like this."

"I understand."

Ami stood. "I'll be in my room."

He passed his guest as he walked down the aisle to the back of the plane.

Rahman Salek looked up from the book he was reading. "Is everything still on schedule?" he asked as Ami stopped by his side.

"Yes," Ami answered, at ease with a blatant lie. "Things are progressing just as I planned. Try to get some rest if you can. It will be just past dawn when we arrive."

Rahman nodded. "I'll try to do that shortly. I've never slept well on planes."

"I can assure you the Duxiana mattress in your room will allow you to sleep like a baby. It's like you're floating on air."

"Which I am, in fact," Rahman said.

"Indeed."

"You're heading off to bed then?"

"Yes, I'll rest soon, but plan to meet you for breakfast an hour before we land," Ami said as he walked away.

"Till then," Rahman replied.

Inside the privacy of his opulent bedroom in the back of the plane, Ami picked up the secure phone line. The phone rang several times before a raspy voice answered on the other end.

"Yes," the other person said.

"We may have a complication," Ami stated in a firm yet direct tone.

"I'm listening. What seems to be the problem?"

"It appears likely the Americans know about the location of the nuke I've just sold. I'm on my way to retrieve the device from Babylon."

"Is the buyer with you?"

"Yes," Ami replied.

"And are the Americans headed there as well?"

"Not sure, but it seems probable."

"Naseefa?"

"Dead or the Americans have him, which is the same."

"What do you want to do about it?"

Ami stroked his chin. "I need time to think about my options."

"Okay."

"But at the very least, I need the asset in D.C. on standby," Ami said.

"Is it that serious?"

"Like we've discussed, if something were to happen to me, I need the Reprisal Protocol activated."

"You sure the situation is that dire?"

"Maybe. If I were to die, I want him to target the D.C. area. Specifically, Joint Base Andrews, but the fallout and destruction will encompass the whole District of Columbia."

"Joint Base Andrews? Still holding a grudge after all these years?"

"As the book of Exodus says ..." Ami started before his voice trailed off.

"Eye for an eye," the man said on the other end of the phone.

"Precisely, if they want to come after me, I'll hit them back one thousand times greater. If you don't hear that I'm safe by sundown tomorrow, I want the asset to start the twenty-four-hour countdown."

A discernible pause occurred as the man on the other line considered the repercussions of Ami's proposal. "I understand."

"You'll see that he's notified?" Ami demanded in a harsh tone.

"I'll take care of it personally. If you go, I go. That was always my plan."

"I've never asked that of you."

"You didn't have to. It's my duty."

Ami smiled. "I knew I could count on you, brother."

"Hopefully, this path isn't needed."

"One can certainly hope, but in the meantime, it's best to be prepared," Ami said. "I intend to live a long life and die in my bed one day in the company of a naked woman much younger than I with a smile plastered on my wrinkly face ... but just in case."

47

AT CRUISING ALTITUDE

BOEING 757-200

Toward the front of the plane, a man with a thick black beard and an equally thick head of hair pulled the earpiece from his left ear as Ami's call ended. He had planted the listening device in Ami's private room months before. As soon as the call started, he recognized the person Ami conversed with just by the sound of the raspy voice. He had many interactions with the man over the years and knew his allegiance to Ami would be unbreakable. The conversation confirmed that the United States would be in dire straits if Ami perished while recovering the nuclear device. *But how do I contact the US to warn them of the attack? Can I get in touch with them in time?*

He thought about the interaction with the American he approached outside Ami's compound. *What would have happened if I had climbed into that Range Rover?* He quickly dismissed the thought. His fate was sealed a long time ago. He told himself *I need to protect Ami and prevent the Reprisal Protocol.* He hoped if somehow he relayed valuable intel to the Americans while at the same time their intelligence agencies found the clues hidden in Ami's files it would be enough to locate the second nuke and prevent any attack.

⸺⬦⸺

A familiar face took the seat next to him a few minutes later.

"Penny, for your thoughts?" Ami asked as he sat down, noticing how deep in contemplation the man appeared.

"Just considering what might unfold in Iraq. The events at the compound have me concerned for your safety. Especially since the Americans are behind all of this. I don't like that we have to go there and wonder what kind of shitstorm might be awaiting us."

"Trust me, I don't want to go there either, but we need this sale to go through. Made some calls, and reinforcements are on their way. They will meet us in Babylon."

"We don't have a choice, do we? Not going isn't an option, right?"

"No, we don't have a choice. This sale is too lucrative, and the transaction must be completed. I'll certainly need you by my side in Babylon." Ami paused and stroked his chin as he appeared deep in thought. "I would rather that weapon goes off and kill us all than let it fall back into the American's hands."

"I understand," the man with the thick beard replied.

"You've been a faithful associate, Benjamin. I'm sorry I doubted your allegiance during the purge."

Benjamin thought back to the torture he endured when the associates who worked for Ami were rounded up and systematically tortured before being killed in heinous ways. Benjamin almost cracked more than once during the interrogations but somehow kept it together. His reward was his life.

"You had a mole, Ami, and did what you felt best." Benjamin bit at his lower lip. "If the price of finding that mole would have been me giving up my life, well, that's a cost I was willing to pay."

Ami reached over and touched his shoulder. "The loyalty you've displayed does not go unnoticed, my friend. When all this is behind us, you'll be rewarded for what you have given me and my organization."

"I'm happy to serve."

"If the Americans try to take the weapon, we must fight till our last breath." Ami paused. "You agree with that, don't you, Benjamin?"

Benjamin nodded profusely. "With all of my heart. And we will survive, Ami. Allah will protect us."

48

AT CRUISING ALTITUDE

GULFSTREAM G450

Once inside the small cabin at the rear of the plane, the colonel sat on the narrow single bed and took off his boots. His feet were sore, and stretching his toes for a few minutes felt good. Once he got comfortable and had two shots of the liquid the stewardess left for him on the side table, he placed three calls.

First, he dialed the SecDef to fill him in personally on the events that transpired in Accra. SecDef Wastradowski sounded pleased that the mission had succeeded up to that point but voiced his concern about what might happen in Babylon. The colonel assured him the Omegas had things under control, and come hell or high water, they would secure the nuke.

Next, he called the DNI to request additional assets on site when they landed in Iraq. Most of the big Army resources were limited to FOBs and joint task force bases scattered around the war-torn country. However, the agency still had an impressive number of personnel in the country, and the colonel knew he might need to leverage those bodies and assets if things went south.

Finally, the colonel called a group based in Virginia that technically didn't exist. At least not according to the United States government. This small but highly effective team excelled in ways government agencies failed miserably. When the colonel needed answers fast, he bypassed the alphabet agencies and went straight to them. He called earlier in the week as soon as he left Iraq and headed for Washington, D.C., so they could begin the task of finding out who targeted his team. Enough time passed, and now he expected answers, not excuses.

As soon as the man on the other end answered, the colonel got straight to business. "What have you learned, Mr. Grey?"

Used to the gruffness, Mr. Grey couldn't help himself. "Nice to hear your voice as well, sir. I'm doing great. Not slept in thirty-six hours, but thanks for asking."

"I don't have time for your shit. Give me a damn update, now."

"Let me open the file." A few seconds of silence took place before his exacerbated voice spoke again. "We've actually discovered much since the last time you called."

"Such as?" the colonel asked.

"My team positively identified all fourteen men who attacked your team in Iraq."

"Nationalities?"

"All over the board. A couple of Saudis, a Syrian, a Pakistani, a few Afghan fighters, but the majority were Iraqi."

"Mercenaries?"

"Yes."

"And who hired them?"

A pause took place before Mr. Grey responded. "Not the person you thought."

"Oh really? Well, enlighten me."

"Does the name Dimitri Petrikov sound familiar?"

The colonel searched his memory bank, but the name didn't ring a bell. "No, and you're right, that's not the name I expected to hear."

"I know, and from what we can tell, the man you thought was responsible didn't order the hit."

"You're saying he had absolutely nothing to do with it?"

"I didn't say that. I said he didn't order the hit. If he had something to do with the attack on The Omega Group, we have yet to uncover evidence implicating him."

"Keep digging," the colonel demanded.

"Of course, sir."

"Tell me more about this, Dimitri Petrikov. Who the hell is he, and why did he hire these men to kill me and my men?"

"He's Russian ..."

"Obviously," the colonel interrupted.

"He's a Russian oligarch who owns one of Russia's largest natural gas businesses. Former KGB—"

"Ain't they all." The colonel sighed.

"Dimitri maintains close ties to the FSB, and it appears he's good friends with the president of Russia himself. His brother Sergei is their Minister of Energy. Basically, his hands are all over the energy sector in the former Soviet Union."

"Wonderful." The colonel spoke in a clearly sarcastic tone. "But why does he have a hard-on for me and my team?"

"We're still working out all the specifics, but his motivation appears to point back to the operation earlier this year in St. Petersburg."

The colonel delved into the recesses of his mind and retrieved the mission parameters for what occurred in January. His defining memory included how damn cold St. Petersburg was that time of year. "Okay, we took out six men who were trying to sabotage the natural gas pipeline that ran into Belarus from Russia." The colonel recalled. "I would think Dimitri would want to thank us, not kill us."

"It's complicated," Mr. Grey replied. "We've been able to confirm so far that one man killed was related to Dimitri."

"So, this is about revenge, then?"

"Yes and no."

The colonel released a drawn-out breath. "Explain."

"As I said, it's complicated, and we've just scratched the surface."

"Keep digging. I need more details."

"We will get to the bottom of it, sir. The team always does."

Colonel Marshall cleared his throat. "In the meantime, was the attack in Iraq a one-time event, or is this son of a bitch coming after us again."

"From what we can tell, the attack in Iraq will not be a one-off. Dimitri has taken a liking to you guys, and not in a good way. He wants you all dead because of what happened."

"Great," the colonel stated. "Another shithead who wants us snuffed out. Add him to the list. Any intel as to when he may take another shot at us?"

"Negative. We've intercepted chatter, but no specifics."

"That still doesn't explain the photos we found in Iraq. Those pics had Charlie in them as well, but she wasn't part of the mission in St. Petersburg. The timing on all this is dubious at best."

"I know, sir."

"Then my question is, how the hell did they get the pictures, and why include her?"

"Last part first. I believe Charlie just got grouped together with the team. She appears to be collateral damage in their minds. As for how they got the photos, you won't be surprised to learn the agency has a mole who provided the images to Dimitri."

The colonel's blood pressure rose. "You know who this person is?"

"We do. He works at Langley on the seventh floor. We have his home address, family bio, and a full dossier worked up on him."

"Seventh floor? He must be a big wig at the agency. Put a fucking tail on him."

"Already done, sir. Mr. Blue arranged everything."

"Good. Is Mr. Blue there now?" the colonel asked.

"No, he went home already. He worked forty-eight hours straight before I took over."

"Okay, I guess everyone needs to sleep eventually. Does Dimitri have any direct contact with 'you know who'?"

"Indirectly, yes."

"And the evidence against this seventh-floor agency prick is airtight?"

"We're one hundred percent sure he provided the photos to Dimitri and his mercenaries. He tried to cover his tracks and did a damn good job of it. We just happen to be better."

"Once this rogue nuke is handled, I'll deal with this traitorous piece of shit myself," the colonel said with a snarl. "Then The Omega Group will move on to Dimitri."

"You really have no other choice," Mr. Grey said. "Snuff or be snuffed when it comes to these Russians."

"Good work. Keep digging on the other stuff. I'll be in touch soon."

With that, the colonel disconnected the call and stared at the floor for several minutes, lost in his thoughts. It seemed too many of the missions they undertook resulted in blowback. Yes, one could say it came with the territory, but that didn't mean he liked it. Not one bit.

49

AT CRUISING ALTITUDE

GULFSTREAM G450

After not nearly enough rack time, the entire team, including Charlie, huddled around the first two rows at the front of the plane. Each of them nursed a piping hot cup of coffee in their hands. The sleep helped, but they all could have been out for twelve hours straight under different circumstances.

The subsequent discussions and planning lasted exactly eighty-eight minutes.

Colonel Marshall looked down at his black G-Shock watch and nodded. A wide grin formed at the corner of his mouth. "Good job, team. You finished two minutes early."

From the cockpit, Captain Messick's voice carried through the fuselage. "We'll be on the ground in fifteen minutes, Omegas."

"Roger that," Troy bellowed.

Charlie sat next to Troy during the intel briefing; they had not talked since they left Ghana.

"You owe me that answer." She nudged him with her elbow.

"What answer?" Troy asked in a surprised tone.

"Remember our conversation on the plane from Paris to Ghana?"

"I think not," he replied as he scratched his head, wondering where she was going with this.

"I asked if you loved her still. The woman named Cate."

"Oh yeah, that conversation." He rolled his eyes.

"You said if we lived through the events at Ami's without being chopped up into fertilizer and fed to the sharks, you'd tell me, so I'm waiting."

Troy smiled. Charlie sure as hell acted tenaciously, but there wasn't time to get into that discussion. "The quick answer is yes, while the longer one ... well, it's very complicated."

"No, it's not."

"What's not?"

"Complicated. It's always simpler than we think. We make things seem too complex so we can keep our guard up."

"I won't argue with you there."

"And I still expect the longer answer one of these days."

"Stateside, when we're back, but you may not like me as much when you hear the ending."

Charlie's eyebrows raised. "And if I want to meet her?"

Troy's grin slanted down to an unapproving grimace. "You're pushing your luck."

"I don't know any other way to live, Cap," Charlie replied.

"Hate to interrupt your love connection," the colonel said.

"Whoa, sir." Troy raised his hands. "It's not what you think is going on here."

"Uh-huh," the colonel replied doubtfully as his gaze left Troy and Charlie and settled on Digger. "Do we have any ETA on where and when Ami will land?"

"No way to know for sure, sir," Digger said. He sat in the opposite row alongside Sarge. "Satellite images indicate he left shortly after we did. However, that being said, we'll be landing at a secret facility maintained by the agency that is very close to Babylon. Once we hit the ground, we should be at the Ishtar Gate within thirty to forty-five minutes. While we aren't sure where Ami will land, we feel certain he'll have a longer transport time when he arrives. There are limited places he can land a 757 in that part of Iraq unless he tries to put it down on Freeway 1."

"Now I'd like to see that shit," the Jackal replied from a row back.

"How many men will he have with him?" the colonel asked as he ignored the Jackal's comment. A common occurrence.

"Not sure, but we must assume he will come with enough men and plenty of weapons. We should also consider that he has people on site."

With a nod, the colonel replied, "We all know what needs to be done. Get to that nuke first, secure it, and then we'll call in the cavalry."

"Yes, sir," Troy answered for the entire team.

"You forgot to add, and don't die in the process, Colonel," Harry added.

"Well, if someone has to get shot ..." The colonel turned and glared intently at the Jackal.

"If the colonel gets his wish and I die, I'm coming back as a hemorrhoid for all your turds," the Jackal said with an audible laugh.

"Classy," Charlie quipped.

50

AL-HILLAH, IRAQ

SECRET CIA AIRFIELD

The heat, my God, the heat. The phrase ran through Troy's brain like a re-run of an old Seinfeld episode.

Troy really hated the sandbox. As he stepped off the plane and his feet touched the concrete tarmac, the wind, filled with granules of sand, smacked him against the side of the face, causing his cheek to sting. He took it as Iraq's way of saying *fuck you* one more time.

Dammit, he thought, *Back again. Why couldn't the global war on terrorism be fought in Fiji, Bora Bora, or Tahiti? Instead, these asshats choose oil fields in the middle of the God-forsaken desert.*

Curiously, his mind wandered back to Drexel, Idaho, where he grew up. The harsh climate of Iraq made him miss the quaint town and long for the days of his youth. Quickly, he pushed those thoughts aside and walked a step behind the colonel.

As the entire team approached the large metal building before them, a man emerged from the slightly ajar hangar doors and approached the colonel.

"Colonel Marshall, glad you and your team made it safe." The tall man with a lean face and dirty blond hair said. "I'm John Lawson."

"You work for Pat O'Shea?"

John's face shifted. "Well, no, technically, I'm part of Section Seven, but I've been tasked with assisting the NNSA's Accident Response Group (ARG) based on the sensitive nature of this incident. The rest of the ARG team is waiting for us inside. I know you're in a rush to get to Babylon and secure the nuke, but the team needs to go over some things quickly. Won't take more than five minutes."

Colonel Marshall formed The Omega Group at the bequest of Section Seven's director several years ago. The mysterious agency was buried deep within a subset of the Department of Homeland Security, and few people in the federal government had ever heard of it. Of those who knew of its existence, even fewer asked questions about it. William knew the drill and just smiled and nodded at the mention of the words, *Section Seven*. "Lead the way, John," the colonel said as he and the rest of the Omegas followed behind.

True to his word, John kept the conversation brief and told The Omega Group only what they needed to know about the nuke. Five minutes later, the team stepped through the open hangar door and back into the harsh sunlight.

"Fellas, grab the gear from the plane," the colonel said as his head tilted toward the Gulfstream.

"Hold up! Where's the armored SUVs the agency promised?" Troy asked.

"No clue." The colonel looked around the barren airfield. "We need to grab one of the spooks that work at this hellhole. They were supposed to meet us when we landed. That's who I thought John Lawson was at first."

With two camouflaged colored, unarmored Humvees parked close to the hangar, a runway, and fifty yards away, a two-story concrete building that was the entirety of the complex. The colonel could see several black Suburbans parked just beyond the concrete structure. A man emerged from the building a minute later and walked toward the team with a timid look.

"Hey! Are you with the agency? We're looking for our vehicles," the colonel barked to the man as he got close.

"They're right there." The man pointed to the Humvees.

"Can't be! I was assured several armored Mercedes would be ready for us." The colonel responded with a scowl spread across his face. "Not those IED magnets."

"I don't know anything about that, sir. I was told those Humvees were for your team."

"Where the hell is the CIA station chief?" the colonel demanded. "He was supposed to meet my team here and assist with any help we needed."

"He got called back to Baghdad on an urgent matter a few hours ago, sir."

Colonel Marshall was pissed off. He knew immediately that the Director of the CIA just dicked him over. They had a love/hate relationship over the years, and for the past several, it certainly stayed firmly on the hate end of the spectrum.

The colonel pointed to the two black Suburbans behind the building. "Are those armored?"

"Of course, we're in Iraq, not Disneyworld!"

"And who do those vehicles belong to, smartass?"

Shaking his head back and forth, the man said. "No way, Colonel. There's a HUMINT meeting going on inside with senior agency staff. Those are part of the station chief's convoy and for their use only."

"We'll see about that," the colonel said. "I need the keys."

"Not gonna happen, sir. If you'll excuse me ..." the man replied as he turned and trotted toward the concrete structure and away from the team.

"Sarge," the colonel barked as he tilted his head toward the fleeing man and arched his eyebrows.

"Got him, boss."

Sarge moved at lightning speed and overtook the man in seconds. With his massive arms wrapped around the man's neck, he had him subdued and unconscious a minute later. After patting him down, he groaned and ran back to the colonel.

"No keys, boss. Just a 9mm and a cell phone," Sarge said.

"How are we going to get the vehicles now?" Charlie asked in a frustrated tone.

Troy looked at Jesús. "Time for you to work your magic, brother."

"Gotcha six, Cap," Jesús as he sprinted to the vehicles about a hundred feet away.

"What's he going to do? Hotwire them?" Charlie asked in a skeptical tone.

"Precisely," Troy said.

She arched her eyebrows. "Jesús knows how to hotwire cars?"

"Yes," Digger said. "He was a damn fine car thief back in the days around East L.A."

"I heard that," Jesús bellowed as he opened the door to the first Suburban. "Don't forget I was a drug dealer, too," he yelled over his shoulder.

"You weren't aware that Jesús didn't always walk the straight and narrow?" The Jackal touched Charlie's elbow.

"Not a clue." Charlie shook her head. "I thought he was just a good ole' Christian with a heart of gold who got stuck with you morons."

"Sometimes you have to dance with the devil before you roll with the saints," Troy said with his tongue firmly planted in his cheek.

"Man, you guys are all jacked the hell up, aren't you?" Charlie asked.

She didn't get any answers, just a few smirks.

Three minutes later, the first SUV pulled up next to the team. "Load up the gear, Ese's!" Jesús exclaimed with a wide grin on his face as he pointed at the rear of the Suburban. "I'll go grab the other one."

"Good job, Jesús," Troy said.

"Yup, the real Jesus and his faithful servant Jesús save our asses from time to time." The Jackal said in a mocking tone just to yank Jesús's chain.

"Watch it, heathen." Jesús turned and glared at the Jackal.

Troy looked at Charlie, whose eyes grew wide. "I take it Jesús doesn't like the sacrilegious stuff much."

"Find a weakness, then exploit it," the Jackal said before adding, "That's what I learned in Sunday School."

"You're such a manchild," Charlie said as she shook her head. "And I'm not sure the carpenter from Nazareth has you in his good book."

"You gotta start as a sinner before you can graduate to being a saint." The Jackal winked at Charlie.

Troy shook his head as he looked from the Jackal and then over to Charlie. "Just don't ask what church he grew up in."

"I'll take Anton LaVay for a thousand, Alex," Charlie replied.

The Jackal laughed at her comment. "Nope! Born and bred Baptist, my dear. I still have my Awana vest at home in my mom's hope chest!"

Charlie's face contorted into a questioning scowl. "Awana. Do I want to know?"

Troy shrugged. "No clue."

"It's a kids club for the Bible thumpers' offspring," the Jackal said.

"And they let you in it?"

The Jackal smiled. "My teacher always said sometimes a wolf hides amongst the sheep."

"Perceptive teacher," Charlie said.

"Yeah, she was like twenty and hot, too." The Jackal let out an elongated whistle.

"I don't want to know any more of this story." She covered her ears.

"Welcome to our world," Troy said.

Jesús returned with the second vehicle a few minutes later, and the supplies were loaded. The team split equally amongst the two vehicles and left the airfield at Al-Hillah, traveling fifteen minutes down Highway 8 toward the ruins of Babylon.

51

AT CRUISING ALTITUDE

BOEING 757-200

Ami tried to rest on the flight to Iraq. However, sleep eluded him. He spent most of his adult life building a criminal enterprise with international arms sales as his most lucrative income source. With far more riches than he could have ever dreamed of obtaining, it was never enough. A drive within always whispered a single word. *More.* No matter how much he accumulated or how big of a deal he secured, it never satisfied the gnawing hunger just below the surface.

Born to an Israeli mother and German father, Ami grew up mostly middle class, but because of his mixed heritage, he faced difficulty in school. The taunts and jeers only fed his insatiable desire to do something different and achieve a notoriety beyond anyone he knew as an adolescent. A chance encounter with someone who sold goods on the black market while attending university significantly altered Ami's path.

The excitement of the illegal acts and financial rewards he earned slowly over time deluded any moral qualms he may have about the questionable legality of the activities he took part in. Because of his growing wealth, he could have any woman and buy any vehicle or garments he desired. The allure of what might be possible overwhelmed his last string of morality as he gave into the intoxicating lifestyle he became accustomed to enjoying.

When he was only twenty-six, he took a life for the first time. The victim was a petty thief who stole something of little value from him, a watch worth only a few hundred dollars. The act of murder did not sear his conscience, and in some ways, he quite enjoyed seeing the life drain from the man as he repeatedly stabbed the robber to death. Over the years, physical violence toward those who crossed him increased, and his ways of seeking retribution became more dubious.

Life's spiral from mediocrity within the realm of civil obedience to dreams of grandeur under the pretense of invisibility proved to be a slippery slope for Ami Sulzer.

As he opened the door and walked out of his private cabin, he arrived at the front of the jet, where Benjamin worked at his laptop. The glare of the screen illuminated his face.

Benjamin nodded as his boss took the seat across from him.

"Did they arrive?" Ami asked just as the plane touched down in Iraq.

"Our contact at the CIA facility in Al-Hillah just called to say their plane is on its final approach," Benjamin replied.

"We must move quickly and load the gear into the helicopter," Ami stated.

Benjamin pursed his lips. "The men know what we need done."

"How far behind will we be?"

"At least thirty minutes."

"How about the other men?"

Benjamin shrugged. "Martyrs are hard to find on short notice, even in Iraq."

"Did they not find us any?"

"They found a handful. They should arrive before we do. I expect around twenty men should be onsite, including Rahman and his guards."

"He won't be happy when I tell him what's about to happen," Ami said.

"If he wants his nuke bad enough, he'll have to deal with the reality that awaits us all."

"Agreed," Ami said. "And how about the four men at the site? Are they ready?"

"They said they were, but I think we both know what fate has in store for them."

"Without question," Ami said. "They'll be slaughtered like pigs."

"Maybe it will slow the Americans down slightly, or even one of them may get lucky."

Ami frowned and raised a single finger. "Benjamin, Benjamin, Benjamin ... as I've told you over the years, luck is for the poor and weak-minded. A real man forges his own path, creates his own destiny, and doesn't rely on such mumbo jumbo as luck or put his fate in the hands of lesser beings."

Benjamin shook his head. "So I've heard you say."

52

BABYLON, IRAQ

ISHTAR GATE

The road leading off Highway 8 to Babylon was covered with a thick layer of sand after a sandstorm moved its way across the region overnight. Troy drove the lead vehicle and had difficulty locating the pavement as he raced down the two-lane road much too fast. Only the signs sprinkled along the side of the road sporadically gave him any indication of where the pavement ended and the desert landscape began.

Troy had visited Babylon on two separate occasions during his many deployments to Iraq. He had done so primarily for the ancient city's historical significance, but knowing the area's layout now proved valuable.

As the wind continued to whip across the desert landscape, the roadway ahead once again became visible as the sand retreated from the asphalt. In the distance, a seven-meter-high dune blocked the view of Babylon. It also gave Troy an idea; he recalled that the Ishtar Gate stood less than a quarter mile beyond the dune.

"Digger," he barked into his comms.

"Yes, Cap," came the reply from the vehicle directly behind him.

"There's a sand dune directly ahead. I need you and the Jackal on top of it for overwatch."

"Roger that, Cap."

Thirty seconds later, the two vehicles quickly stopped at the base of the dune. The Jackal jumped out from the lead vehicle while Digger climbed out of the other, and they scaled the steep pile of desert sand. Within two minutes, Digger had his sniper rifle in place and his first round chambered. The Jackal maintained a similar pose next to him and used his spotter optics to acquire targets.

Once they were both in position, Digger gave Troy the go-ahead to proceed. Troy accelerated the Suburban as the sand flew out from under the back tires and, within a few seconds, made his way around the dune. The Ishtar Gate became visible, its blue-painted bricks providing a splash of color in the dull monochrome palette of the Iraqi landscape. Troy saw the man with his hand out and the orange traffic cone in the road at the same time as Digger's voice breached the silence.

"Cap, we got an armed guard two hundred yards ahead blocking the road," Digger warned.

"Copy that, I see him." Troy looked to his right at the colonel. "We were told no guards, right?"

"Correct." The colonel's eyes narrowed as he frowned. "The Iraqis assured the agency all guards would be ordered to stand down."

"Then he must be treated as a hostile," Troy replied.

Colonel Marshall agreed. "I concur. Omegas, you have permission to engage. As usual, you gents and the lady have full operational authority."

"See anyone else visible, Digger?" Troy asked.

"Negative, Cap. We are scanning the structures nearby. Do you want me to engage the target?"

Troy reached to his right side and removed his Kimber 1911 .45. With a round always chambered, he removed the thumb safety and held the gun against his left thigh as he continued to steer with his left hand. "No, I'll handle him. You guys see if we have any other threats or if we're driving into an ambush."

"Roger that."

The colonel looked at Troy. "You think Ami arrived already?"

"Doubt it," Troy said. "But it's highly likely he dispatched a team here to protect the site."

"I'd be shocked if he didn't."

Troy bit at his lower lip. "Game time, ladies and gentlemen," he said after he activated his comm unit. "Make sure you're cocked, locked, and ready to rock."

"Hooah!" The simultaneous words uttered by the Omegas came over the comms.

Troy slowed as he approached the man whose outstretched hand demanded they stop. The vehicle stood high enough off the ground that the man could only see from the chest up as he approached the driver's side window. Troy lowered the window and returned the icy glare the man provided.

After years of experience, the tell-tale signs to watch for were obvious. The eyes, it always came down to the eyes. The guard's eyes darted to each person in the vehicle and narrowed ever so slightly. Not in a way you assess if something is a threat but calculating how to eliminate an acknowledged threat.

"Ishtar Gate is closed. You must turn around," the man ordered in broken English. He wore a white helmet, tan uniform, and black boots that looked much too new for an Iraqi soldier. An AK-47 slung across his chest, while a large caliber sidearm hung on his right hip.

"You don't get it, bud. We must pass," Troy replied in a calm, cool tone. "It's official government business."

Just then, Digger's voice interrupted the exchange. "Contact, I have three weapons trained on your position ..."

The guard's response was rapid but still not fast enough. As he reached to his right hip and gripped the handgun that hung to his side, Troy raised the 1911 with a lightning-quick motion. As soon as the barrel cleared the door trim, Troy fired one solitary round. The large .45 caliber round struck the man in the bridge of his nose and left a dime-sized hole in his face. When the hollow-point round emerged, half the back of his head exploded. The sound inside the vehicle was nearly deafening.

Suddenly, rounds began hitting the front grill of the armored Suburban and traveled up the hood. Troy rolled up the window and mashed the gas pedal to the floor. Successive bullets struck the front hood and smacked into the bulletproof windshield, splintering the polycarbonate but not breaking the toughened glass.

"Anytime, fellas," Troy yelled as the engine whined and the vehicle accelerated.

Digger fired one round after another. Within five seconds, the three shooters were neutralized.

Both Suburbans came to a screeching halt before the Ishtar Gate as the team jumped out and took up defensive positions, not knowing what other threats they may face.

"We clear?" Troy asked.

"Roger that, Cap," Digger answered from his overwatch spot atop the sand dune.

"Then double-time it and get your asses to the gate."

The colonel stood at Troy's side as they scanned the area for hostiles.

Troy rubbed his fingers against the rough pock marks splattered across the smooth hood. "Glad we didn't take those POS Humvees the spooks left us."

With a visible grimace, the colonel replied, "The director and I will have fierce words when I get back to D.C. after this is over."

Troy nodded before he raised his voice. "Move out, everyone, and stay alert."

With his weapon pointed forward, Troy led the group as he approached the left side of the structure. He immediately noticed the large stone blocks that Naseefa described. They were huge sandstone blocks that made up the wall constructed by Saddam on top of the existing Babylonian antiquity wall. A large gap big enough to place a finger inside ran along the top of each three-foot-square block. In many places, the gap had been filled by papers and stones stuffed into the slits by tourists and locals.

It took a couple of passes, but Troy ran his finger inside the third block and finally felt the two locking pins set several inches back, hidden inside the stone. With both index fingers inserted, he simultaneously pushed the two pins, and a metallic *click* sound indicated the mechanism keeping the block in place was disengaged. His fingers gripped the smooth stone, and it easily swung toward him, revealing a blackened shaft that led underground.

Digger and the Jackal arrived just as Troy shined his flashlight into the pitch-dark abyss.

"Someone hold onto me so I can get a better look." Troy lowered his head and torso into the shaft. He abandoned the flashlight, flipped down his GPNVG optics, and used an IR illuminator to boost the light. Sarge and Jesús each held tight to his legs as Troy looked down the long tunnel bathed in a greenish hue.

"What's it look like?" Sarge asked as they pulled him back up.

"Not much to report." Troy stood and felt the blood rush out of his head. "It appears to be at least a hundred feet long and dead ends right here. Metal ladder rungs lead down to the ground. Looks like there's a locking mechanism in place so the hatch can be sealed from the inside."

"What's at the other end of the tunnel?" Sarge asked.

Troy shrugged. "Guess we're about to find out." He then turned to his right and locked eyes with Harry. "Doc, I need you to stay topside and watch our six, okay?"

"Copy that, Cap."

"Let us know if you see anyone coming toward the gate."

Harry nodded.

"Everyone else, follow me. You'll need your NVGs and IR illuminators," Troy said before he paused. "Oh, who's got the cooler?"

"I got it." The colonel patted the blue Igloo cooler.

"Won't get far without that."

They made their way down the ladder rungs one at a time, with Troy taking the lead.

Jesús paused momentarily and bowed his head before starting down the opening.

The Jackal saw him and muttered, "Hope you mention me in your chats with the man upstairs."

"Always, brother," Jesús said, then added with a wink, "For you more than the others," before he quickly disappeared down the hole.

"Ladies first." The Jackal swung his arm at the opening as Charlie sidled next to him.

"Well, aren't you just a gentleman," she responded with an exquisite southern drawl rolling off her tongue. Next thing he knew, she crouched down, grabbed hold of the top of the shaft, and swung her body over the opening, dropping straight down to the darkness below. Her movements were like an elegant dancer as she twisted her body and slipped flawlessly out of sight.

"Show off." The Jackal shook his head slightly. *Damn, that girl is hot*, he thought as he watched her disappear.

53

KARBALA, IRAQ

As the helicopter gained altitude and climbed into the gleaming Arab sky, Ami felt a slight tap on his leg. He looked at Benjamin, who touched his hand on his headset and then put up two fingers. This indicated that Ami needed to switch to channel two. Whatever he needed to say, clearly, he didn't want any of the others in the helicopter to hear. Rahman Salek had his back to both men, so it wouldn't be a problem keeping him out of the loop.

"Yes?" Ami asked.

"Our men in Babylon just made contact with the Americans?" Benjamin said.

"And?"

"As expected, the one manning the checkpoint didn't last long."

"What about the others?"

"They engaged the two vehicles that approached, but the call ended abruptly with an immense amount of gunfire."

"Have you called them back?"

"No answer. I tried repeatedly, but ..."

Ami shook his head. "They're dead. What about the other team? Did they make it?"

Benjamin shook his head. "They hit a roadside checkpoint south of Baghdad. Made it through okay, but it caused a delay."

"When will they arrive?"

"Just about the same time we'll land." He looked at his watch. "In about fifteen minutes."

Ami was quiet for a moment as he considered the options. "We'll need to flush out the Americans before they can secure the nuke and bring reinforcements."

"Agreed. Do you want to gas them?"

As he considered the question, Ami knew the answer. A team that could make it into his compound and steal critical info would be not only well disciplined but highly prepared. "No," he replied. "They're sure to have masks. We'll have to rely on superior firepower."

"I suspect marksmanship will be in their favor."

"True. That's why we'll send in the Iraqis first. They're dispensable."

Benjamin nodded. "Are you sure you want to enter the facility? You could wait until the Americans are dead and the area is secure."

Ami's upper lip rose into a noticeable snarl. "My future and financial security rests under Babylon. I'm not sitting idly by while you and the others go down there and deal with the Americans and secure the nuke for Rahman. You know I'm a man of action, Benjamin, and I don't live in fear of what may happen. Plus, I'm likely a better shot than most of the mercenaries we hired. You can't afford to leave an expert marksman behind when so much is at stake."

"Of course, Ami."

"Anyway, if something were to happen to me and the Americans recovered the nuke, my death would seal the fate of many of their fellow citizens."

54

— • —

BABYLON

UNDER THE ANCIENT CITY

From the moment they entered the pitch-black tunnel, the ground sloped downward with a steep grade. As the team reached the end, Troy put his hand up to motion everyone to hold up. With two quick gestures, he indicated for Sarge and Jesús to check the left and right sides of the opening. They moved in rapid steps, and both swung out in tandem. In low voices, both replied, "Clear."

The team continued to move forward with the Jackal and Charlie on their six. With two long hallways, the complex closely formed the shape of an X, and a series of rooms lined each passageway. In the very center of the X, the schematic showed the vault. With quickened paces, the team cleared each of the eight rooms they encountered and moved forward before reaching the center room.

A large forty-foot by forty-foot room with a ceiling close to fifteen feet high greeted them as they entered. The four hallways that made up the facility extended from the corners of the sizeable room. A sense of relief spread across Troy as he immediately took note of the vault, which was precisely where the diagram said it should be. As they approached the vault door, the team kept at least one gun on each of the three remaining halls they hadn't cleared.

Troy approached the vault first. He noticed a control panel with a dusty digital keypad and biometric hand pad to the right of the door. The stainless-steel rounded vault door was massive and had a polished five-spoke handle. It looked like one of those doors in the basement of an old bank in NYC or any major city during the early 1900s. Clearly, it's not something anyone expected to come across under a four-thousand-year-old archaeological site.

How the hell did they even get this door down here? Troy shook his head in amazement.

The colonel handed him the blue Igloo cooler. "Open her up and make sure the nuke is inside. We need to keep moving. We'll split up and clear the remaining three hallways."

Troy nodded as the Omegas quickly disappeared down the three darkened hallways. He put the cooler on the concrete floor and flipped open the lid. There, in a greenish light, he saw Naseefa's severed hand. He picked up the cold-to-the-touch, clammy hand he had cut off just above the wrist. Touching dead bodies never bothered Troy, but for an unknown reason, holding the hand within his own seemed creepy.

With his left hand, Troy entered the twelve-digit code 0-1-2-4-0-7-0-9-0-5-1-1. The light above the keypad flickered green and stayed that color as the code was accepted. Next, he placed Naseefa's hand on the keypad. A digital scan head passed under the glass and registered the handprint pressed against the surface. The second green light illuminated, and a deep metallic clang and cranking sound indicated the metal cylinders retreated from the door frame. With a dull thud at the end, the door could be opened.

Troy stepped to the center of the door and, turned the five spoke handle counter clockwise and heard the hiss of pressure being released from the vault's seal. He then pulled the heavy door as it pivoted open and crept toward him. Giving it a firm tug, momentum took over, and the door fully opened. Troy looked inside the vault chamber and saw the prize.

The nuclear warhead sat in the center of the space in a custom-designed cradle. A second cradle next to it sat empty. Troy stepped inside and stood next to the device. His mind raced back to years before when he stood inside a vault not much different from where he found himself. At the time when he was younger, a similar-sized nuclear weapon greeted his eyes. For some, it would be a thrilling moment, but for Troy, seeing another warhead brought back only memories of pain and loss. He never wanted to see another weapon of mass destruction as long as he lived.

As he stood there and stared at the weapon for a few moments, the rest of the team returned from clearing the facility and entered the chamber.

"All clear," the colonel said. He whistled noticeably and stepped into the vault. "Damn, that's a big ass nuke." As he spoke, he saw anguish spread across Troy's face. "You did good, Cap. Really good."

"Yes, sir," Troy answered. "The whole team did."

Sarge stepped close to Troy and put his hand on his shoulder. "Not many people get to find one of these things in their lifetime, let alone two."

Troy shook his head. "Tell me about it. A dubious honor I wish I didn't hold."

The Jackal walked up to the weapon and, without warning, climbed on top of it with a full straddle and started his best impression from Dr. Strangelove. Taking off his helmet, he waved it around and let out a few "howls" and "yee-haws" as he gyrated wildly, much to the amusement of everyone on the team. Even the colonel, who normally appeared ever so stoic, cracked a wide smile.

Jesús rolled his eyes at the antics.

"Now, that's some potent power between my legs," the Jackal stated.

Quickly, the colonel returned to his grumpy self after the Jackal carried on for a few extra seconds. "That's enough. Get your skinny ass off the thermonuclear device before you somehow activate it and blow us all to kingdom come."

The Jackal climbed off it. "I always wanted to do that ever since I was a little boy."

"And I'm sure you've done worse," Digger said.

The Jackal smiled from ear to ear. "Ahh, you remember the story I told you about what I did in every single one of Saddam's palaces?"

"Sadly, yes," Digger answered. "Will never get that mental image out of mind, either."

"I don't want to know," Charlie said as she raised her hands to stop Digger from going further. "And remind me to never bring a black light into one of those palaces."

"Bingo!" the Jackal said.

The banter and lightheadedness disappeared instantly as Harry's voice caused everyone's muscles to tighten.

"We have several vehicles approaching at a high rate of speed and also a chopper flying low, which appears to be landing."

"Ami?" Troy asked.

"Not sure," Harry replied. "But whoever it is, I'm pretty sure they spotted me."

"Get down here, close the hatch, and lock it from the inside," Troy commanded. "We're in the middle room inside the vault. The hallway is clear when you get down here."

"Copy that," Harry said. "On my way, and I hope I'm not climbing down into my own tomb."

"We need to seal the vault and set up defensive positions," Troy said. "Find anything you can to give us cover. Meet back here in four minutes."

Troy knew Ami could be ruthless and had access to even greater firepower than The Omega Group at the moment. So, they had to fight smarter, not harder. One of the packs they carried underground contained over twenty-five pounds of M112 (military grade C4) and dozens of detonators. As half the team gathered and arranged obstacles, the others strategically placed the blocks of plastic explosives throughout the three hallways they just cleared.

As Troy pushed the vault door shut and engaged the locking mechanism, something concerned him. Indecisiveness was something Troy never struggled with in life. Planning came naturally to him from an early age. When he formulated a strategy, more times than not, it proved to be exactly the right decision. However, a voice within him welled up and convinced him to change tactics. *Ami's gonna come at us with everything in his arsenal,* he thought. *And what if it's too much?* Troy's mind raced: *RPGs, grenades, who knows what other explosives he would use that could inflict serious damage on us. We need to be proactive, not reactive.*

55

—— • ——

BABYLON

Rahman Salek could be left in the dark no longer. A few minutes before they landed in Babylon, Ami told him the Americans were making a play for the weapon. As expected, Rahman responded with rage when Ami admitted to misleading him. However, Ami cared not, and he clarified that if Rahman wanted the weapon, they would need to deal with the Americans in order to secure the device.

As usual, Ami lied when Rahman questioned what awaited them. It became such a habit over the years that he had difficulty separating fact from fiction in his own mind. *It's not a lie if you believe it*, he reminded himself. He assured Rahman they had superior numbers and could defeat the Americans. Ami was correct; they held a three-to-one advantage regarding the sheer number of bodies available. However, the comparison meant little since Ami knew the enemy they faced could fight off a small army given the right conditions. Pride stood between Ami's intellect and reasoning abilities, and he couldn't just walk away. Letting the Americans retrieve the weapon would be an unacceptable outcome in his mind.

When Ami and his men arrived at the Ishtar Gate, there was no sign of the American soldier his men spotted when they landed. As his men converged on the gate, they discovered the hidden entrance on the right side had been locked from the inside. It mattered not since Ami knew of other ways to enter the subterranean structure. It did mean that the team would be prepared for their arrival and were guaranteed to be ready for any onslaught. Ami had some tricks up his sleeve and convinced himself they could get the upper hand.

"Bring all the gear," Ami told his men.

"All of it?" one of his men asked. "It's quite heavy."

"Yes, and it may very well save our lives today."

Two hundred yards past the gate, Ami located the hatch he used the one time he visited the site with Naseefa. He brushed away the sand that covered the opening and shielded it from prying eyes. Next to it, a metal cover hid a keypad. Ami flipped it up and entered the six-digit number 0-4-0-8-5-3.

After the locking mechanism disengaged, one of his men pulled open the heavy steel hatch. It gave a loud creaking sound as it slowly opened. Looking down into the abyss, his eyes saw only darkness. "Either they haven't located the lights, or they are choosing to operate in the shadows," the man who opened the hatch stated.

"We need every advantage we can take," Ami said. "And using optics will only aid the Americans. They are experts at being silent warriors and thrive in this type of realm. Once inside, we must turn on the lights. Using the NVGs during the battle will put us at a strategic disadvantage."

"But if we turn on the lights, they'll know we're here."

Ami narrowed his gaze. "Trust me, that's already the case."

One after another, the men climbed down the ladder that led to the passage below. Once everyone made it inside, Ami followed behind and shut the hatch. He did so as quietly as possible, but it still made a dull thud that echoed down the hallway.

At the bottom of the ladder, Benjamin stayed close to Ami. "Don't leave my side, boss," he said.

Ami nodded. "I wasn't planning to do so."

56

BABYLON

When everyone returned, Troy briefly stated his concerns about the defensive position they erected.

"Your call, Cap," Sarge said. "If that famous gut of yours is acting up, I, for one, say we listen to it."

The others, including Charlie, nodded.

Troy felt certain the hunted needed to become the hunters.

In the distance, the sound of the hatch opening echoed down the hall. The battle for the nuke would start soon.

"We're not alone ... they're here," Troy said. "Get ready and watch for my signals."

Positioned directly in front of the vault door, Troy had several thick stainless desks aligned to provide him the best cover while also being able to maintain a visual on his team. He said a quick prayer and, as always, asked not for his safety but for his men.

His brothers and now his sister, Charlie, came first.

Two minutes later, a distinct thud reverberated down the hall at the ten o'clock position from where Troy crouched. The sound confirmed which hallway Ami's men used to enter the subterranean facility. He gestured for the rest of the team with his hands and indicated which direction the assault would come. Then, it became a waiting game. Troy had no line of sight down the hallway, but Digger had the perfect angle.

Troy broke radio silence to give quick instructions in a whisper to Digger. "Ami will lead from the rear. Those expendable to him will come first. Take them out so we can thin the herd."

"Copy that," Digger replied.

Everything became eerily quiet.

With a keen eye, Digger saw movement halfway down the hall and made two clicks on his comms. That was the signal for the Jackal, who had the detonator in his right hand. When he heard the clicks, he squeezed the handle tight and depressed the black button on top.

A loud explosion and the subsequent shock wave carried down the hall as dust and debris spewed into the large room. Hearing groaning and screams, Troy stood and led his team forward.

◆

The wave of energy reverberated down the narrow hallway, striking Ami in the chest and knocking his feet out from under him. He landed with a dull thud flat on his back. *Dammit*, he thought as he hit the cold, hard concrete. He never saw it coming. Ami expected the Americans would dig in and use defensive methods to combat his men's attack, but not go on the offensive.

I should've known better.

Up ahead, he heard groaning but could see nothing since the force of the explosion knocked his optics from the top of his head. As he rolled over to his hands and knees, he frantically felt along the cold concrete for the night vision goggles. Shards of metal and concrete punctured his skin and gouged his knees as he moved around. Then he remembered the light switches he passed a few feet away on the wall.

Two firm hands grabbed his collar, and a powerful grip pulled him to his feet.

"Ami, are you okay?"

Even with his head spinning, Ami recognized the voice. "Yes, I think I'm okay."

"Good," Benjamin said. "We need to find shelter in one of these rooms. The Americans are making an assault."

"No," Ami replied forcefully. "Push the men forward."

"But ..." Benjamin replied. "The men will be slaughtered."

Ami would hear none of it. "Now," he demanded and marched forward, much to the chagrin of the man at his side. In the pitch black, he slipped on a pool of blood that filled the center of the hall, the slick pool of coagulated liquid from the bodies littered all over the floor.

Ami fell once again. Four of the Iraqi mercenaries took direct hits from the plastic explosives when they detonated. Little was left besides chunks of flesh and a few intact limbs and torsos.

Benjamin located the optics and handed them to Ami as he rose to his feet.

Crouched down on all fours, Rahman Salek appeared bloodied but miraculously sustained no life-threatening injuries. Ami approached him. Both of Rahman's dismembered bodyguards were scattered across the tunnel.

"Get in this room," Ami growled as he pulled Rahman's arm and led him to the doorway. "Stay in there until I come for you, and if anyone besides me or my men enter, shoot them in the head. I'm going to get your nuke."

Rahman looked to have suffered a concussion by the force of the explosion, but he shook his head and acknowledged the instructions. "Okay," he muttered as his eyes rolled around.

"Lights, turn on the damn lights," Ami demanded as he swung back to Benjamin. "The switch is on the wall just past the opening to the room."

"Are you sure?" Benjamin asked.

"Just do it," Ami hissed. "These men are much better when the lights are out. We need to mount an offensive, and the darkness is not our ally, but it is theirs. Grab the RPGs and follow me."

57

BABYLON

Troy and his team moved to the far end of the room with their backs pressed against the wall. Everyone knew the drill: Keep Ami alive. Indiscriminately setting off C-4 explosives in the hallway would render that objective highly improbable. The first one they detonated was a calculated risk, as Troy figured Ami would not be leading his group through the tunnel.

This severely tied their hands and limited how they could respond. He also knew Ami would have no such restrictions.

With several hand gestures, Troy directed the team to move down the hallway and face Ami's force head-on. As he shifted away from the limited safety afforded by the wall, his body froze as a distinct hum emanated from the ceiling. Just like that, the room was bathed in incandescent light as the fixtures throughout the room and up and down the hallway suddenly came to life. With the lights back on, Troy and the rest of the team pressed themselves against the wall and flipped up their night optics.

Clever, Troy thought. *Levels the playing field a bit. Smart move, Ami.* He considered shooting out the lights, but getting them all wouldn't be feasible.

Sarge stood across from him against the wall on the other side of the opening. He mouthed the words, *What do we do now?* At the same time, he brought his finger across his neck in a quick motion.

Troy shook his head, indicating *no.* There would be no turning back. They must move forward. As he gave hand signals to begin the offensive push, a distinct swoosh reverberated down the hallway. The unmistakable sound announced a warhead careening toward them. Instinctively, they all turned to the wall and crouched low to expose the least amount of their flesh to the destructive ordnance possible. The 93 mm HEAT warhead screamed through the room and struck just to the left of the vault door back behind their position. Pieces of hot, jagged metal littered the room but miraculously caused no injury to the team.

"Now," Troy said, knowing a tit-for-tat exchange of explosives between the two forces would only result in loss of life or serious injury. He had to stop the carnage before it began.

The Jackal and Sarge stood on opposite sides of the doorway leading to the hallway. When Troy gave the signal, they threw two flash bangs down the hall as far as they could. The canisters clanged against the concrete floor several times, followed by four successive explosions. With weapons raised, the Omega Group members flooded into the hallway and acquired targets.

Three men staggered in a dazed fashion about a quarter way down the hall. With three-round bursts fired rapidly from multiple weapons, the men were struck and crumpled to the ground. Two other bodies lay close by, one of them twitching and convulsing. Subsequent shots stopped the one body from moving while insurance rounds were pumped into the others to ensure no threat existed as they moved forward.

No other targets appeared down the corridor, indicating Ami and the rest of his men took shelter in the rooms that dotted the hallway. They needed to clear each room and do it before Ami's team could respond with more lead or bigger ordnances.

Before the second RPG could be fired, the four flashbangs detonated about twenty feet away from Ami and Benjamin. As the stun grenades went off, Benjamin shielded Ami from the blast, then quickly shoved him into an adjacent room. The remaining men fighting for Ami took cover in the various rooms up and down the hallway. Less than a dozen of the original force Ami brought into the facility remained alive.

"We stay in here, we die," Ami yelled in a livid tone as Benjamin pushed him into the room against his will.

Benjamin couldn't disagree with the sentiment, but he also knew death would greet them much faster if they remained out in the open.

"What do you suggest? If we step outside this door, we're dead even faster."

Even though that made sense, Ami shook his head and tried to clear his mind. Then it occurred to him. "Use the corner shot. Take out as many of them as you can. I'll radio the others to use their grenades."

With a nod, Benjamin shifted the weapon strapped to his back around to his chest.

Using the relative safety of the room, he stood a foot from the doorway and adjusted the angle, cocked the weapon, and prepared to fire. Killing the Americans was not his intent, but at the same time, he couldn't refuse the order to shoot. As he extended the weapon around the door frame, his viewfinder located a target. With two quick pulls of the trigger, the man dropped and swung the weapon to the right slightly and took aim at the next soldier. The bullseye settled on the chest, but before he could pull the trigger, a barrage of bullets struck the door frame and hit the weapon, dislodging it from his hands and rendering it useless as several rounds struck the barrel.

"One down," he yelled for Ami's benefit as he drew his sidearm.

"Rush the hallway," Ami screamed into his radio. "Use the grenades."

<hr>

Digger saw the black metal protrude from the distant doorway but didn't react fast enough. By the time he realized it was a corner shot weapon, the two rounds went *pop-pop.* It felt like a sledgehammer hit him directly in the solar plexus, one after another. With the wind knocked out of him, he fell to the ground and grabbed at his chest.

Charlie and the Jackal watched him drop as they each unloaded full mags into the doorway where the shots were fired.

Digger lay on the ground and gasped for breath, as it felt like an elephant was lying on his chest. He sustained many injuries in his ten years with the military, but getting shot hadn't made the list. Fortunately, his body armor saved his life as both rounds struck squarely in the middle of the protective plate. But it still hurt like hell.

Harry stood over him a few seconds later and checked his vitals before leading him back toward the end of the hallway.

"I'm fine," Digger replied in quick, short breaths as he tried to break free of Harry's arm wrapped around his waist.

"Like hell you are. You just took two to the chest."

"And if we don't stay in the fight, the next rounds may find soft tissue. We push through, and we end this just like Cap said. I'm not part of the "B" team after all, I'm with the "A" team bitch, all the way, and I'll follow Hannibal to the gates of hell if need be."

⚬

The Omega Group watched the original A-Team television show, which ran from 1983-1987, countless times while on deployments. Troy had bought the complete series DVD's one night stateside on a 2 a.m Wally World run. There were too many Omegas to assume the identities of all the characters from the show, but everyone agreed Troy was most certainly Hannibal. Sarge acted like and had the brawn of B.A. Baracus, "Mr. T." While the Jackal said he had the look of "Face," yet the Omegas said he most certainly acted like "Howling Mad Murdock" at times.

Troy, Sarge, and Jesús entered the first room to the right, and after a brief exchange, the three men they encountered died with headshots. It took them less than five seconds to secure the room. Next, they proceeded back out and quietly made their way down the hall to the next room.

Harry stayed back to watch their six in case anyone else entered the subterranean structure via one of the other tunnels, and since he got shot Digger stayed with him per Cap's orders.

Charlie, Colonel Marshall, and the Jackal entered the room on the left as two grenades rolled across the floor toward them. In unison, they dove behind a large stainless steel examining table to their right and pulled it down as a shield. A second later, the explosion ripped through the middle of the room. Shrapnel riddled the outside of the table with a series of *clanging* sounds but didn't penetrate the thick steel. Ami's two men who tossed the grenades stood no chance as the trio popped up from behind the table and cut the men down one after the other from the shelter they took before tossing the grenades.

They were down to three rooms to search.

One of them must contain Ami.

58

BABYLON

As Troy stood outside the next room, he gave a nod to Sarge, and they both threw flashbangs inside and counted to three. As soon as the two back-to-back explosions went off, they rushed into the room with Jesús on Troy's six.

Troy heard the shot before he felt it. A burning sensation and a twinge of pain shot up his arm. His mind immediately recognized he'd been hit. Wasn't the first time, and he doubted it would be the last. He still gripped his weapon tightly and engaged the person at the far end of the room who fired the shot. With a three-round burst to the face, the man dropped in a heap. Another man lay on the ground, stunned since one of the flash bangs exploded at his feet. Sarge drilled him with a burst from his rifle, and Jesús took out the third man in the corner, who managed to get off a few rounds that sailed above Sarge's head.

Clearing the room, they moved back toward the door. Then Jesús saw the beads at the end of Troy's elbow that fell to the ground in crimson droplets.

"Cap," he called out as he reached for his friend. "You've been hit."

Troy shook his head. "Just a flesh wound. The round went through near the biceps. I'm fine. We need to push on. Only a few rooms to clear, and Ami must be in one of them."

They stepped outside into the hallway and met up with the others. Two rooms remained. One was much closer to the right, and the other was at the far end of the hall on the left. With hand gestures, Troy indicated he wanted Charlie, the colonel, and the Jackal to take the closest room.

Ami heard sporadic bursts of gunfire and multiple explosions. Based on the sound, it mainly came from the Americans. The HK416, favored by the American special operation groups, made a distinct sound, and Ami had a keen ear for distinguishing one weapon from another. He correctly assumed most of his men had been slaughtered. Their likelihood of getting the nuclear weapon slipped by as each spent shell casing struck the cold concrete floor. With a steely resolve, he grabbed a vest from the black duffel bag near the door and put it on. Benjamin had never seen it before, but once he noticed what it was, his heart sank.

"I can't be taken alive," Ami proclaimed as he zipped up the vest and toggled a switch on the black cigarette-shaped box attached to the top right. In his hand, he held a detonator.

Benjamin's mind raced. He never took Ami for being a martyr. Ami cared for one person and had one singular cause: himself. He simply couldn't grasp that Ami would choose such an action. "You can't go out like that," he pleaded. "You're a survivor."

"We either recover that nuke, or we don't make it out." Ami spoke with clear conviction. "I won't let those bastards put me in Guantanamo Bay or, worse yet, ADX Florence. And if we fail and I die in a blaze of glory, the Americans will pay with their lives. Millions of them will suffer for the sins of their government. Their blood will be on the filth that leads the agency, not me." He noticed the concern displayed in Benjamin's eyes. "Why? Are you afraid to die?" Ami asked as a grim look spread across his face.

Benjamin's mind raced. The ante just got raised. "Of course not."

"Good, then we finish this and hit them with everything we have left." Ami raised his assault rifle and held it with his right hand while the left gripped the black cylinder-shaped detonator.

Realizing there was no way he could warn the Americans, Benjamin's only chance to avert a nuclear disaster lay in keeping Ami alive.

"Throw two grenades," Ami said. "Then we rush the hallway and give them hell."

Benjamin tried to step in front of Ami, but he pushed his subordinate aside.

"Me first," Ami stated.

59

—・—

BABYLON

Metal striking concrete makes a distinct sound. Troy heard it before he noticed the two spherical objects *clanging* across the ground and rolling in their direction.

"Frag out!" he screamed as the entire team took cover where there really wasn't any to find since they were all out in the open. The best they could do was dive into the closest room. Most of them moved fast enough before the two explosions ripped through the hallway. Troy didn't have the time and would never take shelter before his folks found it first. He turned away from the grenades while he pressed his body as tight to the wall as he could. The deafening sound so close rattled his fillings while shards of metal struck the wall all around him, but aside from a few fragments sticking him in the back and lower leg, he escaped without serious injury.

Between getting shot, the RPG, and the grenade, he wasn't having his best day. However, clearly the good Lord was keeping an eye out for him.

At once, he spun back around toward the opening where the grenades were lobbed as two figures emerged from the door. He recognized Ami in a fraction of a second as he watched the gun he held sweep toward him. Troy didn't hesitate. He put the first three-round burst into the ball of Ami's shoulder while he placed two more shots into each kneecap. Ami screamed out in pain and fell forward, his left hand suspiciously extended.

Right behind him, a second person emerged. Troy recognized the face and knew it was the agency asset he encountered in Ami's compound. He hesitated to take the shot even though the man held an assault rifle. The weapon didn't raise, and Troy wasn't about to shoot the man who provided them with so much intelligence unless it was absolutely necessary.

Sarge and the Jackal stepped out from the shelter they found in time to watch as Troy fired the second round into Ami's kneecap. As he hit the ground and the other man stepped out behind him, neither one hesitated when they saw the weapon he held. With lightning-fast trigger pulls, they both put a burst into the man's chest.

Troy watched as the asset grabbed his chest. He yelled *cease-fire*, but it was already too late.

⸺⸺◆⸺⸺

Benjamin felt the very life get sucked out of him as the multiple rounds tore through his flesh and left him with a searing pain that spread out from his chest in every direction. He wore a flak jacket, but two rounds struck where no Kevlar covered his chest just below his collarbone. As he fell forward, he saw Ami's extended hand and finger precariously close to the detonator. With the ground fast approaching, Benjamin took his arm and swatted at Ami's hand in one quick motion. He connected and hit hard enough to dislodge the trigger from Ami's grip as it fell to the ground out of reach.

⸺⸺◆⸺⸺

The colonel, Charlie, and Jesús cleared the last room. Inside, they found Rahman Salek cowering in the corner, crouched down, rocking back and forth on the balls of his feet as he let out a high-pitched scream. His hands raised high in the air as he hysterically shouted, "Don't shoot me, please don't shoot me. My father, he's a powerful man."

"I know who your father is," the colonel said. He learned all about Rahman and his father on the flight from Accra to Iraq. "And he'll pay dearly if he ever wants to see you alive again."

The Jackal approached the two bodies lying about twenty feet down the hall. Charlie followed close behind him as they rushed forward. Several steps behind came Troy. An echoing scream from down the hall distracted the Jackal, and his head turned back toward the sound.

Ami's body accelerated into shock, and his limbs screamed out in horrific pain as he lay on the ground in torment. Benjamin landed just in front of him and blocked both his assault rifle and also the way to blow himself up. He couldn't even see the Americans with Benjamin directly in front of him, blocking his line of sight. As his body slipped into a state of shock, he kept telling himself, *I can't let them take me alive.* Ami's right shoulder burned with a searing pain he never felt before, and he knew it would take all his strength to reach out with his left hand and reach for the detonator.

Lying flat on the ground, his neck craned to the left, and his eyes made contact with Benjamin. A few seconds passed, and he saw the blank expression on Benjamin's face change. He seemed to come to life and blink repeatedly, and his face contorted into a grimace.

"Traitor," Ami hissed, knowing that the man he trusted had betrayed him and knocked the detonator away.

A slight smile formed at the corner of Benjamin's lips as blood seeped through his teeth. With great effort, he mustered the strength to reply. "You'll live ... which means the bomb won't go off ... I've saved you, and that's all that matters."

"They won't take me alive," Ami said in a defiant tone. He reached over Benjamin's body and grabbed the rifle. The detonator was too far away, and he knew no matter how far he reached, he couldn't grab it before the men rushing toward him arrived. He raised the weapon, pointed it at the closest person in his field of vision, and pulled back on the trigger.

The rifle recoiled as a single round spat from the end of the barrel.

60

BABYLON

Charlie saw the arm reach over the larger body and grip the assault rifle. In one smooth motion, the weapon raised as Ami took dead aim at the closest person who approached his position.

The Jackal.

Charlie didn't think. She only reacted like a reflex, and her motion was based on muscle memory. If she hesitated, the Jackal would die. Only one part of Ami was exposed as he lay on the ground, with the other man blocking most of his body.

She knew the shape of his face all too well. Ami had unmistakable eyes and facial features. Charlie knew the orders. *Ami must be kept alive at all costs.*

Yet one of her own was in his bullseye. All these thoughts occurred in a fraction of a second, and during the time it takes someone to blink, her brain gave her finger one simple command: *Pull the damn trigger.*

Which she did.

Her free hand, the one not holding her rifle, kept a tight grip on the back of the Jackal. She did the only thing she could do as her other hand fired the weapon.

Charlie pulled the Jackal toward the ground with all her strength.

Ami saw her. A woman. The American woman who pretended to be Madeline Lapointe. She had him sighted in. The eyes—he could recognize her eyes anywhere. The same second he finished the trigger pull, he watched as the end of her gun exploded in a reddish/orange hue. His head snapped back, and the light in his eyes dimmed until the darkness engulfed him forever.

His head exploded in a red mist as the three-round burst tore through his forehead.

The Jackal stumbled to the ground as Ami's bullet sailed less than an inch over his head and harmlessly embedded in the concrete roof of the tunnel.

Troy watched as Ami's life passed from him and rushed toward the two bodies. Ami was clearly dead, without question, as the back of his head blew completely off. As he flipped over the asset, Troy checked his vital signs. He felt a pulse, although the man's eyes rolled back, and he appeared to have laborious breaths. With a firm shake, Troy jostled him back to the present reality. The colonel arrived a second later and stood just behind Troy and to the left.

The assets' eyes suddenly opened and moved first from Troy, then down toward Ami. "Ami ..." he said as droplets of blood formed on the corner of his mouth and dripped down the side of his cheek.

"He's dead," Troy replied.

With short breaths that came in rapid succession, the asset replied, "The bomb ... it will go off ... tomorrow ... before sunset ... your country is doomed."

"The intelligence agencies are looking through the files, but they've not found anything that has led them to the weapon yet."

"I ... I overheard Ami ... on the ... plane."

"What did you hear?" Troy asked.

"Andrews ... the target is Andrews."

"Joint Base Andrews?" Troy's mind swirled. It didn't make any sense. *Of all places to nuke, why Andrews?*

The asset nodded, then touched his chest. "Benjamin ... that's my name."

"What else did you overhear, Benjamin?"

"Ami's brother ... he will detonate ... the weapon ... near the front gate."

Troy's face contorted into a dumbfounded look. He had read Ami's bio and knew almost all he could know about the man. Ami's brother had died twenty years ago when his sports car slid off a hairpin turn in Monaco and plunged several hundred feet to the rocks below. There were numerous witnesses to the tragic crash. "That's not possible. I read all the intel. His brother's dead."

With a slight motion, Benjamin shook his head. "I met him ... in D.C. just last month. He's alive ... I swear it." His voice became fainter.

Troy wasn't sure what to think. "Where did you see him in Washington?"

"Suburbs. South ... don't know the address ... close to the beltway." With each passing breath, his voice became weaker, and the pauses between phrases grew longer.

"His brother was named Joseph Sulzer. I take it he uses an alias."

Benjamin nodded. "Yes ... an alias."

"What is it? What name does he go by?"

As his eyes rolled back into his head, Benjamin only got three words out, "His ... name ... is ..." Then his mouth stopped moving as the last gust of air passed from his lungs.

Troy felt for a pulse. He found one, but it was weak. "Harry," he screamed.

A few seconds later, Harry sprinted down the hallway and crouched low next to him.

"Keep him alive, Harry. We need the name he was about to tell me."

Harry nodded and got to work on the mostly dead man. "We need to evac him stat. He needs blood and a surgeon if he's gonna stand any chance."

"I'm going topside to call for the nuke recovery team and also get a SORT (Special Operations Resuscitation Team) team here ASAP for Benjamin," the colonel said.

Troy nodded. "You better warn the SecDef as well. They'll need to implement Operation Rapture."

Troy felt her presence and looked over his shoulder. Truthfully, he could smell her. The sweet aroma of her skin was unmistakable. His fierce gaze zeroed in on her as the weight of what she had done struck him.

"Cap, it was him or the Jackal. If I had any other choice ..." Her voice trailed off as she didn't know what else to say.

His expression softened, but he didn't reply. Deep down, he knew she was right. There was no denying that he would have done the exact same thing. His frustration at losing Ami gave way to one nagging question.

How the hell do we stop the attack in time?

Charlie instinctively knew she had made the correct call and could tell from how Troy's countenance changed. He agreed.

The Jackal stood next to her and gripped her right shoulder, giving it a firm squeeze. Charlie turned toward him as he mouthed the words, *Thank you.*

She smiled, coupled her hand over his and squeezed. Next she nodded before she leaned in close and whispered, "Now we're even. I've got no more red in my ledger." Charlie stood up and gave him a little pat on the backside with her right hand as she turned and walked down the tunnel.

With the nuke secured, Troy and Digger entered the vault and proceeded to follow the instructions relayed to them by the man in the black suit back in the United States before they left. The instructions were succinct, and the item in question was exactly where he said they would find it. Removing it was quick and simple.

Once the item was in their possession, Troy and the rest of the team sealed the vault and waited for the recovery team to arrive and take possession of the nuclear device.

Time seemed to slow as Sarge tapped Troy on the elbow. "This shit just got real, Cap."

Troy slowly nodded. "One down and one more to go, my friend."

"We better bat a thousand," Sarge said.

"We will," Troy paused. "We will ..."

61

WEST FALLS CHURCH, VIRGINIA

Levi Sulzer looked down at his watch and silently swore to himself once more. His brother should have called fifteen minutes ago, which meant he was late, and that could only mean something went terribly wrong.

The Americans, he thought. *They must have prevented Ami from retrieving the weapon.*

A bead of sweat formed on his temple and slowly followed the deep contours of his wrinkles down his bronze-colored face toward his square jaw.

But is he dead? Captured? Or just running late?

His mind swam with the possibilities, and a fierce anger boiled deep inside and slowly rose to the surface.

Ami had been clear when he spoke with his brother: *If I don't call it means something has happened to me. Which means I need the Reprisal Protocol initiated.*

Tapping his finger nervously on the desk, Levi stared intently at his iPhone, almost willing it to ring. When ten more minutes passed, and it did not make a peep, he considered his next move. Deep down, he knew what must have happened. Even though it was a break of protocol, he needed to place a few phone calls. Knowing the powers of the NSA, he dared not do it from his cell phone or landline. Grabbing his wallet and keys, he headed out the front door. His destination was 7/11, only three blocks from the townhouse, right off State Highway 50 in West Falls Church, Virginia.

As a teenager, he began smoking. At first, it was to be cool and fit in with the older crowd. Soon, he became addicted and could never shake the habit as he got older. He admitted to his brother Ami that as he aged, it was a nasty habit, and he even figured it would likely be the death of him one day. Now, as he walked down the tree-lined block, he pondered whether the Turkish cigarette dangling from his lips wouldn't be the reason he left planet Earth after all. As he took a long drag, he considered what he must do if Ami didn't call, which seemed even more likely as the minutes passed.

Twenty minutes later, he walked out of the convenience store with five burner cell phones in a brown paper bag. As he proceeded down the busy road, he placed one call after another to various numbers. Dismay crept up like a stiff wind as none of the people he called answered. After dialing the last number, he was surprised when the line connected, and a man replied in a soft tone, almost speaking in a whisper.

"What happened?" Levi asked.

The whispering said, "You should not have called. It could jeopardize both of us."

"I'm on a burner. It's fine. Where's my brother? What happened?"

A slight pause occurred as the man wasn't sure what to say. After a few awkward seconds, he replied, "They failed. The Americans recovered the device."

"And Ami?"

"I'm sorry, but your brother is dead."

"You saw his body?" Levi asked.

"No, but Ami and his men entered the facility, and only the Americans came back out. Lots of body bags came out, but not your brother. One of my men working with the Americans said Ami was killed."

Even though he prepared himself for the possibility, the stark reality of his brother being killed struck him like a sucker punch to the gut. "Then I know what to do."

"Do what you must," the man said in a low voice.

"So no one survive?" Levi asked.

"Yes, two men made it out of Babylon alive."

"Who?"

"The man with the thick black beard, an associate of your brother's, I believe ..."

He knew in an instant the man spoke of Benjamin. Cutting him off, he asked, "I know who you speak of. What's his condition?"

"He was critically injured. I heard they were flying him to Baghdad but didn't know if he would survive the chopper ride."

"And the other?" Levi asked.

"It was the man who purchased the device."

"The Saudi?"

"Yes, that's correct," the man said.

"Was he hurt as well?"

"No, he's fine. The Americans have him."

"Where are they? The men who killed my brother." Levi asked.

"I don't know. They boarded a plane and left quickly."

"Destination?"

"Unknown. Nobody is saying much about them. All I know is they're pissed off at the agency."

Ami's brother ignored the statement. "Thanks for confirming."

"I'm sorry for your loss."

"Not as sorry as the United States will be." Levi disconnected the line and threw the used burner phone in the nearest green trash can on the side of Arlington Boulevard. He then lit up another cigarette and took a long drag. He sucked the smoke into his lungs as the sweet aroma aroused his senses. Rage, pure unadulterated rage, boiled in the pit of his soul, and he knew what the outlet would be. As he passed others on the road, his mind repeatedly said, *You have no idea of the inferno I am about to unleash,* to each one as they continued on their way, oblivious to what would soon occur.

62

— · —

AT CRUISING ALTITUDE

GULFSTREAM G450

Troy winced as Harry applied the disinfectant to the open gunshot wound near his biceps. The adrenaline had worn off, and now there was a flash of pain every time he made even a subtle movement with his arm. Harry bandaged the wound with precision care.

"Thanks for fixing me up," Troy said through gritted teeth.

"You still need to be checked out by a doctor when we arrive in D.C. What I did is temporary. I'm not too worried about an infection, but I still want to have it cleaned out by someone who's not 34,000 feet in the air working from a first aid kit."

"I got it, Doc. We have five more hours to Barcelona to refuel, then another seven and a half hours to Andrews. I'll survive until then."

"More than likely," Harry said with a smile.

Troy walked up several aisles and took a seat across from Charlie and the Jackal, who appeared deep in conversation.

"Am I interrupting anything?" Troy rubbed his arm gently.

Charlie smirked. "Just listening to Studley Dudley here tell me about the time he took a bullet for you."

Troy laughed out loud, which caused a twinge of pain. "I seem to recall the event slightly differently."

"You don't say?" Charlie looked over at the Jackal with eyebrows raised.

"Hey, I still have the scar to prove it." The Jackal lifted his shirt, revealing his sculpted six-pack.

"Dude, keep your shirt on," Troy said with his hand outstretched.

"You afraid he'll prove he's right?" Charlie asked.

"Hell no." Troy shook his head. "I've known this filthy, rotten piece of trash for a while and know firsthand he never takes off just his shirt ..."

"That's me," the Jackal replied. "A male gigolo."

Before the conversation could slide further down the gutter, the colonel walked up the aisle and stopped next to Troy.

"How's your wing?"

"I'll be fine. Nothing a few Advil can't fix, sir."

"Good. I need you on a conference call."

"Absolutely. Anyone important?"

"Not really." The colonel said with arched eyebrows. "Unless you would consider POTUS, the SecDef, and the rest of the NSC important people."

"Sounds fun," Troy said in a mocking tone.

"Well, aren't you special." Charlie gave Troy a big grin.

"Don't get his head any bigger than it already is," the colonel stated with a sideways grin as he turned and walked toward the rear of the plane. Halfway down the aisle, he bellowed, "Shake a leg, Cap."

Troy stood. "Right behind you, sir." He looked over at Charlie and the Jackal. "This oughta be fun. Not!"

——◆——

As they got to the back of the plane, Troy looked at the last row of seats where Rahman Salek sat slumped against the fuselage. His hands were bound and flex-cuffed to the armrests. "What about Rahman?" he asked the colonel.

"We'll turn him over when we get to Andrews."

"Is his dad aware we have him?"

Colonel Marshall shrugged. "Not sure, but he'll find out soon enough."

"Hard thing to keep from the House of Saud."

"That's the president's battle to fight, but since every POTUS for the past several decades has been in bed with the Saudis, I'm sure they'll let him go pretty quickly."

"Doesn't that piss you off?" Troy asked.

"Considering fifteen of the nineteen hijackers on 9/11 were Saudi, you bet your ass it does. But again, politics trumps logic in this day and age, Cap. I choose my battles carefully, and frankly, Rahman isn't worth the fight."

"He didn't have to survive, you know."

"Trust me, I considered putting a couple of rounds in his head while we were in Babylon, but then I had a thought."

"And that was?"

"I've got some folks who want to talk with him before we turn him over."

"Pump him for all his intel?" Troy asked.

"Something like that." The colonel shook his head.

"Interesting."

"You didn't hear that, by the way."

"Hear what?" Troy asked with a sly grin.

"Exactly."

———◆○◆———

"Wouldn't most people be thrilled to be on a call with the POTUS and NSC?" Charlie asked after Troy had left.

The Jackal shrugged. "Not Cap, this isn't his first rodeo. He has sort of a love vs. hate relationship with the leadership in Washington, no matter which party is in charge. He spent a lot of time in D.C. as a kid and rubbed shoulders with the who's who many times. The Evans family was close with a senator from their home state in Idaho. Cap knows D.C. like the back of his hand."

"So, you're saying he's seen raw power up close and personal, and now he's jaded?"

"I don't know. Does Dolly Parton have to sleep on her back?"

Charlie laughed out loud and shook her head. "You're such a juvenile."

"Girl, don't you just say the sweetest things." The Jackal winked.

"Uh-huh." Charlie sighed.

Thirty minutes later, the colonel and Troy walked from the back of the airplane with serious expressions plastered across their faces. The colonel went straight to Digger.

"What are they saying from the hospital? Did he wake up yet?"

Digger shook his head. "The last report I got said Benjamin is still in surgery and sedated."

"His odds of making it?" the colonel asked.

"The doctor told our contact at the embassy less than ten percent."

Shaking his head, the colonel replied, "We need that name. He needs to pull through."

"Agreed, sir," Digger replied.

The colonel stood there for a moment, lost in his thoughts before he looked back at Digger. "By the way, you okay, son? Taking two in the chest had to hurt like hell."

Digger pulled up his shirt to reveal two golf ball-sized purple welts above his sternum. "I'll be fine. Guess I got a little souvenir, but it's not permanent like Cap's."

Troy touched his biceps and winced slightly. "They tell me chicks dig scars."

"False!" Charlie yelled from a few aisles behind them. "Chicks dig guys smart enough not to get shot in the first place."

Troy looked back at Digger. "Scratch that, some chicks dig scars."

"The dumb ones," Charlie hollered once more.

Troy smirked. "She fits right in with this motley crew."

"Call the embassy and see if you can get an update from whoever is monitoring the surgical team," the colonel said. "They know to call us as soon as he's conscious, right?"

"Yes, sir, they do, but I'll give them a jingle to get an update."

"Good." The colonel turned to head to the back of the plane. He stopped next to Charlie.

She felt his gaze and wasn't sure what he might say.

"You made the right call in Babylon, Charlie. We protect our own, and don't let anyone give you any shit for doing just that."

"Thank you, sir," Charlie said with a sense of pride displayed on her face.

"Even if it was the Jackal whose ass you saved," he added with a huff before he marched down the aisle.

"He doesn't like you much, does he?" Charlie asked as she gazed at the Jackal.

The Jackal raised his right cheek and shoulder. "We've had a few frank disagreements about my behavior on missions from time to time."

"By a few, numbnuts here means every time we're on a deployment, they get into it over something or other." Troy now stood in the aisle next to Charlie.

"Grumpy needs to chill out," the Jackal said. "So, I like to have a little fun. And yes, it might be at another's expense."

"And by fun, you're referring to the time you accidentally shot Jesús in the right ass cheek during that mission in Kabul?"

"Oh, thanks, you just had to bring that one up, huh?"

"My butt still hurts every time I sit down on the crapper!" Jesús exclaimed from the next aisle.

With his hands stretched out, the Jackal replied, "It was an accidental discharge, I swear, and anyway, Jesús got me back."

"When?" Jesús asked in a surprised tone.

"At that chalet in Anzère," the Jackal replied.

"Where?" Charlie asked.

"Switzerland. That was quite the mission," Troy said.

Jesús frowned. "Dude, I didn't get you back."

"Oh, yeah," the Jackal replied. "I've even got the scar to prove it." He grabbed the top of his pants.

"Whoa, now!" Troy stretched his arms out with his palms facing toward the Jackal. "Keep those drawers on, yo. Mr. Johnson does not have authorization to clear the polyester enclosure."

"I believe you," Charlie said as she gently touched the Jackal's arm.

The back-and-forth banter was broken up as Digger, currently on the sat phone, frantically snapped his raised fingers high in the air. Everyone grew silent as they heard him say, "Thanks for the information, Doc. I'm sorry he didn't make it."

Troy rushed to his side. "Benjamin? He's dead?"

Digger shook his head. "Surgery ended about ten minutes ago. He crashed almost immediately, and they just called it."

"Dammit." Troy's anger swelled as he swore a few more times. "We needed that name. The agency and NSA are no closer to finding that nuke based on the data we retrieved."

"Cap!" Digger exclaimed. "You cut me off, man. I didn't get to finish."

"Finish what?"

"Benjamin's gone, but he woke up briefly before his heart gave out."

"And?"

"He gave the doctors a name before he kicked it."

Troy's angry expression quickly subsided. "And what name was that?"

63

FORT MEADE, MARYLAND

Dave Buzan sat back in his no-frills government-issued office chair and let out a loud yawn. As Director of the National Security Operation Center (NSOC), he and his team had been working around the clock with members of Homeland Security, the FBI, the NNSA, and the CIA on analyzing the data found on Ami Sulzer's hard drive. His dimly lit office contained several discarded pizza boxes, piles of papers on the desk, and even a couch with a pillow and blanket so he could snag a quick nap every several hours. After years in retail management, he thought moving over to the government sector would be a pleasant change of pace. However, little did he know the change would throw him from the firing pan into the proverbial fire.

His office space looked more like a lair where you would find a hibernating creature than an office where someone provided rapid intelligence for the highest level of decision-makers at the NSA. So far, he and his team had uncovered a treasure trove of intelligence, but none of it led them to the location of the nuclear device hidden somewhere within the United States.

With only four or five hours of sleep in the past thirty-six hours, the stress and sleep deprivation showed. As Dave placed his feet on the desk and leaned back, he closed his eyes and dreamed of his own bed, ergonomic pillow, and hours and hours of uninterrupted sleep. The obnoxious ringtone from his landline jostled him back to reality. Putting his feet back on the floor and leaning toward the desk, he answered the call on the fourth ring.

"Director Buzan."

"Dave, it's William Marshall."

Buzan sighed slightly since he knew why the colonel was calling. "I'm sorry, sir, but we still don't have any updates for you. Everyone at the NSA and our sister agency ..."

The colonel cut him off before he could finish. "I'm not looking for an update, Dave."

"Okay. What can I do for you, colonel?"

"I have something for you. A name."

Dave was now fully awake. His heart raced, and his body tensed. "Ami's associate survived the surgery?"

"He woke up long enough to give us what we needed before he passed. The name he provided, we need you to run through it your super-duper computers in Fort Meade."

Dave grabbed a legal pad and a blue pen. "I'm ready."

"Amos Zogg, that's the alias Ami's brother used while in the United States."

Dave wrote the name and underlined it once. "That's a fairly unique name. Can't imagine there are tons of Amos Zogg's in the database."

"I concur."

"We'll get right on it," Director Buzan said.

"Dave, this is Troy Evans."

Cap was on the call as well.

"Yes, Captain," Dave said. He had spoken with Troy several times on the flight from Accra to Babylon.

"Try having your team run that name through the data we got from Ami's laptop. Maybe we'll get lucky, and Ami sent something to his brother that's on an invoice or something. Anything that will help us nail down his precise location."

"We're on it. I'll call you back in thirty minutes with an update."

<hr>

The call ended, and the colonel looked at Troy. "You think this name is legit?"

Troy nodded. "We need a lucky break right now. The analysts aren't finding enough to go on, at least regarding helping us narrow down the location of the device. I have faith we're gonna find this thing, and my gut says the name will be the catalyst to get the snowball rolling."

"Well, your gut hasn't failed us yet."

"And I hope it won't start now," Troy replied.

The colonel nodded. "Me too."

"Can I ask you something, sir?"

"Of course, Cap. What is it?"

"Of all the places to target, why did Ami choose Joint Base Andrews? It makes no sense. I could understand the National Mall, New York City, Philadelphia, or any other major metropolis, but Andrews seems so random."

Colonel Marshall shrugged. "I asked on the last call I was on with the National Security Team. If they know, they aren't telling me. But I agree the location is quite odd."

"Don't ask questions, just save the world. The usual beltway secrecy, huh, sir?"

"Exactly."

⚬

Twenty minutes later, the phone rang.

The colonel answered. Yes?"

"It's Dave."

"Find him in the database?"

"There's no evidence of an Amos Zogg in the federal database. He doesn't exist."

"Dammit." The colonel smacked his fist against the flimsy desktop, causing it to make a splintering sound.

"But," Dave continued. "When we ran the name through the data collected from Ami's laptop, we got hits, lots of them. They are providing us actionable intel. Good call by Captain Evans."

"That's great news. Do we have an address?"

"We do. Ami shipped numerous items to an address in West Falls Church, Virginia. The name Amos Zogg is on the detailed shipping manifest but not the mailing address. That's very close to the Beltway. Property records indicate the home is owned by an LLC out of Antigua. One with ties to Ami."

"We have eyes on the house yet?"

"It's a townhouse, actually, and no, not yet. The bureau has a surveillance team on its way. They should be in place and operational in the next ten minutes."

"Can you get us patched into their feed when it comes online?"

"Will do, sir."

"Good work, Dave."

"The Omega Group gets the lion's share of the credit."

"Nonsense, my guys know they only get to kick down doors and exterminate the bad guys thanks to the tremendous resources provided by so many others in a support role. We succeed together, Mr. Director."

"Kind of you to say," Dave said. "We'll have a real-time data and audio feed set up by the agents on the ground so that every agency involved can be on the same page."

"Looking forward to it. This is the break we needed."

64

West Falls Church

The FBI used the 24/7 satellite coverage over Washington, D.C., to determine what type of vehicles lined the road near the townhouse where the person suspected to be Ami's brother, Levi Sulzer, received shipments. They had no intention of screwing things up, and getting the vehicle right could be critical. Suburbans screamed FED, so it wasn't a smart move to park one near the townhouse for reconnaissance. With an Amazon delivery truck belonging to one of the residences in the neighborhood, the FBI paid the man a visit and immediately took over the inside of the delivery vehicle. The Amazon delivery driver was handsomely compensated for the inconvenience and shifted to another vehicle to deliver his packages.

Several vehicles down from the Amazon delivery vehicle, two FBI agents parked across the street from the townhouse and tried to act casual as they leaned back in the leather seats of the plush silver Audi A8 four-door sedan with heavily tinted windows. The luxurious sedan belonged to one of the bureau's deputy directors, who reluctantly loaned it out for such a critical surveillance mission. The vehicle was an exact match for one owned by a local doctor and normally parked on the road just down from the townhouse.

Rubbing his rough hands against the smooth leather of the vehicle's passenger seat, Special Agent Ryan West stated, "Not too shabby. A little different from my Ford, but I could get used to this."

"Yeah, well, don't. The SES pay scale is slightly higher than your measly GS 11," Special Agent Marcus Carter said from the driver's seat.

"Hey! You're a GS 11." Ryan looked over and frowned at the perceived insult from his partner. "So why are you knocking our pay scale?"

"I'm not the one fawning over a ninety-thousand-dollar plus car I'll never be able to afford," Marcus stated.

Ryan heard the voice in his right ear, instructions from an agent hidden inside the Amazon vehicle. He interrupted his partner. "We got movement down the block. A man is approaching from the south."

"Get the camera ready," Marcus said. "Take the pics, but be discreet."

"On it," Ryan said as he took rapid snapshots of the man who approached with a cigarette dangling from his lips. "It might be him. He fits the MO." He zoomed in with the telescopic lens and took one pic after another.

Marcus pressed the comm button attached to the center buttons of his shirt. "We've got possible eyes on the target."

After a few seconds, a response came. "Copy that. Upload the photos, and sit tight for further instructions," the gravelly voice on the other end said.

The man with thinning gray hair came toward them along the opposite side of the street and paused as he reached the steps leading to the red brick townhouse.

⸺◆O◆⸺

Levi Sulzer stood at the base of the steps. He took one more drag from his Turkish cigarette and dropped it to the sidewalk while his left foot ground what was left to a pulp. He took one more deep breath of fresh air and looked up and down the road. Everything looked normal, nothing out of the ordinary. Ever since he spoke to his brother, he'd been paranoid that somehow the Americans would discover the plan and stop the attack.

The left side of his brain, where his logic originated, believed his concerns were foolish. Yet, the right side, where his creative juices flowed, imagined all sorts of scenarios where the Americans and their behemoth intelligence apparatus might foil the plot. As he stood on the bottom step and his mind raced, he considered indulging in one more smoke, but with so much to do, he thought better of it. After all, he needed to complete the night's tasks and stick to his brother's timetable.

His thoughts turned to his brother. He remembered the time as teenagers when they snuck out of their parents' home and made their way to a nightclub. Ami had fake IDs made for both of them, and they were good enough forgeries to get the two clearly underage brothers inside the club. The bartender provided both boys enough alcohol to get them both wildly blitzed out of their minds. Stumbling back home, they climbed up the lattice on the side of their house and threw up all over their shared room before both boys passed out on the carpet between their two single beds. They woke hours later to the sound of their mother's scolding voice. Besides cleaning up the vomit, their punishment was a month of doing the dishes, laundry, and scrubbing the toilet bowl with toothbrushes. The next month, the boys did it again, careful to throw up in the neighbor's yard before climbing the lattice and foregoing their mother's wrath.

The memory brought a smile to Levi's face as he climbed the stairs. At the top step, he looked skyward and considered his own mortality or lack thereof in light of the events that would occur. Finally, he unlocked the deadbolt, stepped inside, and quickly closed the door behind him.

65

— • —

AT CRUISING ALTITUDE

GULFSTREAM G450

"Your team did great." Pat O'Shea said.

"Thanks, Pat," Troy said. He was grateful to hear his friend's voice. "I'm just glad we retrieved it. One down, one to go."

"What's this fuss about you getting shot?"

"Just a graze, actually. Nothing to get worked up over."

"Even a bullet can't stop Captain Troy Evans, huh?"

"As my dad used to remind me as a kid, you can't hurt steel," Troy said with a slight chuckle. As he flexed his biceps, a twinge of pain shot up his arm and traveled into his shoulder. Apparently, steel could feel something, even if it couldn't be hurt.

"What's your ETA?" Pat asked.

Troy looked down at his MTM Gray Silencer watch, a gift from a powerful family friend when he graduated from Special Forces Qualification Course (SFQC). "Five hours till we touch down at Andrews."

"Did you see the pictures of Levi?"

"Yeah, they sent us several images. We're told facial recognition software pegs it at a ninety-six percent chance it's him."

"The intel is coming in fast and furious now," Pat said. "I'm going to be on the NSC call in thirty minutes. Will you and Colonel Marshall be on it?"

"Yes, we will," Troy replied. "We've heard Operation Rapture is proceeding smoothly."

"From what I know, much of the senior leadership has already left D.C. some are already underground while others are headed that way. Most of the cabinet is settled in at Mount Weather. The VP is in Colorado at NORAD, while the Speaker of the House is secure inside the Raven Rock (Site R) facility not far from Camp David. The hardest part is trying to keep the press out of the loop. If they get wind there's a rogue nuke loose, the city would descend into chaos, and chances are Levi would set it off."

Troy asked, "Where's POTUS?"

"Still in Washington. His family has been moved already, but the president plans to stay in D.C. a little longer."

"Secret Service is letting him stay? That's ballsy considering what we know."

"POTUS is safe. He's in the Deep Underground Command Center (DUCC) Obama built under the north lawn, just accessible via the west wing. If the nuke went off, he'd be fine. Besides, they can get him out of town via the tunnels if necessary."

"Guess you didn't get the invite for the DUCC and will get to die with the rest of us poor schlubs if we fail and the nuke goes off later today."

"No way, buddy. I'm already back at the Y-12 with my wife and kiddos, far away from the blast radius."

"Seriously?" Troy asked in an incredulous tone.

Pat laughed. "No, just yanking your chain. Me? Miss out on another adventure with the famous Troy Evans as he attempts to stop one more nuclear disaster on American soil. Not on your life."

"You mean infamous, and if I fail, it may cost you a life, your own."

"Then I'll die with you, my friend. Can't think of a better way to go."

"I can. You could be in the sack with your hot wife and die with a smile on your old, wrinkly face."

"Well, there's that," Pat said with a hearty laugh. "And Eva is still pretty smoking hot, even after all these years. I'll pass along your compliment of her appearance."

"I'd rather you not." Troy paused. "This is one screwed-up world, Pat. Doesn't it freak you out as a parent? Makes me wonder if I'll ever be able to settle down and bring kids into this chaos."

"We've always had evil with us, Troy, and it's taken on many faces throughout human history. Sure, as a parent, it's disconcerting, but I also see the good in people and truly believe the future of mankind can be bright once more. The shining city on a hill is not an impossibility, even now. But it would be more attainable if you keep that nuke from going off."

"I guess," Troy replied with very little conviction. He was running on fumes, and optimism didn't rate high on his list when exhaustion set in.

"And as for settling down, I not only encourage you to do so, but I know exactly the right person for you."

Troy sighed. "Don't go there, Pat."

"I think it's time you stop running around saving the world and settle down with her. You ain't getting any younger after all."

"That ship sailed. You know that."

"I bumped into her a few months ago while at the Hoover Building for a meeting with the Director."

Troy felt his pulse race as his face flushed. "Really?"

"Sure did. I wasn't gonna tell you with all these crazy missions you've been on lately. But since you're going on about your own mortality and this nuke possibly going off, it might be my last chance."

"How'd she look?" Troy asked before regretting the question.

"Good, really good, my friend. Cate's like a fine wine and is only getting better with age."

Troy was quiet. His mind went back to ten years before, and a flood of memories overwhelmed his senses.

The phone line grew quiet.

"Earth to Troy, did I lose you?" Pat asked.

A few silent moments passed before Troy replied, "No, I'm here. Just lost in my thoughts."

"I know it's not my place to say it, but you two have unfinished business. You know that, right?"

"Yes, I know," Troy said before a twinge of concern made his body shudder. "Do me a favor."

"Anything," Pat replied.

"Make some calls and get her out of D.C. ASAP."

Pat considered the request. "I'll see what I can do, Troy."

"Just make it happen."

"I'll pull a few strings with the director's office."

"Thanks, Pat. I owe you."

"You don't owe me a thing. After all, we are all human, and having concerns about those we care about is a fact of life. But Troy, don't let doubt creep in. We will stop Levi. Keep the faith."

Troy let out a long sigh. "It's never left me."

66

THE WHITE HOUSE

DUCC

POTUS sat with several of his key advisors in the DUCC and listened as the Security Council meeting moved along quickly. Many of his senior leadership attended via conference call in secure locations.

"Mr. President," Pat O'Shea said. "The NNSA has made two dozen passes by the townhouse with Geiger counters over the past hour, and every time, the count rate jumps as we approach the garage and drops back down soon after we move away."

"How sure are we that the nuke is inside the garage?" POTUS asked.

"We can't be one hundred percent sure, sir. But based on the intel we've gathered, the consensus is nearly ninety percent," the SecDef said.

"And we don't want to breach the townhouse and take Levi Sulzer down right now?" POTUS asked.

"There are too many variables, sir," the SecDef answered. "We've run through a litany of scenarios in our simulations and feel our best chance to prevent the device from going off is to take it in transit while they are on the move. Thermal imaging confirms there are two people in the residence. One appears to be near the garage, close to a vehicle. If we move in, there's a chance they can detonate the device before we can stop them."

The president considered the words and countered. "What about eliminating the entire townhouse?"

"You mean with an airstrike, Mr. President?"

"Yes, take out the entire block if need be. Make sure the surrounding residences have been evacuated and blow the entire block to kingdom come."

"Too risky, sir, plus evacuating area homes may alert Levi to our presence. Also, we can't be sure the weapon won't go off in the event of an airstrike, sir. You know about the incident in 1961 in Goldsboro, North Carolina. The only reason that nuke didn't go off was thanks to one low voltage switch. All but one of the safety switches failed in that case, sir."

"But this is a different technology from 1961," the president said.

"Agreed, Mr. President," the SecDef replied. "If you give the order, we will absolutely level the entire city block. But based on the data we have reviewed, I highly suggest we stick with our initial plan."

"Take them down during transport to Andrews?"

"Yes, sir."

"And which team will be responsible for the takedown?"

"The Omega Group, Mr. President. They are inbound from Iraq."

"Colonel Marshall, you're still on the line, right?" the president asked.

"Yes, sir. Myself and Captain Troy Evans are on the call," the colonel said in a firm tone.

"William, are you sure your team is up for this after all the action you've seen over the past forty-eight hours? We can bring in others very easily."

"Yes sir, Mr. President," the colonel said. "My men are rested, and they would be honored to complete the mission they started."

A moment of silence occurred as the president rubbed his thumb and index finger in a circular motion, and his eyes darted around the conference room, which was buried deep under the White House. "Very well, I trust the judgment of everyone on this call. Make it so, recover the nuke." He paused. "And Omegas?"

"Yes, Mr. President?" the colonel asked.

"Don't fail me."

The colonel replied in an authoritarian voice. "We won't, Mr. President."

As the line clicked off, the SecDef leaned over to the Chairman of the Joint Chiefs of Staff (CJCS), who sat to his right and whispered in his ear. "I want an AH-64 Apache in the air following the box van after it leaves. If we get even a sniff of this takedown going south, I want that vehicle blown to hell."

The CJCS nodded. "You got it. And what about if the airstrike detonates the bomb?"

"We might have no choice but to roll the dice."

"Very well, Mr. Secretary. We'll be ready."

67

WEST FALLS CHURCH

Across the street from Levi Sulzer's townhouse stood a three-story sandstone-colored apartment complex. The two-bedroom, eleven-hundred-square-foot apartment on the top floor had two bay windows that provided a perfect vantage point overlooking the townhouse. Twenty federal agents, comprised of various agencies, crammed into the apartment. They set up countless technological gadgets to record every piece of audio and capture photos and videos from Levi's townhouse.

Every word uttered by Levi and the other man was recorded and scrutinized by floors of analysts in various buildings throughout the D.C. metro area. One thing was for sure: they confirmed not only the target but also the delivery method. Conversations uttered inside the house even discussed the route they would take. That invaluable intel made its way to everyone who needed to know, including the members of The Omega Group.

Levi poured himself another espresso and savored the sweetness and aroma of the EL Injerto Guatemalan coffee. A wide grin formed as he took his first sip.

"You've had quite a lot of those, have you not?"

"Hmph!" Levi looked at the short, balding Pakistani man before him with a derisive facial expression. "Why the hell should I deny myself pleasure right now? We'll both be dead in a few hours, anyway."

Tahir Bhutto nodded and looked at the floor. "I guess I see your point," he replied as strands from his thinning, combed-over hair drifted over his plump face.

"Have you talked to your family?" Levi asked.

"No, I'll call them soon."

"I want you to know my brother was a man of his word. The money transfer has already taken place. Your family will never want for anything ever again."

"It makes me happy knowing my sacrifice will provide them with a life I could never offer while we were together in Karachi."

"The passports have been sent as well. They will be free to leave Pakistan and travel anywhere they like very soon."

"My wife always wanted to visit New Zealand. She is fascinated by those Lord of the Rings movies," Tahir replied. Although Levi couldn't see it, a tear formed in the corner of the man's eyes. Knowing he would never again feel the touch of his wife's skin cut him to the core. Tahir confided that he missed the smell of her hair, the softness of her skin, and the flavor of her lips as they tenderly pressed against his own. "I hope she gets to visit all the places I couldn't take her in this life."

Levi noticed Tahir's emotions. "She will get to do that and more, Tahir. All thanks to the sacrifice you're about to make."

"I know." Tahir lowered his voice as he blinked rapidly to keep the tears from escaping.

Levi steered the conversation back to the bomb. "Let's go downstairs to the van. Show me once more how the mechanism works. I want it to be second nature to me as we approach the main gate."

"I understand," Tahir said.

"Also, show me the switch on the center console. Is it simple to operate?"

"Designed it myself. There's not much to it. You simply depress the button on the switch, and the nuke detonates. Can't get more straightforward than that." The nuclear physicist thought of his wife and children as he stood and headed for the back stairs.

Levi took a long sip, finished the rest of the espresso, placed the white ceramic glass on the bar, and then followed Tahir toward the stairs. Before he made it down the first step, his taste buds told him it was time for another one of his Turkish cigarettes. For whatever reason, coffee and cigarettes always seemed to go well together.

As they made their way down the stairs, Levi said, "So, the blast radius. You're sure it will cover the area we discussed?"

"Without a doubt. This bomb is quite large. The fallout will be tremendous. Loss of life will be on a scale the United States cannot even fathom."

"Go big or go home," Levi muttered to himself. A phrase his brother Ami often said when they were kids.

"What?" Tahir asked.

He repeated himself. "Go big ..." but stopped mid-phrase. "Never mind, just a stupid American phrase I must have picked up."

As they reached the last step, Tahir turned to Levi. "Are you afraid to die?"

Levi did not want to make light of the question but merely shrugged in his response at first. "Not really. After all, everybody dies eventually."

"But you are young and still have much life inside you."

"I've lived more lifetimes than most Tahir and am at peace with my decision to see my brother's wishes carried out. I'm ready to rest."

"And the afterlife?" Tahir probed.

"There is no afterlife," Levi barked as a fit of anger burst from him, and his skin visibly turned a shade of red. "All we are is flesh and blood. When we die, there's nothing but a dark void."

⁕

Tahir didn't utter another word, but his soul wrestled with the statement. Not necessarily a religious man, he wasn't an atheist either. Once the call came the day before, a palpable uneasiness stirred deep inside. He felt torn like a piece of frayed cloth. His scientific-oriented mind questioned the possibility of an afterlife while another part of him struggled with the concept that after death came nothing but a "dark void," as Levi said. Something within him wrestled with the actions he set in motion, and his thoughts focused on his wife and family. He missed them so much, and it caused his heart to ache, knowing he would never have the chance to be with them again.

68

— · —

On Final Approach

Gulfstream G450

The Gulfstream cut through the clouds and peeked out from the billowy, white void. The greenery of the landscape revealed itself in a magnificent array of colors and shapes.

Troy needed rest as his muscles and joints cried out for relief. If the opportunity presented itself, he could sleep for a week straight. Standing up in the center aisle of the plane, he raised his voice and, with an authoritarian tone, spoke to the team. "Okay, Omegas. Let's go over this one more time."

Before he could get out another word, the colonel walked out of the back room and made his way down the aisle with heavy footfalls. "Keep talking, Cap. Don't let me interfere with what you have to say." The colonel took a seat a few rows back next to Harry.

"Everything still on schedule, sir?" Troy gave his commanding officer a quizzical look.

"Correct, no changes in intel. We proceed as planned."

"Very good," Troy said. "The 11th wing has a hangar all ready for our arrival, and we'll meet up with the other members of our strike team at that time." He spoke for a few minutes and covered a few changes that came up during the final call he had with the colonel and the security council. "Any questions?" he asked.

"What's the significance of 3:33?" Sarge asked in his deep baritone voice.

Troy shook his head. "They don't know yet why Ami wanted the nuke to go off at that time, but we're lucky the FBI caught that audio soundbite from the feed. Knowing the specific timeframe is invaluable."

"And the president isn't evacuating D.C. why?" Digger asked.

Colonel Marshall answered. "The Secret Service wanted to move the president to a bunker in the mid-west, but he insisted on staying put, at least for the time being. Knowing the president that could change at any moment though. The DUCC is impregnable and can survive a nuclear blast and the subsequent fallout. I even asked POTUS myself, and he believes in us and the larger team that's been assembled. He has enough faith in our abilities to stay put. That's high praise coming from our Commander-In-Chief." He took a deep breath. "I know we won't let him down cause if we do, it's the last thing any of us will do on this planet."

"No pressure or anything, boss," the Jackal said in his typical sarcastic tone.

"You guys better not be the death of me," Charlie added.

There were a few more questions about operational authority before Captain Messick voice came over the PA and interrupted the lively conversation. The captain said they were on final approach and instructed Troy to take a seat.

—◆◇◆—

Five minutes later, the team arrived at Joint Base Andrews, made their way across the tarmac and inside the cavernous hangar. Troy was the last one to leave and stopped in the cockpit before descending the stairs.

"Thanks for the ride, Mickey."

"You got it, Cap. My pleasure as always."

"Can I have one last request?" Troy asked.

"Of course, anything."

"Take this jet and get the hell out of D.C. airspace as quick as possible."

Mickey looked at Troy with his eyebrows raised. "And why would I do that?"

"In case we fail. You know what happens if we don't succeed."

"No can do, Cap. I know what you and the Omegas are capable of. You guys and gal won't fail!" Mickey said before he added. "You can't. There's too much at stake."

"That's the plan, Mickey, but we both know this mission is no slam dunk."

"I appreciate the concern, but I'll be right here at Andrews waiting for you guys to get back so I can fly the whole team to Joint Base Lewis-McChord."

"Look, my friend, you've got a wife and two kids just down the road. Pick them up. Bring um' somewhere safe, just in case. Humor me, at least."

Mickey shook his head. "No can do, Cap. We're all in this together. Besides, I sent the wife and kids down south yesterday to be with her family in Greenville, South Carolina. They'll be safe. I'm relying on you to do the same for me."

"You're stubborn," Troy retorted as a warm smile spread across his face. "But I do appreciate the vote of confidence."

"That bottle of Woodford Reserve is waiting for us when you get back."

"Sounds like a deal."

"Godspeed, Cap."

Troy patted his friend's shoulder, nodded, then turned and proceeded down the stairs to join the others in the hangar. As he reached the base of the steps, his eyes glanced to his right, and he saw the distinct blue and white paint job of the plane with the tail number 28000, better known as Air Force One when the president was aboard. The 747-200B was parked inside the adjacent hangar to where he walked. With his gaze squarely on the massive jetliner, a pushback tug began to pull the plane slowly from the hangar to the tarmac as a frenzy of activity and agents scurried about in every direction. The flurry of movements reminded him of countless ants running around their hill, completing tasks. *Clearly, POTUS will be on the move soon*, Troy thought. *Maybe he decided to bug out and leave D.C. after all.*

The scene around the plane appeared chaotic, but Troy knew better. Anytime the president moved, the motions by those around him were well-choreographed actions with one stated goal behind every move: Protect the Office of the President at all costs.

69

— · —

WEST FALLS CHURCH

A feeling of unease encircled Levi's thoughts, although he couldn't place why he felt that way. A lump formed in his throat, and he found it hard to swallow even after he took several large gulps of spring water from the liter-sized bottle he held. Maybe it was his looming death. Regrets for what he was about to give up. He pushed aside those lingering doubts. The townhouse, which had felt like a sanctuary for so long, now felt restrictive. Knowing they still had at least forty-five minutes before they needed to leave for Joint Base Andrews, his skin felt like it was crawling with bugs. An intense desire to leave and get on the road washed over him like a cold, stinging wave.

Levi yelled down to Tahir, who worked diligently in the van a floor below inside the garage, making final preparations. "Tahir! It's time to go."

Tahir looked at his watch and shook his head. *Something isn't right*, he thought before he verbalized those concerns. "But we still have time. It's too early to leave." His voice echoed along the narrow stairway.

"Change of plans, we leave now," Levi commanded. "Is everything ready?"

"Yes, I guess so. Although I'd like to check things one last time." Tahir's pulse throbbed. He climbed out of the vehicle's passenger seat and faced Levi, who bounded down the stairs with a concerned look. "What is it? Why are we leaving early?"

Levi shook his head. "I don't know. Something just came over me. Don't ask me to explain it. I just know we need to leave. You've got less than ten minutes to do whatever you need to do."

Tahir tapped his watch. "We'll arrive much sooner than 3:33 if we go now."

"That doesn't matter right now. The only thing that concerns me is completing our task. My brother is dead, and we will both be soon enough as well. The time at this stage is less important than success. Ami is gone. He'd have no way of knowing if the nuke went off before the time he instructed."

Swallowing hard, Tahir nodded. "As you wish. I'll double-check the connections and arm the device, and then we can be on our way in ten minutes or less."

Levi headed back up the stairs and disappeared inside the townhouse.

Tahir climbed into the back of the van and checked everything one more time. It would take him about seven minutes to verify all the wires were in place and connected to the devices appropriately. Large beads of sweat formed on his forehead and rolled down his face as he completed each task. Several yellow Post-it Notes on the floorboard near the weapon provided a final checklist to ensure nothing was missed. He used the side of his arm to wipe the moisture from his face, ensuring nothing dripped on any part of the nuclear weapon or the other components.

In those final moments, his thoughts turned to his family. The money would provide the life they could never have, but in every way, it seemed hollow since he could not enjoy the moments of life with them after the bomb detonated.

He pushed himself to stay on task, but the dread of his impending demise gnawed at him from within.

What I do is for them! He reminded himself over and over as the bile tried to climb up his throat and reach his mouth. Tahir took a deep breath and slowly exhaled. *What I do is for them!*

70

JOINT BASE ANDREWS

Pain shot through Troy's arm like an errant hammer striking a thumb instead of a nail head. He visibly grimaced, and his arm involuntarily pulled close to his torso as a self-defense mechanism that turned out to be woefully too late. "Ahhh," he said out loud as the pain radiated down to his fingertips and up to the ball of his shoulder.

"Oh damn!" Pat exclaimed as he eased his firm grip on Troy's thick biceps. "Is that where you got shot?"

Troy turned to see the sheepish expression plastered all over Pat's face. "Uh, yeah."

"I'm so sorry about that, Troy." Pat's tone was drenched in sincerity.

Troy's pained expression faded. "It's okay, Pat. And thanks for reminding me that the two Advil must've worn off."

"Wait? You got shot in the arm and all's they gave you was a couple ibuprofen?"

Troy's face wore a, *What do you think?* expression as he simply looked back and nodded. "Good to see you too, Pat, even if you are an inconsiderate dick occasionally." He followed the words with a slight chuckle.

"Seriously, my bad. And if I had known it was your bum arm, I would have gripped it with both hands."

"Sure you would've." Troy raised his still throbbing arm around Pat's shoulder and pulled him in closer as they walked toward the rear of the hangar, where a large group of people gathered. The longtime friends exchanged a few more words before they arrived at the mass of men and women from an assortment of agencies. Troy affectionately said, "The alphabet soup is gathered to chime in," as he and Pat approached.

A surprised expression formed on Troy's face as he saw the SecDef step out from the group and approach him and Pat.

"Good to see you again, Captain," the SecDef said.

"Sir." Troy gave the SecDef a salute. "I figured you'd be gone by now. In some secured location."

The SecDef nodded. "My ride is close by." He gestured behind Troy toward the hangar doors. "There's someone who wants to have a word with your team before we leave."

Troy turned to see the beast, as the presidential limo is affectionately referred to, come to a stop just outside. Once the Secret Service confirmed the area was clear, they opened the heavy, eight-inch-thick armor-plated doors and outstepped the President of the United States. He walked with an air of authority and confidence toward the group of people near the rear of the hangar.

"Where's The Omega Group?" he asked in a slow, methodical tone as he got closer.

Colonel Marshall and the team stepped out from the others and joined Troy. Pat moved a few steps back.

The president went straight to Troy. "Captain Evans, it's a pleasure to finally meet."

"An honor, Mr. President," Troy said.

"This nation owes you and your team a debt I fear we will never repay."

"Just doing our job, sir."

"Well, we have one more task for you and your team to complete today."

"The Omegas won't fail the American people, sir."

The president smiled and turned his attention to the colonel. "William, good to see you again."

"Likewise, Mr. President."

One by one, the president made his way down the line, shook hands, and thanked each member of the team. As he reached Charlie, his smile widened, and his contact elongated. A minute later, he turned away. "I must be going. I don't want to keep my pilot waiting."

SecDef Wastradowski followed close behind the president, and within a few minutes, both men climbed the air stairs and disappeared deep inside Air Force One.

The entire incident felt surreal to Troy as he watched the swirl of people make final preparations to get the president out of Joint Base Andrews and into the perceived safety of the skies above. While The Omega Group and the others in the hangar watched, the well-oiled machine worked at a frantic pace to usher the president away from the harm of the nuclear device.

Troy cocked his head towards the colonel. "Guess he decided to get out of dodge after all."

"Yeah, his faith in us might not be that rock solid." Colonel Marshall said.

"He's smarter than I thought," the Jackal added.

The comment got more than a few frowns amongst the team.

A couple of minutes later, the plane taxied away from the hangar, and The Omega Group joined the others in the hangar as they formed an oblong circle shape. Pat moved toward the center of the group and relayed instructions one after another. The SecDef tasked him to lead the strike in his absence. Close to sixty people listened intently as Pat spoke. Represented were personnel from the FBI, Homeland Security, CIA, NSA, NNSA, and other obscure departments.

Members of Seal Team Six stood just to the right of Troy. Lieutenant Commander Frank Fitzgerald led the red squadron and had worked closely with Troy over the years during joint operations. When Troy was asked to pick a team to back them up, he didn't hesitate. Frank and his team were the best in the business, and Troy trusted them implicitly.

Pat quickly reviewed the plan, which had many details. As he wrapped up the specifics, he let everyone know they needed to be out of Joint Base Andrews and in their designated places along the Beltway within thirty minutes.

Then Pat's phone rang, and the bottom fell out of the well-choreographed plan.

71

WEST FALLS CHURCH

FBI Special Agent Susan Swedberg bit her lower lip as she glanced at her watch. "I think they are getting ready to move," she said over the secure comms.

George Alexander was several pay grades above her and scoffed at the statement. "It's too early, Susan. You must have misheard what they said."

"Negative, George. I'm telling you they are leaving now. Something must have spooked Levi. He just said they needed to go."

"Standby," George replied in a skeptical tone. "We need confirmation."

Several minutes passed as tensions rose across several agencies. The resources were not prepared for Levi's early departure.

The sound of an engine turning over came from the garage, and a moment later, the heavy wooden garage door made its ascent upward as it rolled along the metal track toward the ceiling in one smooth motion.

"Damn, they are early," George said once he received confirmation from a spotter.

"Told yeah," Susan replied. "I know what I heard."

"Get the team at Joint Base Andrews on the line," George hollered. "They need to move now, or they'll never make it in time."

Organized panic set in when the box van's hood slowly emerged from the garage as rays of magnificent sunlight came down and shone upon the white hood.

Fear sprang to life within Pat's eyes as he heard from the team conducting over-watch at the townhouse.

"Listen up!" Pat yelled at the throng of people around him. "Levi's early. The vehicle is leaving the townhouse right now."

"Dammit," Troy said.

"We'll never get to the South Van Dorn Street interchange in time," Digger replied.

"Is everybody else in place?" Troy asked as he stared intently at Pat.

Pat shook his head. "Not yet. The sharpshooters and tactical (TAC) team just left the command center. Nobody's ready since Levi jumped the gun."

The Jackal looked at Charlie sitting in a folding chair across from him. "Told them to hit the townhouse."

Charlie shrugged.

"Everybody, get in the vehicles, now!" Troy commanded. "We'll have to improvise on the fly and take them in transit farther down the Beltway than we planned."

Like a school of fish, when someone sticks their hand in a shallow pond, everyone scattered all at once and made their way to their vehicles.

Pat grabbed Troy's arm as he moved away, careful not to reach for the injured biceps a second time. "You need to know something."

"I don't have time to talk. What is it?" Troy asked. Time was working against him.

"Cap, you better take them down before the van reaches the Potomac."

Troy saw the look on his friend's face. "Drone or chopper?"

Pat frowned. "Not sure, maybe both. All I know is there's a standing order to not let that vehicle cross the river. Teams already have tacit approval to use whatever force is necessary to stop the vehicle before it reaches the bridge."

Troy shook his head. "Copy that. Will a direct hit from a hellfire set off the device?"

Pat shrugged. "Nobody knows for sure, and let's ensure we don't need to find out."

"Hooah!" Troy exclaimed.

"Good luck," Pat said.

"You're not coming with us?"

Pat shook his head. "No, I've been told to stay here and coordinate the movements of the team."

"Understood." Troy smacked the top of Pat's shoulder as he sprinted for his vehicle.

Pat watched as the convoy of vehicles squealed their tires and barreled out of the hangar seconds later. He made the sign of the cross as the last vehicle disappeared. "God be with you, Omegas." He turned back to the group assembled inside the hangar. "Okay, team, let's give them every assistance we can muster so they complete their mission. I don't think I need to remind any of you if the Omegas fail. We're all toast. Literally!"

72

IN TRANSIT

The white box van merged into traffic as it pulled onto Arlington Boulevard. The other drivers on the road going about their business were completely oblivious to what was transported in the back of the van. Kids were late to ball practice, mothers were making a grocery store runs for dinner, and fathers were getting gas to mow the lawn before the rain meteorologists predicted would arrive the next day. Each person going about their daily routines, unaware that those simple tasks might end forever with the push of a button you could buy on Amazon.

Levi gripped the wheel in a steely manner. His knuckles turned a shade of white as he virtually strangled the steering wheel while he drove. Tahir anxiously sat in the passenger seat as he pulled his shirt back and forth at the collar. The air conditioner pushed cold air into the cab, yet beads of sweat continued to pour down Tahir's face in a constant stream.

"Take deep breaths. Breathe in and breathe out. Do this slowly." Levi instructed Tahir in a firm tone as he looked over at the heavyset Pakistani man. "It will all be over very soon. For both of us."

"I know, and we won't feel a thing," Tahir muttered.

"That's right. Death will be instantaneous."

"While I know this. I still fear the end."

Levi acknowledged the sentiment. "Fear of the unknown is normal. And being apprehensive right before it all ends is to be expected. But don't let the fear pulsating through your veins paralyze your judgment or inhibit your actions. Every man will die, Tahir. But few men give their lives for a greater cause. Our path is just. What you do will richly reward your family. Think of them and how your actions will transform their lives."

"I know, but I won't be ..." Tahir's voice trailed off.

Based on Tahir's words and bodily movements, Levi knew he needed to distract the man, or his growing fear could compromise the mission. "The device is armed? You double-checked everything?"

Tahir looked at Levi. "Yes, of course."

"And the biometric switch?"

Tahir touched his chest with a gentle tap at the breastbone. A wire stuck out from his shirt sleeve and led to the floor. There, it coiled up like a viper before it led toward the back of the vehicle and out of sight. "It's all plugged in."

"Don't have a heart attack before we arrive." Levi looked over at Tahir and smiled to reassure him.

"I'll try not to." Tahir's heart thumped so very hard with every frantic beat.

Levi nodded and glanced at the side mirrors. Nothing appeared out of the ordinary. Truth be told, he was quite surprised. He fully expected the Americans to make a play for the weapon as soon as he learned of Ami's passing. Even though he didn't have any concrete proof to indicate they knew the full plan, he assumed in the deep recesses of his mind they had found out. Somehow, they had to know.

It's also why he wanted to use a biometric trigger as a failsafe. If the Americans tried to take them out in transit, the weapon would detonate. He also decided it best to have the switch attached to Tahir's pulse and not his own. Levi figured if they did take the vehicle in transit, they would likely expect it would be him who would have some sort of kill switch, but not Tahir. Again, as best he could, Levi tried to plan for every contingency. No matter what, the bomb would detonate at or before arriving at Joint Base Andrews. Of this, he had no doubt.

As he pulled onto Arlington Boulevard, then a minute later onto the 495 Outer Beltway, a calm enveloped him. He constantly looked back and forth to the side mirrors to look for a tail, but he saw nothing.

Surely, they would have taken us out by now if they knew we had the device. He accelerated while quickly merging with traffic heading east. Traffic was fairly light at that time of day.

Only thirty-four minutes.

He kept his speed pegged right at the posted limit, as he didn't want to draw the attention of the police and be forced to detonate the weapon early.

Be proud, brother. He touched the necklace that hung around his neck.

The gold chain had been a present from his brother, Ami, on his twenty-first birthday.

They're about to pay for what they did to you, brother. And, of course, what they did to Father all those years back.

73

Joint Base Andrews

The activity level inside the Strategic Information and Operations Center (SIOC) at the FBI headquarters in Washington, D.C. could best be described as organized mayhem. Real-time images, video feeds, and all communications from the various agency members involved were routed through the large room filled with wall-to-wall digital displays. The staff members who were on site 24/7 acted as a central clearinghouse for all intel and routed pertinent info straight to the agents in the field.

Pat acted as the central link between the SIOC and the boots on the ground and wore two earpieces. One was a direct feed from SIOC, while the other relayed the comms from his teams converging on the Beltway. His brain was pulled in two directions as voices came at him from both ears and converged in the center. He did his best to piece together actionable intel versus just plain chatter. One of his biggest struggles was activating the correct mic whenever he needed to speak to those in the SIOC or the field.

His iPhone ringing on his hip added a new layer of chaos. He knew the number and whipped the SIOC earpiece out of his left ear while answering the call.

"Kinda busy at the moment, Dave. What is it?"

"Just found something on Ami's server." The analyst had been pouring over invoices, and shipping manifests with others for almost forty-eight hours straight.

"I'm listening, Dave. Talk faster."

"An item was shipped to Levi's townhouse that piqued our interest."

"What type of item?"

"Easiest way to describe it would be a biometric dead man's switch."

Pat's face contorted into a look of confusion. "A what?"

"Listen clearly," Dave said. "What I'm about to tell you may make the difference between the nuke going off or not."

Pat immediately pulled the second earpiece from his other ear. "You've got my undivided attention."

***

Troy would have rather been in a Charger SRT or something that didn't scream the word *FEDS* as they barreled down the Interstate 495 Beltway at an obscene rate of speed in the black Suburban. "Try not to kill us," he barked at the Jackal from the second row of seats.

"You mean before the nuke vaporizes us?" The sarcastic reply rolled off the Jackal's tongue as he drove the Suburban like an avatar from the video game *Grand Theft Auto*.

"Touché," Troy replied.

A constant chatter came over the comms by the various teams converging on the new intercept location. The interchange at Telegraph Road was where they now planned to acquire the device. Sharpshooters would be in place in time, but the only question remaining was whether The Omega Group would make it there. If they couldn't, the TAC team would have to step in and take their place. Troy didn't like that one bit. No disrespect to the TAC team, but this was their mission, and he wanted his team to see it to the very end.

"On second thought," Troy said. "Drop the pedal through the damn floor."

"Now you're talking," the Jackal replied as he mashed the pedal flush against the Suburban's floorboard.

Sarge sat in the front passenger seat while Charlie sat next to Troy. Behind them, Jesús, who appeared lost in his thoughts, had the third row all to himself.

Charlie saw the concerned look on Troy's face and nudged him with her elbow. "We'll get there in time, Cap, and stop this thing."

He smiled back, but it was clearly a nervous smile. "No doubt," he uttered in response.

A second, identical vehicle followed directly behind, with Digger, Harry, and the colonel, who had his cell phone glued to his head as he made one call after another as the vehicle weaved in and out of traffic along the Beltway, heading westbound.

The airspace around the Beltway was cleared of all air traffic while three helicopters and four drones monitored the van's progress. The aerial reconnaissance assets beamed high-quality images of the cab back to the various teams for constant analysis. Two AH-64 Apache attack helicopters hovered close by, with explicit instructions not to allow the white box van to reach the Woodrow Wilson Memorial Bridge.

"They just crossed the 395 interchange," a deep voice on the comms proclaimed.

"Copy that," Troy said.

Another voice said, "You're two and a half miles from the crossover, just past the South Van Dorn Street exit."

"Understood," Troy replied.

The next thirty seconds remained quiet until Pat's voice broke the silence. "Troy?"

"Yeah, Pat," he answered.

"We've got a problem."

"What kind of problem?" Troy asked.

"We just confirmed they have a second dead man switch."

"You mean Levi and the other guy each have one?"

"It's more complicated than that. We know they have one switch in the cab. The drones recorded an image clear enough to show it was attached to the center console. Close enough for either man to reach."

"Right," Troy said. "We know about that one. We need to kill them before they can click it."

"But there's a second switch, and it's biometric."

"What's that even mean?"

"It means the switch is physically attached to one of them and continually monitors their vital signs. If whoever is wearing it dies, the device will go off."

"Damn," Troy replied. "Which one of them is it attached to?"

"We don't know yet. We are repositioning the drones to give us a better angle into the cab, but we are running out of time."

"Well, there goes the plan of slowing them down and giving the both of them a rat-tat-tat-tat," Jesús said from the back seat.

"Yeah, this just got a hell of a lot more complicated," Charlie added.

"Tell the Apache pilots to stand down," Colonel Marshall commanded. "There will be no failsafe of blowing up the van before it reaches the bridge with a biometric kill switch in place."

"Copy that," Pat replied. "Relaying instructions now."

Another voice interrupted everyone. "They're just passing you guys headed eastbound."

Troy stared intently as he watched the white box van approach and then whiz by in the opposite lanes. "Saw them," he acknowledged. He then noticed the crossover one hundred and fifty yards ahead. "There's our turn." He pointed at the off-ramp.

"Roger that, Cap, I see it," the Jackal replied.

"How many surveillance vehicles do we currently have?" Troy asked whoever would answer.

"There's three of us in front of them and four tailing them." One of the agents answered from fifty feet in front of the van. "There are four lanes. They just moved from the far-right lane to the second lane from the right a few miles back."

"Roger that. We are taking the crossover now," Troy said as the sound of tires squealing drowned out most other noises. "Clear the right lane. We're headed toward them, and coming in hot."

One of the agents tailing the van replied, "We're on it."

"Pat," Troy pleaded. "We really need to know which one has the biometric device."

"I know, Cap. They're working on the images as fast as they can."

"We can try non-lethal shots to both of them, but I can't guarantee it will stop either one from hitting that center switch."

"Understood. Wait for my word before you take them down."

"Only a few miles from the Potomac," Troy said.

"We know," Pat replied, his voice strained.

74

THE CAPITAL BELTWAY

I-495

"I need an answer, now!" Pat demanded as the frustration in his voice proved impossible to mask. Nobody had ever faced the pressures of a rogue nuke on US soil only a handful of minutes from detonation. People with lesser resolve may have cracked under the strain.

Back at the SIOC, a dozen people stood in front of several large monitors on the wall. The assembled staff pointed and offered conjecture about what they saw from the various images plastered over the screens. Normally, the analysts had ample time to extrapolate data, but now they were expected to offer their opinions in mere seconds. If they were wrong, the consequences could prove cataclysmic.

"Understood. We just got fresh images from the drones, and we're analyzing the data now," a voice from the SIOC replied to Pat.

Pat let out a rush of air. "No time left to analyze the real-time images. We must know right now whether it's the driver or passenger that's hooked up to the biometric device."

"We know, and the team is going over every detail possible from the footage we have. Give us sixty seconds, Pat."

"You've got thirty seconds before The Omega Group intercepts," Pat said. "We're about out of time."

Pat heard the chatter from his right earpiece. The Omegas were almost even with the van.

It would be close, maybe too close.

"I need an answer now," Pat urged one last time.

A few seconds of silence greeted the request. "I think we got it. There's a wire coiled on the floorboard between the two men. But we can just make out which person the wire leads to."

"Driver or passenger?" Pat asked.

◄O►

The Telegraph Road interchange was less than a quarter mile away. They were just about out of time. Even though the Apaches would not fire if the white van reached the bridge, at this point, his concern was squarely on the fact that either Levi or Tahir could detonate the weapon at any moment, even though Joint Base Andrews was still several miles away. There was zero guarantee Levi would wait until the base, regardless of what the intel said.

Troy yelled into his comm unit. "Which one, Pat? Time's up. We're stopping that van."

"Hold on, Troy, they're confirming who has it now. Ten seconds is all we need. Slow them down somehow but do not intercept yet. The answer is coming."

"You heard em' fellas," Troy said to not only the Omegas but, more importantly, the surveillance vehicle teams. "One of the recon vehicles needs to grind the Beltway to a halt, but don't make it obvious what you are doing."

An FBI agent who drove a silver Toyota 4Runner directly in front of the white van replied. "Copy that. We'll stop traffic." The agent motioned to the vehicle next to him, also driven by an agent, cut the wheel hard to the left, and made solid contact with the red Nissan Altima in the next lane.

The sound of crunching metal and the screech of locking brakes as the 4Runner with oversized tires crashed into the Altima altered the flow of traffic immediately.

All the vehicles behind the 4Runner and Altima hit their brakes as they witnessed the accident unfold only a few feet in front of them. In an instant, the Beltway was awash in a sea of red taillights and turned from a steadily moving road to a parking lot.

The Jackal had the black Suburban matching speed with the white box van as he shadowed them to the right. He glanced over and saw Levi and the fat Pakistani, who appeared to have beads of sweat rolling down his face, soaking his shirt. His eyes darted back and forth between the white box van and the vehicles in front of them as they suddenly crashed into each other. With traffic grinding to a halt, the Jackal rapidly applied pressure to the brakes as he made sure he kept pace with Levi, who also decelerated.

"We have confirmation of who has the biometric device," the voice said through the comms as the Suburban said.

"Commencing takedown," Troy said. "Tell us who not to shoot in the face."

75

THE CAPITAL BELTWAY

I-495

The drive to Prince George's County had been uneventful for Levi, and the uneasiness he felt at the townhouse slowly dissipated as they made their way east along the 495 Beltway. An inner peace overcame him as the miles clicked off. The fact that it would be the last few miles he would be alive seemed to not faze him. He kept the vehicle at or below the posted speed limit and stuck to one lane while rarely deviating from it. Nothing looked out of the ordinary as his eyes constantly scanned the road.

He visualized where he would press the button and detonate the nuke. Since he had no clearance or badge that would allow him access to the actual base, he could not get onto it. So, the main gate under the *Joint Base Andrews* sign next to one of the security checkpoints that looked like toll booths would have to work.

His right hand touched the gold necklace hanging from his T-shirt. He felt certain Ami, wherever his spirit might be, would be proud of what he was about to do.

Levi glanced to his right, and his gaze focused on the last living person he would see in this life. Tahir acted like a nervous wreck the entire drive. Levi kept assuring him they were almost at the base. More than once, he thought, *This fool is going to have a stroke or heart attack before we even reach the Potomac.* His assurances seemed of little or no help to the Pakistani, who clearly looked like he was having second thoughts.

Too bad. Your fate is sealed. As is mine.

Levi's eyes stared ahead as the traffic slowly built up around them.

Then he saw it. His brain recognized the errant swerve before his hands could react. *Fool*, he thought as he watched the silver 4Runner slam into the red Altima directly in front of them.

What's he doing? His mind screamed. Over the years, he witnessed many accidents, but the timing of this one couldn't be worse.

Instinctively, he yanked his foot from the accelerator and pushed hard on the brake. The van shimmied and shuddered as it quickly went from sixty-five miles per hour to almost nothing in several seconds. Behind them, similar screeches told him others were trying their best to come to a sudden stop without crashing into the vehicles ahead of them.

The black Suburban next to them came into his peripheral vision as he heard them lock up their brakes as they attempted to slow down as well.

As both vehicles stopped side-by-side, the Suburban's front and rear doors opened, and the movement startled him. Confused by the accident, his mind grappled with the commotion that ensued just to the right.

76

THE CAPITAL BELTWAY

I-495

Troy lunged out the rear driver's side door the second Pat's voice reverberated through his earpiece for everyone to hear. "Take out Levi. The biometric device is attached to the Pakistani Tahir. Repeat: do not kill Tahir."

With his weapon raised, Troy saw Levi's eyes register the threat and reach for the center console. The three-round burst spat out of Troy's weapon at the speed of sound and shattered the passenger side window. The explosion of the window sprayed the inside of the cab with shards of glass. All three rounds found their mark, and Levi's head exploded like a melon, sending pieces of his skull and brains all over the white wall of the van's cab.

For Troy, the events seemed to happen in slow motion. He had run through the takedown dozens of ways as they converged on Levi's location, and Troy visualized each shot he might need to take.

Tahir's hand left his lap and moved out away from his body. Thinking he may be reaching for the switch on the center console, Troy fired a burst into the man's wrist, which shattered like a clay pigeon. Behind them, from the overpass, a long-range rifle shot cracked as a bullet punctured the man's left shoulder, and blood sprayed out in a fine mist.

"Cease fire," Troy commanded as he saw the Pakistani grimace in pain. "Cease fire," he repeated once more.

He had the passenger's side door opened a fraction of a second later and grabbed the badly mangled left hand, which was hanging by just strands of loose skin. He pulled what remained toward the man's lap while at the same time grabbing his right hand. "Flex cuff him," he screamed to Charlie, who stood just to his left. "And put a tourniquet on his left arm above the wrist."

Blood flowed freely from both wounds from Troy and the sniper. Charlie used the zip-tie-like flex cuffs and looped them into the assist handle above the passenger side door. This elevated Tahir's hands above his head, preventing him from reaching the switch mounted on the center console.

"Harry, get a tourniquet on the left arm stat and keep this piece of shit alive until the NNSA team arrives to defuse the bomb."

"On it," Harry said. He was only a step behind Charlie as she administered the flex cuffs.

"Status?" Pat asked as his voice echoed from the comms.

Troy quickly looked around the cab as a myriad of agents swarmed the vehicle from every side. "Tahir is alive, and we'll keep him that way. Levi is dead."

"And the device?" Pat asked.

"Making our way to the back of the van now." There was a pause as Troy and the others ran to the rear of the vehicle and flung open the doors. There, in all its glory, lay a perfectly intact nuclear device.

Troy had now seen three in his lifetime. Three too many if you asked him.

The device was a sister device to the one Troy and the team had recovered less than twenty-four hours before in Babylon. "We have it." Troy let out an audible sigh. The weapon appears undamaged, and I can confirm it's armed. Get your team here to disable it right now."

"Chopper is sixty seconds out. Our response team is on board. They'll have it disabled within minutes."

77

JOINT BASE ANDREWS

As with the first device, Troy and Digger removed the item from the second nuke after it was disarmed but before the recovery team took possession of the weapon.

The next ninety minutes passed like a blur for the entire team.

Troy found himself finally alone with only his thoughts as he was back at Joint Base Andrews, sitting on a metal folding chair in the rear of the dimly lit hangar. With his head firmly in his hands, he leaned forward and took deep breaths. The adrenaline high of the past few hours wore off, and he had a few minutes of relative silence to think about what had occurred. His wounded arm ached as the pain meds and adrenaline wore off around the same time.

The respite proved brief as the colonel made his way back to him with a wide grin on his face.

"You okay back here?" the colonel asked.

"Yes, sir. Just thinking."

"Yeah, thought I saw smoke."

"Hardy, har, har."

"As always, you and the team performed flawlessly, Cap."

Troy ignored the compliment. "Can we head home now, sir? I think we need that leave you promised us."

"Sorry, Cap. Not yet. After action review at the Pentagon for the mission, and before that, we need to get your arm looked at and the wound cleaned out."

"I'll be fine," Troy said, rubbing his biceps gently.

"It wasn't a question. A chopper is standing by. You and I will head to Walter Reed to get the wound properly taken care of. Then they'll get us over to the Pentagon after they clear you."

"Gonna be a long night, huh?"

"Always is, but I think I can get you and the rest of the team home by mid-day tomorrow."

"What about you?"

"I'm staying in D.C. a little longer."

"You have to deal with the Rahman fallout?"

"Yes and no. I have something else to take care of while I'm here besides Rahman. Trust me when I say it's for the good of the entire team."

"Sound mysterious."

"No, just necessary." The colonel quickly changed the subject. "You'll be okay after what happened?"

Troy was quiet for a moment. "Yeah, I'll be fine. I just don't want to see another nuclear bomb as long as I live."

"Third one wasn't a charm?"

"Pfft. Something like that, sir." Troy's thoughts drifted back to the year 2002.

The colonel lightly touched the top of his arm. "After the Pentagon briefing, you'll need to take care of the last piece. You want me to come?"

"No, sir. I can handle it solo."

"You sure?"

"Yes, it will be quick. I got this."

"Okay, Cap. Let's get on with it all then. The Jackal keeps bitching about how he wants to get back for pizza at Salamone's."

Troy chuckled. "I wouldn't mind a slice and a cold one at this point as well."

The colonel nodded. "Soon enough. Let's dot the I's and cross the T's, and we can get you and the Omegas out of D.C. pronto."

78

WALTER REED NATIONAL MILITARY MEDICAL CENTER

Troy made the rounds to thank his team and those assembled in the hangar for a job well done. You were only as good as your weakest link, and everyone did their part to ensure the safe retrieval of the nuke. Troy had a few words with Pat in private, away from the others, before the two men shook hands and parted.

A few minutes later, he climbed aboard the helicopter with Colonel Marshall for the short flight to Walter Reed Medical Center.

Over the years, Troy knew plenty of soldiers who recovered at the facility. He also knew more than a few who perished there because of the injuries they sustained while on the battlefield.

As he walked through the halls, he didn't take it for granted that he could have easily been one of the soldiers admitted to the hospital for wounds sustained while in combat. Or, just as easily, it could have been his flag-draped coffin returned to Joint Base Andrews.

For most who live, a lifespan might be defined by years, but in the world of combat, the difference between living for years or perishing in seconds can often come down to one's proximity in feet or even inches. Although Troy never believed in luck, he was more of a fate type of guy. He would constantly tell the soldiers under him, "We are all dealt a random hand of cards, but we get the choice of how we play each hand."

Memories flooded him as he walked down the hallway a step away from Colonel Marshall. Troy didn't know any of the soldiers currently in the rooms they passed, but he knew those who had been in those very rooms over the years, and a sense of profound grief welled up with each step.

The doctor on call and his staff cleaned the wound and signed off on the paperwork an hour later. Troy thanked them for their professionalism and all they did for his fellow soldiers.

As he and the colonel climbed aboard the helicopter once again, he looked back and hoped it would be the last time he would have to put eyes on Walter Reed.

The flight to the Pentagon was short, and as they landed, the rest of The Omega Group was waiting for them at the heliport. One Joint Chiefs of Staff member met the team and led them to the conference room within the "E" ring where the meeting was to take place. The SecDef led the after-action review, and the entire meeting took close to two hours. Although the questioning was thorough, it proved to be fair. After all, The Omega Group and those in support achieved the objective, retrieving both the nuke in Iraq and the one set to be detonated in D.C.

Each received medals for their actions and bravery, even though what they did fell outside the military hierarchy, and the truth of their top-secret mission would likely never be disclosed to the general public.

Surprisingly, the Jackal made it through the entire meeting with few words and no sarcastic comments. Troy did notice the occasional smile thrown toward Charlie and the fact that she returned the grin on more than one occasion.

With the meeting over, an unmarked SUV was waiting in the below-ground parking structure to whisk Troy away.

"Sure you don't need me to come?" the colonel asked one more time.

"All good, sir," Troy replied as he gestured to the Jackal. "Just keep numbnuts here from causing any havoc in my absence. I should be done quickly, and I'll see you all back at Joint Base Andrews for the flight home."

"I think I behaved admirably in there," the Jackal said.

"Yeah, you did. That's what scares me," Troy replied.

"Food for the flight?" the colonel asked.

"Five guys. Bacon cheeseburger with jalapeños, sautéed onions, mushrooms, and barbecue sauce. Cajun fries, too. Oh, and a strawberry shake as well." He smiled before he added, "Please, and thank you."

"Think you earned at least a good meal or two for your efforts," the colonel said.

Troy gave the members fist bumps before he climbed into the SUV, and it left the underground parking structure.

79

THE WHITE HOUSE

WEST WING

The hairs on Troy's arms stood upright as he walked through the east entrance into the White House.

No matter how often you enter the *People's House*, the experience remains almost religious for most.

The Secret Service agent who escorted Troy inside looked like a spitting image of a character from the movie *Olympus Has Fallen*. Troy re-watched the movie recently and, considering the storyline thought it ironic that the agent was a doppelgänger for an actor in the movie. Troy almost pointed it out, but the agent's stoic persona gave him pause, and he kept the passing thought to himself.

The agent led Troy to the West Wing, where he passed by the entrance to the Oval Office, the door leading into the office firmly closed. The agent ushered Troy to a door only a few steps down the hall from the history-laced office most people think of when they think of the President of the United States.

With his head tilted toward the door and eyebrows raised, the agent indicated Troy should knock. He did so, and a second later, a booming voice said, "Enter."

Troy opened the door and came face to face with the man in the dark suit he met before they left for Iraq.

"Good job, Captain Evans. You and the rest of The Omega Group did phenomenal work. The president sends his regards. I was told you and your men passed on the opportunity to meet with him this evening?"

"We are tired and anyway we saw him briefly before the operation on the beltway. My men want to get back home and rest. It was a challenging operation. Maybe we can have a rain check and meet with the president at another time."

The man in the dark suit nodded. "I'm sure that can be arranged."

"Great," Troy said.

The man held out his hand. "I've been told you have something for me?"

"Ah, yes." Troy removed the wooden box, tucked it under his right arm, and handed it over.

"The President of the United States is grateful for this." He placed the box on his worn desktop.

Troy pursed his lips. "You're not gonna open it and ensure they are both there?"

The man shook his head. "Not my place to do so. And besides, the president trusts you and your team. Colonel Marshall spoke with the president personally after you were back at Joint Base Andrews. That's all the assurance the president needed."

"Interesting," Troy said.

"While you are here, would you like a look around? The president is not in the Oval Office, but I can give you a brief tour. Let you sit behind the Resolute desk if you would like, and get a picture. Or maybe see the tunnels."

"Nah, I'm good. I've done it before when I was younger, and once is enough."

"Ah, yes. I read your file. You've averted the United States from imminent destruction twice now, Captain Evans."

Troy ignored the compliment. "Can I ask a question?"

"Maybe."

"Why did Ami target Joint Base Andrews? It might be where they keep Air Force One, but there's very little chance they could coordinate the president being there at the same time they detonated the nuke. The location just made no sense. Even Colonel Marshall wasn't privy to why Ami and Levi targeted that spot."

"You read Ami's file, correct?"

"Of course."

"And you know his father was German, and his mother was Israeli."

"Yes."

"Well, what the file does not say is that, several decades ago, besides being a military installation, Andrews had a black site hidden within the property."

"Black site as in jail? Like what we don't allow on US soil anymore?"

"Correct. Well, in the nineteen-nineties, we had no such qualms about having facilities like that spread around the globe. One such place existed at Andrews, and Ami's father was a guest at the facility for a period of time."

"So I am to believe Ami targeted Andrews, became his dad was held there against his will at some point?"

"Troy, you can believe what you want. All I can say is Ami's dad spent thirty-three days at the facility starting in March of 1997. Even though Ami eventually worked for the agency in some capacity, he never forgave the former president for doing what was done to his father."

"Okay. Seems like a stretch, but if you say so."

"As the saying goes, *Truth is often stranger than fiction*, Captain Evans."

"Well, thanks for that, but can I ask one more question?"

"Can't guarantee an answer, but as long as it's not more details about Ami's father, you can certainly ask."

"Fair enough. When we met in Crystal City, you wouldn't reveal your name. Now that my men and I have recovered the nukes and retrieved the items for POTUS, it would be nice to have a name to go with the dark suit." Troy extended his right hand out to the man. "And you are?"

The man in the dark suit let out a slight laugh before he took the extended hand and gave it a firm yet not overbearing shake with his own hand. "You and your team can call me The Body Man." He pulled a card from his suit pocket and handed the card to Troy. "If you and any members of your team are ever in a pinch, reach out. I'll do what I can."

Troy nodded, turned, and walked out the door. As the agent who escorted him from the east entrance led him back out of the West Wing, Troy stole a quick glance inside the Oval Office. With the door now ajar, it gave him an unobstructed view inside the most famous office in the world. The empty Resolute desk called to him in some weird way as he walked past the open doorway. Troy shifted his gaze forward and kept a steady pace as they exited the White House a few minutes later.

80

AT CRUISING ALTITUDE

GULFSTREAM G450

It had been a long twenty-four hours for the entire team. Finally, after some sleep at Joint Base Andrews, they were back on the jet early in the morning and headed west. Their destination was Joint Base Lewis-McChord southwest of Tacoma, Washington.

An hour into the flight, Charlie came over and sat in the empty seat beside Troy.

"You look like shit," she said with a slight smirk peeking out from the corner of her lips.

"Thanks, feel like it, too. I was surprised to hear you were coming back with us."

"Why?"

"Well, Division S is based at Bragg. Figured you'd be heading back to them now that the mission is over."

"They said I deserved several days of extended leave, and I've got somebody I promised to see out West. Thought I would bum a ride."

Troy shook his head. "Smart move, I guess."

"Plus, I'm ready for it."

"Ready for what?" Troy asked.

"The long answer ..."

"Huh?"

"About Cate. Ring any bells yet, Sherlock?"

"Jeez, you're persistent."

"Sure am. Most women are, Cap."

"You seriously want to know what happened?"

"Yes, and you promised to give me the full scoop."

Troy sighed. "All right, Martin, I'll lay it on you, but I might need a few drinks to lubricate the old memory bank."

"I'll take a few rounds if you're pouring, Cap."

"Of course you will." Troy stood. "I'll be right back."

Troy made his way to the cockpit. "Knock, knock," he said while simultaneously rapping on the side of the cherry cabinet just inside the flight deck.

"Whatcha need, Cap?" Captain Messick turned around in his flight seat.

"Can I borrow that bottle of Woodford Reserve? I'll replace it when we land. You didn't open it yet did you?"

"I might have had a nip while you were preventing the nuke from going off. After all, it may have been my last sip if you had messed up." He held up his index finger and thumb with a small gap between the two.

"By a nip, you mean you drank half the damn bottle, right?"

Mickey smiled. "Ha, I wish. But someone has to be responsible and fly an elite group of soldiers around the world with little to no notice." He looked at his watch. "The bottle is all yours, but you're not usually a day drinker."

"I need to chat with Charlie and might need liquid courage."

"Ruh-roh. About?"

"I promised her on the way to Ghana I'd give her an explanation of what happened with you know who."

"That may take the rest of the bottle," Mickey said with a growing smile. "And why would you make a stupid ass promise like that?"

"Women." Troy sighed and didn't say anymore.

"Ain't that the truth," Mickey said with a chuckle. "And hey, Cap?"

"Yeah, buddy?"

"You guys did great out there. I know you'll never get the appreciation you deserve, but millions of people are indebted to you and the rest of the team. I, for one, am grateful."

"Thanks, Mickey. Sometimes we're more A-team than an elite fighting force, but we seem to get the job done when the shit is about to hit the proverbial fan."

Mickey passed the bottle to Troy. "I'll drink to that. Bottoms up, my friend."

Troy smiled. "Thanks."

"So how do you do it every time?" Mickey asked.

Troy's expression contorted to one of confusion. "Do what?"

"Succeed when the cards are stacked against you?"

With a shrug, Troy answered, "I honestly don't know."

"Is it fate? Divine intervention? Or just plain dumb luck?"

With a laugh, Troy said, "Probably the latter, but I tend to think the man upstairs has our six, as well."

"Whatever it is, I'm glad you guys have it and hope it never leaves you."

"Me too," Troy replied, letting the words sink in. "Catch you later, bud, and thanks for the bottle."

—◆—

Troy sat down next to Charlie and placed two shot glasses on the table. After filling them with the amber-colored nectar, he said, "Bottoms up," as he lifted the glass.

In one smooth motion, before Troy could react, Charlie grabbed her glass and pounded it down. "Ahh, that's smooth!" she exclaimed.

"Impressive," Troy remarked as he watched her take the first shot. "Where should I start?" He took down his shot.

"Start where all stories should begin, silly," Charlie answered. "When a boy meets a girl ..."

81

McLean, Virginia

"Ray! The dog."

"Not now, dear. I'm watching the game."

A few seconds passed before the voice inflection turned up a few notches, and the tone turned less than what any man in his right mind would discern as cordial. "Raymond B. Surrey! The dog."

His wife used his full-given name, which meant if he didn't respond in the affirmative, there would most likely be hell to pay. "Yes, dear," he finally relented. Ray grabbed his coat, put on his boots, and clipped the leash on his Jack Russell terrier named Rufus.

It was almost midnight. The moon lay hidden behind a thick cover of clouds, and the temperature hovered in the low forties.

Ray stepped outside, silently cursed Rufus and his limited bladder retention, and headed down the road away from his house at a quickened pace. The damn dog would never piss in his own yard. He always had to go down the road to the far light pole to lift his leg.

A minute later, a black Lexus quietly approached from behind. As the sleek vehicle hugged the curb, it stopped just to Ray's left. He paused and looked over, curious as to why he didn't recognize the vehicle.

The passenger window lowered, and a firm, non-threatening voice called, "Hey, pal. I think I took a wrong turn, and every road looks identical at this time of night. Can I bother you for directions?"

Ray sighed. He wasn't interested in acting like Google Maps at that moment. Nevertheless, he approached the vehicle and ducked down to look into the open window. As his eyes focused on the darkened interior, his body involuntarily jerked as he realized he was staring down the barrel of a large-caliber handgun. Instinctively, he reached behind his body to the concealed Glock 19 clipped to the waistband of his pants.

With a stern yet calm tone, the man inside the Lexus said, "Ray, if you draw that Glock, your wife Mellie will be scrubbing your brain matter out of Rufus's fur with a fine-tooth comb later tonight."

He withdrew his hand and brought it back into view. "Who the hell are you, and what do you want?"

The ambient lighting came on, illuminating the inside of the plush car. Clear as day, the driver's face and also the full view of the HK45 were on display. The recognition within Ray's eyes was difficult to mask, even for someone who worked at the agency.

"You know who I am," the man said in a matter-of-fact tone.

Try as he may, Ray knew there would be no way to deceive the man before him. He swallowed hard. "Yes, I know who you are, Colonel Marshall."

"Then you also must know why I'm here?"

Ray played stupid. "No, sir, I don't."

"I need you to get in the car. We need to chat."

"And if I refuse."

"Your wife will become a widow, your children fatherless. Rufus will have to find another dude to take him out for his damn piss every night."

"You'd shoot me right here, a block from my home?" Ray asked.

"Try me. You ratted out my team to Dimitri Petrikov."

"It's not as simple as that," Ray retorted. *Damn, how does he know it was me?*

"Rarely is."

He couldn't talk his way out of this. Reluctantly, he climbed into the vehicle, and his body sank into the upscale leather seats. He left the door still ajar. "What about Rufus?"

"He looks like a smart dog. He'll find his way home," Colonel Marshall said before he added, "Close the door, Ray."

Ray did as instructed and pulled the door shut. "My wife will wonder what happened to me if Rufus returns without me. She'll call the agency number ASAP."

"Mellie is the least of your worries. And as for the tracker you have implanted in your body ..." The colonel flicked his wrist, and the knife in his other hand opened. The blade locked in place with a distinct click. "I know where the chip is and how to remove it."

"This is a dangerous path you're headed down, William. You still have time to let me go, and I won't breathe a word of it to the director."

"You're in no position to negotiate with me, Raymond. And besides, don't be a dick. There's no reason why you can't make it out of this alive."

"If I tell you what you need to know. You'll let me go free?"

"Me? No, you won't be talking to me, Ray."

Ray never saw the figure who had been hidden low to the floorboard in the back of the vehicle. The person dressed in all black rose up quickly and silently reached over the seat, then plunged the syringe into Ray's exposed neck. The warm liquid filled his body, and an instant later, everything faded to black.

"How long do we have?" the colonel asked.

"He'll be out for at least ninety minutes," the man with a raspy voice in the rear seat said.

"We better get moving then. It will take us nearly an hour to reach the facility in Culpeper."

EPILOGUE

TACOMA, WASHINGTON

Five and a half hours after they left Washington, the six members of The Omega Group were back where the mission began, at Sarge's house. Charlie said her goodbyes to the team on base. They tried to convince her to come by the house, but she declined. She promised to meet up with the team real soon, which would have to be enough for now.

It was just the guys, a mountain of pizza boxes, and more beer bottles than any of them could count. Around 11:00 p.m., the Jackal got a text message. Troy watched him from the other side of the room as a smile encompassed his face. As the Jackal put down his cell phone, he stood and headed for the door.

"Where you going?" Troy asked.

"Gotta bounce, Cap. Have something I need to do."

"At this time of night?" Troy asked with a surprised look. "I thought we all agreed to crash here? Plus, you've been drinking."

"Yeah, I know, but I've had a slight change of plans. Anyway, I only had a few cokes, no booze."

Troy looked over at Sarge, who nodded. "He's telling the truth, Cap. I thought it was odd myself."

The Jackal winked. "Told you. Oh, and don't wait up for me."

"You're not falling back into the arms of that one, are you?"

"Hah! Nothing like that, Cap. Trust me. I'll be a good boy. I promise."

"Okay," Troy said as he got up, stepped out onto the front porch, and watched the Jackal climb into his 4X4 Tundra. A minute later, the truck taillights disappeared into the darkened night.

"What's that all about?" Sarge asked after Troy closed the door and came back inside.

"Not sure," Troy said.

By 2 a.m., they all gave in to exhaustion and passed out in various rooms throughout the house. Sleep came to Troy, like the others, but it was an uneasy rest. He had crashed on the couch in the living room closest to the front door.

At 6 a.m., he was startled awake when a car door slammed outside. Reaching for his Kimber on the end table, he hopped off the couch and made his way toward the front door. Without looking through the peephole, he thrust the door open, his hand firmly gripping the 1911.

A shocked look formed on his face as he watched the tender kiss between the Jackal and Charlie conclude.

"Good morning, Cap," Charlie said as she smiled and stepped away from the porch. Halfway down the walkway, she looked back and made eye contact with the Jackal. "I'll call you soon," she said.

"Can't wait," the Jackal replied as he watched her climb into the Uber and drive off.

As soon as she was gone, the Jackal let out a short whistle, turned around, and made his way through the open door. A smile from ear to ear covered his face, and he had an unmistakable glow about him.

Troy grabbed his shoulder. "What the hell was that all about?"

With a devilish grin, the Jackal replied, "Sorry, Cap, but a gentleman never tells."

Troy rolled his eyes. "Bullshit! Since when are you a gentleman?"

———◆———

THE END

———◆———

THE OMEGA GROUP WILL RETURN

ACKNOWLEDGMENTS

With the completion of *Babylon Will Rise*, my fourth published work, I'm doing something I've never done before, and writing these acknowledgements from over 32,000 feet as I fly to California. I've lost count on how many times life's journey has brought me to The Golden State. During this visit, I once again plan to visit one of my favorite places on earth, Yosemite National Park. It's my sixth trip to Yosemite since September 2014. In fact, I finished my first (unpublished) novel *Vengeance* during that first visit to Yosemite. The park will forever hold a special place in my heart. I'll work on my 2025 release *Supreme Justice* in the evenings while resting from my adventures in the park, and maybe a few of the experiences from the trip will make their way into future stories. Seeds for story ideas are planted in the most unusual ways, and you never know which one may sprout into an actual tale.

***

Babylon Will Rise started its literary journey as a novella during 2017 and I initially called it *Project Nebuchadnezzar*. I know, I know, I know, that doesn't have a nice ring to it as a title for a novel. Let's go back and discuss the first (unpublished) novel, *Vengeance*. As I mentioned, the book was completed in 2014 during my first visit to Yosemite. It featured The Omega Group, and in particular the protagonist, Troy Evans. From 2014 until 2018 I wrote three complete novels and two novellas that featured Troy as the main character. Fast forward to 2023, and I formed my own Indie publishing company, **BruNoe Media Publishing**. I've grown as a writer since starting this journey in 2014, and I dug back into some of those old stories when I formed the new company. Where possible, I will breathe new life into those old tales. Not all of them may see the light of day, but I'll strive to take the stories I can enhance and release them to entertain my readers! In 2023 I released the novella *Ransomed Daughter* to introduce the world to The Omega Group, and now in 2024 *Babylon Will Rise* is part of the ongoing series. Where will Troy and the rest of the Omegas go next? I'm not telling...yet!

❖

Writing is a very solitary endeavor, yet people help in the overall process from inception to finished product. It's an honor to share in the achievement of publishing books with so many family members, friends, peers, and acquaintances who have supported me over the years. I put these words in most my acknowledgments but it's good to remind my kids, readers, and especially myself that, "Life's A Journey, Not A Destination."

Above all, thank you to **I AM** for the gifts you've bestowed upon me and my family

Bruce and **Noelle**. I love you both. Fulfilling my dreams of publishing books is a blessing, but none of it compares to being your father. Work hard, never settle for less than you deserve, and above all never stop believing anything in life is possible. Many people go through life making excuses as to why they don't succeed. Be the exception to the rule. And never forget I believe in you both, always

My **Mom – Patty**. Nobody has supported me more in my writing career. I love you

My **Dad – Tom**. Thank you for reading thrillers while at S.N.E.T. and giving me the tattered paperbacks. Those novels started my love of reading and eventually turned into a desire to write

Jackie, Shawn, Meadow, Brett, and **Alli.** Love you all

Aunt Sue. You've always supported my dreams

To the rest of my **Family**. Much love

Babylon Will Rise is dedicated to **Andrew Reinertsen** my freshman year college roommate and lifelong friend. During the twenty years he served our nation in the Army, **Andrew** spent much of his time in the Middle East. The real life (or maybe at times tall tales) he shared with me when back stateside helped enhance storylines for The Omega Group and other books I have yet to write. Each time he returned from a deployment; I received a new flag with a story of how he retrieved it. They are prized possessions, and I'm grateful for the pieces of memorabilia he gave me. Most importantly I treasure our friendship. This one is for you **Rino/Filthy Mug**

Max Council/The Pope One of my oldest friends (Literally, geez you're 50 now!)

TC Thompson/Mr. President Hard to believe we met when our sons were in pre-school together, and now they are seniors in high school! Where does the time go?

Noah George Grateful for our occasional cigar chats

In college I flew in a Cessna with **Mickey Messick**, my friend and a business aviation student who lived across the hall. It seemed appropriate for him to fly The Omega Group around the globe this time

John Guarnieri Because of you my podcast, *A Tale Of Two Scribes*, on your SpearTalk Podcast Network became a reality. Bring on the Reaper and our future (shhh) ventures

Thanks to **Eric Bass** of the band **Shinedown** for his encouragement, motivation, and valuable advice to my son

Kathy Lubin My dear friend and 1st editor

There might be a little MIL trash talk in the book I garnered from time spent with **Simon Fraser**. Plus, **Joe Tanguay** always comes to mind when I write anything MIL.

My co-workers, **Shawn Cassidy** and **Carolynn Tolbert**. Grateful to enjoy the beauty of Yosemite with you both this time

Boy Scouts may be over for our sons, but I'm still honored to have friendships with the **Troop 610 Dads: Bud McCall, TC Thompson, Marty Thomas, Dr. David Richards, Mike Webb, Shannon "Radar" Roberts,** and of course, the "Mountain Dew Man" himself who I offed in *The Body Man,* **Wes Russell**

Thankful for my golf trip buddies: **Jim Latina, Brian Wohnig, Bill Esch, Dan "Dano" Reed, Eric "E" Wade, Mickey Harris, Brian Houston,** and **Mike Haggerty (FU)**

———— ◆ ————

I get a lot of joy when including cameos in the pages of my books. For *Babylon Will Rise* I included: **Anke Dul-van Dooren, Shannon "Radar" Roberts, Marcus Carter, Dan Coates, Ryan West, Frank Fitzgerald,** and **Dave Buzan**

———— ◆ ————

Special thanks to **Ama (A.M.) Adair** and **Steve Stratton** for their early reads and constructive feedback regarding *Babylon Will Rise*. I have never served in the military, but hold a deep respect for those that signed up and sacrificed for me and my family. I try my best to get the details right in every story. Grateful for Ama and Steve helping with some military aspects. Any issues/inconsistencies that remain in the final draft are purely from me and not them.

———— ◆ ————

Thank you to **Todd Wilkins** & **Kashif Hussain** at **Best Thriller Books (BTB)** for the *Breach Of Trust* review. Also, thank you to **James Abt** of **BTB** for the *Babylon Will Rise* cover reveal

Excited to work with **Chris Cochrane** of **Machete Comics** on a fun comic book collaboration

I write thrillers thanks to the path forged by **Tom Clancy** & **Vince Flynn**

This year author **Keller Hackbusch/Charles Hack** was instrumental in helping out with ads on Facebook. He learned much on his own, and passed that knowledge on to me, which proved invaluable. Authors helping fellow authors is an amazing thing to be part of. You never know how it may help others. What a community of incredible scribes!

After 10 years of writing, many authors continue to inspire and offer ongoing support/encouragement on my literary journey: **Adam Hamdy, Charles Hack, Joe Goldberg, David Darling, Mike Mason, Brad Meltzer, Sam Whitfield, Terrence McCauley, Matt Leone, Yasmin Angoe, Kyle Steele, Jack Carr, Fred Burton, Dony Jay, Jeff Clark, Ama Adair, Richard Maverick, F.X. Regan, Travis Davis, Laurie Chandlar, Dave Buzan, Tony Tata, Michael Carlson, Lori Twining, J.B. Stevens, Kyle Mills, Steve Stratton, Terrance Layhew, John Stamp,** and **Dr. Jason Piccolo**

The following people graciously agreed to read the *Babylon Will Rise* ARC's. Thank you so much to **Aida Flick, Mark Elliott, Marcus Carter, Daryl Delabbio, Mikael Sandeberg, John Currens, Mike Mason, Matthew Persson, Matt Leone, Sam Whitfield, Nick Stoczanyn,** and **Michael Carlson.**

⸺◆⸺

Thanks to **Jonas Saul** at **Imagine Press Inc.** for my copyedits

Grateful for **Marisia Robus** who gave the novel one final pass

The phenomenal covers for *The Body Man, Breach Of Trust,* and *Babylon Will Rise* were designed by **Momir Borocki**

Bruce Bishop (my son) took my awesome author photos

Blessed to own an Indie publishing imprint, **BruNoe Media Publishing**, and I'm looking forward to everything it will achieve.

⸺◆⸺

Thank you to everyone who picked up copies of *The Body Man*, *Breach of Trust*, *Ransomed Daughter*, and now *Babylon Will Rise* since November 2021. It's beyond humbling to know my words are resonating with readers worldwide. So far, my books have reached over twenty countries and counting! How cool is that? This year, thanks to the advice of author **David Darling**, I put my books on the **Kindle Unlimited (KU)** program, part of **Amazon**. Between January and October 2024, my books had over one million three hundred thousand page reads with KU. The equivalent of roughly 3,500+ books read. What a blessing!

If you read any of my books please take a few minutes and leave an **Amazon** rating and/or review (plus **Goodreads**). It really makes a tremendous difference to me and all writers. Thank you for the support. I'm grateful you've given me a chance to entertain you with my stories. Like I keep saying, I'm just getting started …

Finally, life is a precious gift. You get to choose how you will receive that gift, and what you do with it

Onward and upward, my friends,

Eric P. Bishop

(October 2024)

About the Author

Eric P. Bishop grew up in Connecticut, and relocated to the South after college. Moves to the Rockies and the Pacific Northwest occurred before finally heading back East to raise his family. Part of him never left the West, and he is always grateful to make it back as often as possible.

After many years in corporate America, Eric turned his passion for the written word into reality and chased his dreams of crafting novels.

Eric lives in Western North Carolina with his children, where they explore the great outdoors most weekends, all the while he dreams up his next great adventure. He loves to travel and incorporates what he sees around the world into the stories he crafts.

See www.ericpbishop.com for more about Eric, his novels, and pictures of his amazing journey.

www.ingramcontent.com/pod-product-compliance
Lightning Source LLC
Chambersburg PA
CBHW022020310726
48972CB00006B/1730